Don't Call Me Hero

Don't Call Me Hero
Book 1

Eliza Lentzski

ISBN: 1502912503
ISBN-13: 978-1502912503

Also by Eliza Lentzski

Standalone Novels

Lighthouse Keeper (forthcoming)

Sour Grapes

The Woman in 3B

Sunscreen & Coconuts

The Final Rose

Bittersweet Homecoming

Fragmented

Apophis: Love Story for the End of the World

Second Chances

Date Night

Love, Lust, & Other Mistakes

Diary of a Human

Works as E.L. Blaisdell

Drained: The Lucid (with Nica Curt)

To C

Chapter One

The thing about going away parties is they make you want to stick around a little longer. That was the singular thought on my mind as I sat at a bar top table surrounded by the few friends I'd made since moving to Minneapolis less than a year ago. We were all cops on the city police force, but on that particular night we were just five twenty-somethings having drinks on my last night in town.

Brent, a native Minnesotan whom I'd always thought looked like an authentic Viking, raised his pint glass. "To Cassidy!" he toasted loud enough to be heard over whatever mash-up remix the DJ was playing. His chevron mustache twitched above his top lip. "To one awesome chick and one helluva cop."

Everyone around the table raised their assorted glassware, which ranged from pint glasses to martini funnels, and they echoed Brent's sentiment. Glasses clinked together and beverages sloshed over the rims.

I ducked my head at the gesture. I typically hated being the center of attention, but I was trying to let myself enjoy it. It had been a while since I'd experienced this feeling of belonging or that anyone appreciated my existence.

I looked around the table at the faces of the people who had quickly become like family: Brent the Viking, whose shoulders were broader than a doorframe, but whose heart was just as big; Angie, the dark-skinned woman with the quick smile. She was small in stature, but feistier than anyone I'd ever met, male or female. Adan, a slim Latino man, nursed his gin and tonic. He was the quietest of our group, and as the alcohol flowed more freely, he seemed to sink farther and farther into silent contemplation while his toothy grin grew wider and wider.

At the rank of detective, Rich had the most years in the department, but he was also the most immature of all of us. He reminded me of the guys I'd served with in the Marines—young at heart, but serious and professional when the situation called for it. I was proud to call him friend. In fact, even though I'd only been in the Twin Cities for a little over a year, I was going to miss this place and these people.

Angie echoed my thoughts. "God, I'm gonna miss you, Miller. Without you around, I'll be swimming in testosterone." She took a careful sip of her apple martini.

"Methinks the lady dost protest too much," Rich teased. "Don't let her fool you, Cass. Angie's been counting the days down until she gets all the men to herself."

Angie snorted. "Boy, you've got it twisted if you think Miller and I have the same type."

"You're probably right." Rich ran his hand over his shaved head. "I suppose I don't have enough hair to be on Cassidy's radar."

"Or nice enough tits," Angie countered.

A howl of laughter rose around the table. Rich clutched at his heart, feigning being wounded by her words.

Brent palmed his broad chest over his T-shirt. "What do you think, Cassidy? Are these a solid B cup?"

I smirked and took another pull from my bottled beer. I drank using only my thumb and forefinger. It was an unnatural way to hold the bottle, but it mimicked the motion of pulling a bolt from a rifle. I'd been indoctrinated to drink that way at boot camp on Parris Island. "Dude, your boobs are bigger than mine." I grabbed onto his muscled cleavage and gave it a firm squeeze. "I'm kind of jealous."

A loud chorus of laughter erupted from an adjacent table, rivaling our own volume. I glanced in the direction of the noise and saw five women sitting around a bottle service table. It didn't look like a bachelorette party—there wasn't enough penis paraphernalia for that—so I wondered at the cause for celebration. The VIP seating was too pricey for a simple girls' night out, and in a low-key city like Minneapolis, the need for bottle service seemed out of place.

I'd never been to this particular club before. It was too loud for extended conversation, and the strobe lights were too aggressive for my liking. I preferred dive bars that served cheap beer and gave away free popcorn. But my friends had insisted that this was a special occasion and that we needed to deviate from the norm.

My eyes flicked over each woman's face as I tried to discover the reason behind the party. My innate curiosity had gotten me into trouble over the years, but it had also served me well in combat and on the police force. My investigation came to a halt on one face in particular. When caramel-colored eyes looked up and met my own, I immediately tore my glance away and pretended to be interested in the label on my beer bottle instead.

The boisterous conversation of the going away party continued around me, but I couldn't stop looking back at the other table. It might have been the alcohol starting to talk, but seated at the adjacent table was the most striking woman I'd ever laid eyes on. Her raven-dark hair was styled and cut to frame her heart-shaped face. The ends flipped out just below the edge of her strong jaw line. Dark eyes, accentuated by smoky makeup, smoldered under the lights of the club. Her lips looked impossibly perfect, painted a deep shade of red and tugged up at one corner in an early smirk.

"Could you be anymore obvious?" Angie nudged a well-placed elbow into my ribs.

I snapped my eyes back to my friend. "What?"

"Don't play innocent. You've been gawking at that woman like you're on a stakeout."

"What are you two birds buzzing about?" Brent butted it. He leaned across the table, and his thick blond mane fell across his eyes.

"Nothing," I quickly asserted.

"Miller's got a crush," Angie countered.

"I do not!"

"Where?" Rich grinned eagerly. His eyes swept around the dimly lit club.

"Classy brunette over at the bottle service table," Angie supplied, much to my horror.

Rich and Brent nearly fell over each other trying to get a glimpse of the woman while I couldn't look up from the bottom of my beer bottle.

"Jesus, Miller," Rich chuckled when he spotted the gorgeous brunette with her friends. "You really shoot for the stars, don't you?"

"I'm not doing anything," I defended myself. "I'm just sitting here, you assholes." I chanced another glance in her direction. The distance between our two tables wasn't that much, and I was *sure* she could pick up the topic of our conversation if she had wanted to.

"Which is a problem. You should be sitting over there," Angie pointed unobtrusively in the direction of the nearby table, "charming your way into whatever fancy underwear classy dames like that wear."

"Which *you* would know nothing about, Angie," Brent snorted before draining the rest of his pint.

"You *wish* you could check out my underwear, Olson," Angie returned with a snarl.

"So are you gonna make a move?" Rich egged me on.

"Guys, she's not even gay," I mumbled. Personally, I didn't enjoy labels. I found both sexes attractive, but if pressed I enjoyed being intimate with women more.

"How do you know until you try?" The optimistic statement came from Adan. He was a man of few words, so when he did talk, people usually listened.

"Dude, this is your last night in town," Brent reasoned with me. "What do you have to lose?"

I glanced again in the direction of the VIP section. The woman had her head thrown back, laughing. My eyes were drawn to her mouth, lips painted red and white teeth flashing. I jerked my attention back to my table when I spotted a hand grab my wallet off its surface.

Angie waved down a nearby cocktail waitress. "Bottle of champagne for that table over there, please," she requested. She produced a credit card from my wallet and gave it to the server.

I swiped back my wallet, now one credit card lighter. "What are you doing?"

"Helping you be brave, my friend."

"With my own money?"

I watched in mixed fascination and horror as the cocktail waitress delivered the bottle and five long-stemmed glasses to the adjacent table. The women uniformly appeared confused and waved the waitress away until the server pointed in the direction of our table.

"Jesus." I jerked my stare back down to the tabletop and my visibly shaking hands.

"Hey ladies," Brent called, waving a massively muscled arm. His blond hair wasn't the only thing that looked like it belonged on a Viking; he was physically built like one, too.

"Would you stop it, Olson?" I hissed under my breath. I was thankful for the dim lighting so no one could see the blush I was sure had crept onto my cheeks. I aimed a boot to kick him under the table, but I missed and hit Rich's shin instead.

"Fuck, Miller!" Rich leaned under the table to rub his tender shin.

"You probably deserved it, too," I huffed, refusing to feel guilty about my poor aim.

"If you keep sitting here, I'm gonna keep charging drinks to your card and sending them to that table," Angie threatened. "*Someone* has to make a move."

Brent started to pound on the table in some kind of primal testosterone encouragement. Rich joined, followed by Angie, and even Adan.

"I really hate you idiots," I spit out between ground teeth. I took one more pull from my beer bottle, building up my courage, and stood up on uneasy legs. The pounding on the table turned to victorious whoops and cheers.

I raked my fingers through my loose hair. "What the hell do I even say?" I grumbled to no one in particular.

Rich hopped up from his seat and slung his arm around my shoulder. "Don't worry. I won't let you go in there without backup."

"I'm sure this has nothing to do with the fact that her four friends are equally attractive."

Rich ran his hand over his squared jaw, which was just as closely shaved as his bald head. "Just taking one for the team, Rookie."

We made our way over to the table, Rich's gate exaggerated and mine unsure. I could feel myself start to sweat in the small of my back, but Rich's arm remained slung around my shoulder, keeping me from running off. It felt like it weighed one thousand pounds.

The women were distracted by each other's conversation and didn't notice our approach. We hovered close to the large table, ignored for the moment, until Rich cleared his throat.

"Excuse me, ladies," he announced. "Sorry to interrupt, but I hope you're enjoying the champagne my good friend Cassidy was so generous to send over."

The chattering at the table died down.

A blonde woman with wide-set eyes and an upturned nose was the first to respond. "Thank you, Cassidy." She raised her champagne flute and tilted her head to the side. "What's the occasion?"

I opened my mouth, although I wasn't sure what I was going to say, but Rich beat me to it. "It's Officer Miller's last night in town so we're giving her a kind of *bon voyage* party." He leaned forward and flashed what I thought was a particularly wolfish smile. "How would you ladies like to celebrate with the Twin Cities' finest and help us see our friend off with a bang?"

"You're all cops?" asked a redhead with a spray of freckles across her nose.

"Detective Richard Gammon of the Minneapolis Police Department reporting for duty, Miss." Rich touched his fingers to the rim of an imaginary hat. "Think you've got room at your table for a few more?"

The women looked at each other, wordlessly conferring, before the blonde spokeswoman answered. "Sure, why not?"

I couldn't help but notice with a belly full of misgivings that the woman I had been staring at hadn't participated in the conversation. I was about to excuse Rich and myself—the need to run away building in my body—but he had already waved at our other friends, motioning for them to come over, and the five women were shuffling around the long rectangular table to make room for us.

Rich settled himself between the blonde and the redhead, looking particularly pleased with how things had turned out.

I hesitated, unsure of where to go, until I felt hands firm on the tops of my shoulders planting me in the empty space next to the dark-haired woman whom I had been eyeballing.

"Have a seat, Cass," Adan instructed me in his lightly accented English.

The space was limited and ten people were crammed around the table that was meant for maybe only eight. Beneath the wooden surface, my thigh pressed flush against my crush's and our shoulders knocked together so I wouldn't fall off the end of the cushioned bench. Despite our physical proximity, she continued to stare straight ahead. As I inspected the faces seated around the L-shaped table, she appeared to be the only person upset by the interruption. Even Adan had partnered up with one of her friends and was looking uncharacteristically chatty.

I found myself unable to make eye contact now that I was actually sitting here. Things had escalated too quickly, and I needed a moment to get used to the change in company. I had planned on spending my last evening in town with my closest friends, not making awkward small talk with attractive strangers.

I managed to flag down a cocktail server, and I ordered another bottle of champagne for the table. Uncomfortable with silence, I would ply the table with more alcohol.

"You should slow down." The woman finally acknowledged me.

"Excuse me?"

Dark eyes turned to meet mine. "If you keep ordering bottles like that, your bank account isn't going to thank you in the morning." Her voice was an impossible low burn, and I felt its hum all over my body.

I grimaced at the truth of her words. I hadn't bothered to ask how much the bubbly beverage cost; I'd only been following Angie's lead. I looked for our cocktail waitress, but it was too late to retract my order of the second bottle. I mentally vowed to pace myself in the future.

"I'm really sorry about this," I apologized under my breath. "I didn't mean to crash your party. My friends are idiots."

"They wanted to make sure you had a good time tonight," she supplied. "That doesn't sound so idiotic to me."

"Yeah," I said, appropriately chastised. "I guess so." I let out a shaky breath. I should try to have a conversation. "Do you, um, you live here?"

She twisted her long-stemmed glass on the table. "At the bar?"

"No, no. Of course not." I forced out a nervous laugh. "In the Cities."

"I used to," she confirmed.

She didn't supply any additional information, and my nervousness returned until the second bottle of champagne appeared. I busied myself with the task of filling five more glasses for my friends. I also topped off the woman beside me's glass, but hated the way my hand shook. At least I hadn't poured champagne all over the table.

I slid her refilled glass in front of her. "So what's the occasion? Girl's night out?" I asked. "Or are you celebrating something?"

Her dark, painted lips pursed. "I'm sure I don't know you well enough to reveal that."

"Maybe after a few more glasses of champagne, we'll be best friends," I shrugged.

I didn't think of myself as particularly clever, but she laughed at my comment, and the sound was glorious. As soon as I heard the deep, throaty chuckle, I knew that as long as she continued to talk to me, I would continue to order champagne, regardless of the price.

"I'm Cassidy, by the way—in case you didn't catch it from before."

She shifted beside me, turning her body and attention more in my direction. Her knee bumped lightly into mine beneath the table. "Julia," she returned.

With her hands at the base of her champagne flute and mine on my own, our fingers were nearly touching.

"Can I call you Jules?"

She leaned forward and my pulse quickened. I felt mesmerized as her lush mouth moved to form words: "Absolutely not."

I tilted my head back and laughed, probably a little too loudly. When my palms landed on the table top in my moment of bliss, I promptly knocked over both flutes of champagne. The bubbly liquid tipped down Julia's dress—not *on* her dress: *in* her dress.

I froze and the music in the club seemed to come to a halt, but it was only my overactive imagination. No one had noticed my clumsiness outside of myself and Julia. I would have found the look of horror on her face mildly comical if I hadn't been the party responsible for it. I grabbed fistfuls of cocktail napkins with the intention of helping clean up the mess, but she stood up before I could ply her flesh with tiny squares of paper.

"Oh my God. I'm sorry."

"It's fine," she said stiffly. "I'll just ... clean up in the restroom." She wiggled out from behind the table and stalked away in the direction of an unseen bathroom.

I grappled with indecision. Should I follow her to the bathroom? Or should I give her privacy to put herself back together?

I settled on the latter and sopped up as much of the spilt beverage as I could that covered the table and the space where Julia had sat. I successfully cleaned up the champagne, but an ugly mess of saturated napkins remained heaped on the table as evidence of my ineptitude.

"You okay down there, Rookie?" Rich called down the table.

I could feel a dozen eyeballs on me.

I raised my voice to be heard over the noise of the bar. "Yeah. Everything's fine."

My words were a lie and the mountain of wasted napkins was evidence of that. I tried to catch the attention of the cocktail waitress who'd brought over the bottle of champagne so I could close my tab and escape the awkward situation before Julia returned, but she failed to look in my direction.

"You're not going to make me crawl across your lap, are you?" Julia towered over me. Her lips curved into a small frown.

I scrambled to my feet. The tops of my thighs bumped the table again as I stood up, causing our champagne glasses to wobble, but there was nothing left for me to spill. "I'm *so* sorry," I apologized again.

Julia dismissed me with a wave of her hand and maneuvered past me to return to her place at the table. "Don't worry about it. It's dark in here, and it's not like champagne stains."

"Can I get you another drink?" I offered.

"That depends. Do you plan on dumping this one down my cleavage, too?"

At her words, my eyes drifted to said cleavage. Her black cocktail dress dipped modestly in the front, but it revealed enough to keep my attention. When I realized I was openly staring at her chest, I jerked my eyes away. But it was too late; the smirk on her mouth said she'd caught me.

I waved a hand in the air, and sure enough, this time the waitress immediately saw the motion.

"What'll you have?"

"Dirty martini," Julia ordered. "Three olives."

"Um. Beer," I stumbled out unsophisticatedly.

"What kind?" the waitress asked.

"Surprise me?"

The waitress arched an eyebrow. "Sure thing."

She returned a few, painfully silent minutes later.

"Dirty martini," the cocktail waitress announced, setting Julia's drink down in front of her. "And ... a beer. Enjoy ladies."

I flashed a smile in thanks and the waitress left to check on her other tables.

Julia brought the funnel-shaped glass up to dark red lips. When she returned the drink to the table, her lipstick had left a stain on the glass's edge.

"I don't know how you can drink that stuff," I said, making a face. "Martinis are pure alcohol, aren't they?"

"And olives." She speared one of the olives at the bottom of her glass with a toothpick and sucked the salty fruit into her mouth. Once again I found my gaze drawn to her bee-stung lips, but it was better than me gawking at her breasts.

"I take it you're not picky about your alcohol?" she said, nodding to the beer bottle I worried between idle hands.

"Not really," I admitted. I fiddled with the bottle's paper label, shredding and peeling it out of nervousness. This woman was attractive enough that even without having spilled our drinks on her I would have been tongue tied.

"So what do you do?" I swallowed down a mouthful of whatever beer the waitress had brought me. It tasted like a lager—not my first choice—but I didn't care. It was wet, and it kept my tongue loosened.

"Besides get free drinks from strangers?" She ran an elegant finger along the edge of her martini glass. "I'm a lawyer."

"Wow." I took a second pull from my beer. "That's impressive." It wasn't a line. Anyone who used their brain instead of brute strength for their job was impressive to me.

"Perhaps." She tilted her head to the side. "But no more so

than being a police officer. Isn't that what your friend said you do?"

I nodded and looked down at my hands. I didn't bother telling her that I was no longer a cop with the city and that I was leaving town the very next morning for Bumble-fuck, Minnesota. There was no need to put an expiration date on the evening.

"Yeah. I graduated from the academy last year."

"And you enjoy it?"

I bobbed my head. "Uh huh. Serve and protect and all that." I mentally grimaced. It was just one lame string of sentences after the other. I might as well have been talking about the weather.

"Do you find it difficult being a female cop? I imagine you'd get backlash from some male officers as well as the public who think only men can do a good job."

"It has its challenges, for sure," I acknowledged, "but once you prove yourself, eventually they see you as just one of the guys."

Julia's lips pursed in thought. "Law school was like that, too. Women are still very much a minority in the profession. Plus, I went into criminal law, which is very much a male-dominated specialty. I always felt like I had to be the most prepared person in the room." She shook her head and laughed self-consciously. "I'm sorry. This sounds like a therapy session. I must be boring you."

Every word that came out of that gorgeous mouth was the most interesting thing I'd ever heard.

"I'm starting to feel this alcohol. I can hear myself rambling." She pushed her half-empty glass away. "And no one likes a drunk. It's not attractive."

"I don't think you have anything to worry about there," I said pointedly.

A ghost of a smile played on her painted mouth.

"I can relate though; it was like that when I was enlisted, too," I said. "I had a serious chip on my shoulder after boot camp. The

Marines say soldiers have no gender—we're just Marines—but my experience wasn't genderless at all."

"How long were you in the Marines?"

"Once a Marine, always a Marine." I flashed her a grin. "But I was active duty just shy of ten years."

Her eyebrows rose on her unlined forehead. "Ten years?" she echoed. "That's like half of your life."

"You might be a fancy lawyer, but you're not very good at math," I teased. "I'm twenty-eight." I always got carded when we went out. With my blonde wavy hair, dimples, and wide, toothy smile, I had a bit of a baby-face.

"Well thank goodness for that." Her laughter was like a drug. If given the chance, I'd soon be addicted to the sound. "I was worried I might be corrupting you."

I leaned perceptibly closer and lowered my voice. "I don't think I'd mind that at all."

It hit me all at once: I was pulling this off. I was holding my own, talking to a gorgeous woman; we might have even been flirting.

I didn't want our conversation to stop, but I had to go to the bathroom. I was so worried about the indelicacy of admitting to having a small bladder that for once I didn't worry about my physical awkwardness. My knees bumped the table as I stood up, knocking over our drinks.

Julia's gasp was audible when the drinks spilled across her lap and legs. *Again.*

One accident might have been forgivable, but two? Never.

I kept going without looking back or trying to help, forgetting about my need to use the bathroom, forgetting about my credit card and the open tab, and most definitely forgetting about the woman on whom I'd spilled four drinks.

~

The next morning came too soon. My head pounded and my stomach gurgled from mixing liquors the previous night. It was like a giant mixed cocktail of champagne, beer, and tequila sloshing around inside of my body. The morning sun was too bright, and I stumbled around my nearly empty apartment trying to find a pair of sunglasses that hadn't already been shipped up to Embarrass with the rest of my belongings.

My phone was full of missed calls and text messages from my friends, all worried where I'd disappeared to last night. I would have probably left town without returning anyone's calls, but Angie had left a message that she had my abandoned credit card and would continue to use it unless I came to pick it up.

Meeting up with Angie became my final stop before I left town. We met on a riverboat on the Mississippi River that doubled as a bar. It was more like a glorified double-decker pontoon boat, and the bottled beer was overpriced, but it offered a nice view of the city I was soon leaving. Having grown up in Minnesota, the murky Mississippi River was far from the prettiest waterscape I'd been witness to, but it was an open body of water, and when I'd been stationed in the middle of an ashtray, thousands of miles away, it had been what I'd missed the most about home.

To say that the years between 2004 and 2012 were an interesting time to be a soldier was an understatement at best. The country was fighting a multi-pronged war on terror, and as the memory of 9/11 became farther and farther in the rearview mirror, the war became increasingly unpopular with the people back home. Don't Ask, Don't Tell was repealed, and in July 2010 WikiLeaks released seventy-five thousand secret documents related to the United States and the war in Afghanistan.

I wasn't anything special in the Marines. I didn't go to officer school until after my first tour, and I wasn't doing one-handed pushups like Demi Moore in *G.I. Jane*. I'd signed up in 2004, straight out of high school, on an open contract. That meant the

Marines could put me wherever it needed an extra body. It hadn't mattered to me, though; I just wanted to get away. I wanted adventure. I wanted to get out of Minnesota.

I attended boot camp at Parris Island, just outside of Beaufort, South Carolina, as part of the Fourth Recruit Training Battalion. Although the Marines accepted both men and women, we were separated for training. The Island was gender segregated, but we received the same training: martial arts, close-order drill, pugil sticks, marksmanship, bayonet, gas mark, obstacle courses, rappelling, and combat water survival. I used to think about Swim Week of Phase Two of boot camp when I sat in desert sand so fine that it better resembled moon dust.

After boot camp, I spent two weeks in Marine Combat Training Battalion to learn things like communications, intelligence, electronic warfare, nuclear and biochemical defense, logistics, and vehicle repair. If I'd been a man, I would have gone to a fifty-two day Infantry Training to serve as a grunt: infantry, machine gunners, mortar men, assault, and antitank guided missile men.

Being a female in the Marines was akin to walking a tight rope. If you didn't hang out with the guys in your squad, you were a lesbian. If you palled around with the guys too much, however, you were a slut. The best I could hope for was to be thought of as their little sister.

My first tour was relatively unremarkable. My mosquito wings were freshly stitched on my uniform, and I was admittedly gungy —gung ho, but inexperienced. After witnessing the death of my first Marine, however, they stopped looking at me like a Wookie monster—a female Marine. I was simply a Marine. Sometimes being a woman in Afghanistan was problematic, especially when interacting with village elders. But other times, like when it came to defusing situations between Marines and local women, it came in handy.

I wasn't technically allowed to engage in direct combat until February 2012 when the Pentagon finally changed their ban on women in combat battalions. It was little more than a rubber-stamp of approval on a piece of paper though. I'd been serving as a signal officer through a loophole that allowed me to be attached to a combat unit. A few months later, however, we started to withdraw from the country.

Being a Marine meant working until a job or objective had been completed as expected. At the time, I'd found it ironic that the President was removing troops from Afghanistan. The job wasn't finished. And in my opinion, it hadn't been done the right way.

After my second tour came to an end, I briefly entertained the plan of becoming a Marine security guard for an embassy or consulate. But in the end, I decided to go back to America and be with my family. Marine security guards typically served three rounds of twelve-month long tours. After another three years in the military, I would have been thirty, and I wanted to start the rest of my life before then.

When I ended my service with the Marines, I came home to a hero's welcome. Signs all over town welcomed me back. I even got a parade down Main Street. I'd sat on the back on some stranger's red Corvette convertible like a goddamn beauty queen who wore Marine dress blues instead of a prom dress. There had been a nauseating amount of tiny American flags in the crowd, all stiffly waving as the car carrying me drove by. Kids ran into the streets with their hands on their hips, expecting candy. It was supposed to be a parade, after all. The town did everything short of giving me a key to the city and declaring it Cassidy Miller Day.

During my two tours abroad I'd returned to St. Cloud occasionally, but being back for good was different. Nothing looked the same to my eighteen-year-old self. The only thing relatively unchanged was my parents' house and my childhood bedroom.

VCRs had been replaced with DVD players and tube television sets had been exchanged for flat screens, but that same hideous brown carpet still covered the floor.

I hadn't believed that coming back after all that time in a war zone would be easy, but I'd underestimated the real difficulties of transitioning back to civilian life. War is hell, but the aftermath is endless.

I parked my bike in the small paved parking lot adjacent to the riverboat bar and climbed up the stairs to the second level. Angie was already at a table with a beer in front of her when I showed up.

"You're alive," she observed. She wore sunglasses on the overcast day, which told me how the rest of her night had gone.

I sat down in a plastic lawn chair across from her. "Yeah, I'm sorry about last night."

Angie lifted her sunglasses to her forehead and rubbed at her temples. "Who bails on their own going away party?"

"I know. I'm sorry," I apologized again.

"What are you drinking?" She waved down the bartender. Normally there wasn't table service at a bar like this, but we were the only people on the boat so the bartender made an exception.

"I'm good," I declined the offer. "I've got a long drive ahead of me today."

"You can have one beer. Besides, I'm buying." She pulled out a dark blue credit card, which I recognized as my own.

"Thanks for taking care of that. It saves me the hassle of having to cancel the card." I took the charge card back and returned it to my wallet. "What'd I miss last night?"

"Rich went home with one of those chicks," Angie snorted.

I immediately bristled. My reaction didn't go unnoticed.

"Not your fancy broad, Miller," she reassured. "He's not *that* classless. Besides, she basically clammed up the moment you took off."

"Really?" I didn't know why that information felt so satisfying.

"Also, I may have bought another round with your card." Angie smiled sheepishly. "Sorry."

"It's okay," I dismissed. "That's my punishment for ditching you guys."

"Why *did* you leave?" she pressed.

"I just needed to get out of there."

It was a vague excuse, but my pride wouldn't let me admit the depth of my awkwardness. Besides, it didn't matter anymore. I was leaving the city shortly and chances were I was never going to see that woman again.

Chapter Two

The wheels of my Harley-Davidson Sportster spit up wet gravel as I cruised down the lonely northern Minnesotan county highway. The bike hugged the center double line as I put more and more distance between the Twin Cities and myself. A motorcycle was an impractical vehicle for northern Minnesotan winters, but spring was starting to fade into summer, not that Mother Nature ever paid attention to days on the calendar.

The town was a speck on the map, nestled between national and state parks, about a three and a half-hour's drive north of Minneapolis. A wooden sign that looked like it had been made in a high school woodshop class welcomed me as I rolled into town: *Embarrass, Minnesota. The Cold Spot.*

I tugged at the collar of my leather jacket. The words on the sign hadn't been an empty boast. The bike ride had left me chilled to the bone. A dense fog clung in the sky, making the sleepy town more reminiscent of a costal city than its Midwestern location. It wasn't much past the dinner hour, but the sun had disappeared for the day about halfway into my trip.

I parked my bike in front of a Victorian-style house whose signage indicated it served as a bed and breakfast. It was the first place I saw on my drive into the city limits, so I took a gamble that it would be cheap but bug-free. I could have kept going, but I didn't have much faith that I'd find something better the farther into town I drove. I'd been on the bike for long enough. I just wanted a hot meal and an even hotter shower.

My plan was to stay at the bed and breakfast for only the night. I'd stayed on with Angie longer than I'd originally intended, and I didn't want to bother the town's chief of police at this hour. I would contact him in the morning to get settled. All I had on me was whatever I could fit into the saddlebags on my motorcycle. The majority of my belongings had arrived ahead of me and were sitting in boxes in the rental unit Chief Hart had procured. I was thankful that he'd arranged housing for me; I'd discovered soon after I'd accepted the job that apartments were a rare commodity in the unincorporated town. My sense of Embarrass was a village from which people rarely moved.

A bell rang overhead when I pushed open the front door of the Embarrass Bed & Breakfast. I flared my nostrils; there was a peculiar scent of potpourri or dying roses in the air. It was unpleasant, but it could have been worse. I would get used to the stench eventually, or it would get stuck up my nose.

The inner décor of the Victorian home was like being sucked into a time warp. But instead of turn-of-the-century antiques, the bed and breakfast was filled with artifacts from World War II. Big band music piped in from some unknown location. Old sheet music sat on an upright piano. A worn couch upholstered in imitation velvet was covered with a mountain of Easter Sunday bonnets, and a hand-painted sign announced tea time on Tuesday afternoons. Everything looked a little run down, but at least it was clean.

There was no one at the front desk, so I rang a bell for

service. A small woman in a long jean skirt and white turtleneck walked out from a previously undisclosed location. Her hair was long and dark with grey streaks running through it, and it looked like it had never seen a brush or scissors in her lifetime. When she came closer I saw an embroidered cross on the collar of her turtleneck.

"What can I do for you?" Even from such a small sampling, I heard the thick northern Minnesotan accent.

"I'd like a room. The sign out front said you had vacancies."

The woman laughed at an unvoiced joke. "*Every* room is vacant. It's not tourist season, ya know. How long will you need the room for?" she asked.

"Just tonight."

She pulled out a guest book. "And how will you be paying?"

"Uh, credit card?" The words came out as a question because I had no idea if this place even accepted credit cards.

She pulled out one of those imprinting machines and a multi-layered invoice and filled out the duplicate paperwork while I continued to take in my surroundings. There were kitschy signs hanging on the walls of the lobby, mostly Bible verses.

"Have you owned this place long?" I asked, making idle conversation.

"Long enough. My husband and I took over ownership in 1999."

She returned my credit card and the receipt for the room charge. "I'll be at Mass tomorrow morning, so I won't be here to make you breakfast unless you'd like to wait until I'm back."

"No, that won't be necessary."

"Or you could come to church, too," she suggested. "Mass starts at 9:00 a.m. at the Lutheran church."

"I, uh, I've got to get in contact with Larry Hart in the morning. I don't think I'll have time to make it to church." I wasn't a religious person, and I hoped that wouldn't be a problem in this town.

"What business do you have with the chief of police?" the woman asked.

"I just got hired. I'm the new police officer."

The suspicious look on her face turned into brightened recognition. "Oh! Why didn't you say so? I would have given you a really nice discount on the room."

I looked at the scribbled out bill. She'd only charged me forty-five dollars. I couldn't image anything more discounted than that. "No, this is really fine," I insisted. "You needn't go to that trouble."

She looked like she wanted to argue with me, but she pressed her lips together instead. She handed me a single key and pointed in the direction of a spiral staircase at the front of the house. "Upstairs, last door on the left."

The green carpet was worn like the rest of the interior. I followed it up the twisted stairs, my duffle bag in hand, until I reached my designated room. The key stuck in the lock, and I had to wiggle it until the unlocking mechanism popped free. Inside my rented room the carpeting ended, giving way to dark wooden floors. A queen-sized bed covered with a flowered quilt dominated the modest bedroom and a thin area rug struggled to cover the floor. There was a bookshelf against one wall, stacked high with paperback novels, and a wooden bureau upon which a ceramic pitcher and washbasin had been placed.

I shrugged out of my leather jacket and dropped it on the floor along with my duffle bag. "Thank God," I sighed. The bed beckoned to me, but not as loudly as the porcelain claw-footed tub I found in the connected bathroom.

I shut myself away in the privacy of the bathroom, not trusting that the proprietress wouldn't let herself into my room to leave milk and cookies. I twisted my long, blonde waves into a sloppy bun set high on my scalp and stripped out of dark jeans, cotton top, and mismatched undergarments. When I was in Marines, I'd kept my hair cut just above my shoulders. Females weren't expected to get the same cranial amputation haircut male Marines received at the beginning of boot camp, but I usually tamed my hair into a tight bun like other young female Marines. Now that I was a civilian, I'd let it grow longer.

I inspected the lean, hard lines of my naked body in the full-length dressing mirror on the back of the bathroom door. Nearly a decade of service in the United States Marine Corps had transformed my body from a skinny, awkward teen to the finely muscled woman who stared back at me. I observed the teenage gap between my thighs and settled my palms flat against the swimmer-v on my lower torso that I had maintained long after my high school swim team years. I twisted to the side to regard my profile. My hips were narrow, too boyish I thought, but small, upturned breasts that sat high on my chest in proportion to the rest of my body were evidence of my femininity.

I turned off the bathtub faucet when I deemed the level high enough. First one foot and then the other, as I gingerly sat down in water just a few degrees too hot. My body would acclimate, and it wouldn't be long until the water became too cool. I sat up in the tub, thighs splayed apart, water dripping from my fingertips. Humid air curled the hair at my temples and nape of my neck. I experimentally plugged up the silver faucet with my big toe, stemming the steady drip of the spigot.

The heat of the water penetrated my bones, alleviating the dull ache that the long bike ride had produced. I pushed damp tendrils that had worked their way free from my bun out of my eyes and ran my hand over my face. Eight years in the Marines and another year with the city of Minneapolis police department, but now I was banished to a bed and breakfast in northern Minnesota. In the morning, I would track down Chief Hart and get settled in my new apartment. I didn't know what to expect of my new responsibilities on the Embarrass police force, but anything had to be better than the paper pushing I'd been demoted to in the Twin Cities.

My fingers started to prune and the water had become too cool for comfort. I emerged from the bathtub, feeling moderately refreshed. After toweling my body dry, I checked my cell phone, which I'd left to recharge outside of the bathroom. I had a bevy of text messages from my friends, so wrote them each back a brief message to let them know I'd arrived at the northern outpost in one piece.

I pulled a pair of running shorts and an olive green T-shirt with the word Marines screen-printed across the chest from my duffle bag. I slipped into the clean, but wrinkled clothes, and then between stiff bed sheets. In the military my rack had been about seventy percent the size of a twin bed, forcing me to sleep at the position of attention. Getting to sleep on even a double-sized mattress as a civilian felt like a luxury. As I curled up on my side and shoved my hands beneath the lone down pillow, I wished for a dreamless sleep. I knew it was too much to ask; sleep itself would have to suffice.

~

Afghanistan, 2012

It's July in Afghanistan. My fair, Scandinavian skin has taken a beating these past few years. I used to never leave the house without sunscreen on. Now it's wasted space in my duffle bag. It's a dry heat, like my grandparents explain to us how they can handle the plus-one hundred degree temperatures in their retirement home in Arizona. At least I don't have to worry about trench foot or swamp ass in Afghanistan. It's a small comfort when you're driving down narrow streets, the buildings too tall on both sides and the places where snipers can perch too numerous. I've been at Quantico for the past few months, receiving training to be a communications officer. Then there were train-ups in the Middle East with port calls in Italy and in France. As a female Marine, the extra training is the only way I'll ever see real action and get off the forward operating base.

My second tour is as a member of Task Force Leatherneck in the Second Marine Expeditionary Brigade—Operation *Strike of the Sword* or Operation *Khanjar*—in the Helmand province in southern Afghanistan. Since 2001, Helmand has been considered to be a Taliban stronghold and one of the most dangerous provinces in the country. I'm just one of ten thousand Marines, part of Obama's surge in 2009 into the southern part of the nation.

I met Terrance Pensacola on the transport from the States. Like many other recruits, it's his first time out of the country and there's a nervous, but excited energy about him. Private First Class Pensacola is a black kid from Detroit. We shouldn't have any common ground, but we bond over our geographic similarities and our mutual hatred for the Chicago White Sox. He's bullet bait and gung ho, and I wonder how long it'll be before he realizes that this life is nothing like the movies.

Hurry up and wait—it's the unofficial motto of the armed forces. Pensacola and I play a game of spades. We play a whole lot of card games. Pensacola is a hell of a Euchre partner. If nothing else, I've gotten to be a really good card player in Afghanistan.

"You still glad you re-upped?" he asks me.

I'd submitted my reenlistment packet when my first four-year commitment was almost up. I didn't know what else to do.

I throw down a card. "Well, nothing I can do about it now."

My footsteps creaked down the wooden staircase the next morning. The ground floor was silent except for the ticking of a grandfather clock. The big band music from before had been turned off, and I found myself alone in the bed and breakfast. I still had yet to see the owner's husband, which made me suspicious that she'd made him up or that she had him locked away in the basement and only dusted him off when company came over.

My steps were light as I walked through the eerily quiet front parlor to the dining room. An old chandelier hung from the ceiling, and the floor was covered in the same worn, green carpeting that spanned the entirety of the first floor. Six chairs surrounded a rectangular wooden table, and a white, knitted doily covered the center panel of the polished furniture.

The proprietress had left a plate of still-warm blueberry muffins and a bowl of plain yogurt and granola on the dining room table for me. There was also a handwritten note saying that she'd gone to church, but that I should help myself to any other food I wanted in the kitchen pantry. I shook my head and took an over-sized bite of the muffin. If everyone was so trusting in this town, it was no wonder that Chief Hart needed more police officers. All it would take was one bad egg to corrupt an entire community.

I had to call Chief Hart this morning to receive further information about my future in Embarrass. But first I poured myself a cup of coffee, finished my yogurt and muffins, and enjoyed the near silence of my surroundings. That kind of peace was rare in a combat zone, and I'd learned not to take it for granted.

I found a kitchen attached to the dining room, and I rinsed my breakfast dishes and set them in the sink. The bed and breakfast proprietress had still not returned from church, so I went back to my room and packed up my things before calling the number I had for Chief Hart. I didn't know if he'd be at morning mass with the rest of town, but I could leave a message if no one answered.

A woman picked up after a few rings. "Hello?"

I had been mentally prepared to hear Larry Hart's gravelly voice, and for a moment I worried I'd dialed the wrong number. "Hi, uh, is Chief Hart around?"

"If this is police business," she said sternly, "you should call City Hall."

"No, uh, this is Cassidy Miller. He said I should call when I got into town."

"Cassidy!" The woman's tone immediately brightened. "I'm sorry, dear, I didn't recognize your voice. This is Marilyn. It's been so long."

Marilyn was Chief Hart's wife. Although I hadn't seen her in years, I only had fond memories of the older woman.

"How are you?" she asked. "Did you just get into town?"

"Last night, but it was late. I didn't want to bother you guys."

"Oh, nonsense," she chided. "You're family; you can call whenever."

"Uh, is the Chief available? Or should I call back later?"

"Oh right," she laughed. "You've got official business to discuss and here I am talking your ear off. Let me go get Larry."

I heard her call for her husband, and there was a brief rustling noise as the phone exchanged hands before I heard a man clear his throat. "Larry Hart here."

"Hey Chief, it's Cassidy Miller."

"Cassidy!" I could hear the smile in his voice. "I was expecting your call last night. I was about to put an APB out when I didn't hear from you."

"I got in late last night," I explained. "I didn't want to bother you at home."

"Don't ever worry about that, Cassidy. You call whenever," he echoed his wife's earlier sentiments.

"I was hoping I could get the keys to my apartment today?" The question made me uncomfortable like I was putting him out even though housing was provided for in my new contract.

"Of course. My sergeant, David Addams, is on duty today. He should be hanging out at the police station and can give you the keys to the apartment. If no one's there, call the non-emergency number and he'll meet up with you at City Hall. I'd do it myself, but Marilyn has me roped into playing Bridge with her and some other couples later today. Stop by City Hall tomorrow morning and we'll get you officially set up."

"Sounds great," I said. "I'll see you in the morning."

The police station was located in the basement of City Hall. The three-story, cream-city brick building stuck out among the more modest storefronts on Main Street. The primary entrance was locked because it was Sunday, but I found an alternate door that led directly to the police department in an alley between City Hall and the next-door dentist office. Only a small metal sign with an arrow and the word "Police" indicated I'd found the right place.

My first impression of the police department wasn't flattering. The air felt heavy like rain had recently flooded the basement or ground water had worked its way up through a storm drain in the concrete floor. There was a peculiar scent to the place like burned coffee and motor oil. It reminded me of being at a car mechanic, not a police station.

If it weren't for the small, rectangular windows that dotted the parameter of the walls near the ceiling, no natural light would have reached the sublevel department. Instead, overhead halogen panels ran seamlessly with the drop ceiling and illuminated the space with an unnatural yellow glow.

I knocked on a frosted glass cutout in an old wooden door, and it noisily swung open.

A man who looked no older than myself sat behind a reception desk. He wore a dark brown uniform shirt and pressed pants a shade lighter. He leaned back in his chair with his chunky black boots on top of the desk. His high and tight haircut suggested he'd been military once, but I wasn't ready to swap war stories.

"Can I help you?"

"Are you David Addams?"

"Guilty."

His smile was disarming, and when he brought his arms up to cradle the back of his head so he could lean back even farther in the office chair, I noticed he wore no wedding band. A lot of guys left the jewelry at home when they were on duty, but I sensed that this man was probably Embarrass, Minnesota's most-eligible bachelor.

"I'm Cassidy Miller." It struck me how many times I'd had to say my name already just that morning. But this was only the beginning. I was in a new town full of unfamiliar faces. I'd have to introduce myself a hundred times over.

He dropped his feet off of the desk, and his boots hit the floor with a solid rubber noise. "*You're* Cassidy Miller?"

I raised an eyebrow. "Last time I checked, why?" His reaction had me feeling self-conscious. I smoothed down the front of my wrinkled T-shirt beneath my leather jacket.

"I'm sorry." He shook his head. "When Chief Hart said he'd hired a female police officer to take night shift, I wasn't expecting you'd..." he trailed off.

"Look like a girl?" I finished for him.

He flashed me another boyishly charming smile. "That's pretty horrible of me, right?"

I returned his even smile. "Don't worry; I won't hold it against you." I tended to baulk at stereotypes, but even I'd observed that femininity was a rare commodity in the armed forces and the police academy.

David stood up. "So are you stopping by to check the place out?"

"Kind of." I gave the department another cursory sweep. "Chief Hart said I could get the keys to my apartment?"

"Oh, right." He opened a desk drawer and rummaged around before producing two house keys on a metal ring. "Here you go."

"Thanks." I palmed the gold-colored keys and shoved them into the pocket of my leather jacket. "Think you could point me in the right direction? I have no idea where anything is in this town."

David slapped his hand to his forehead. "Sorry. You must think I'm really thick. Go back the way you came," he said, pointing at the exit, "and take a right out the door. The apartment is in the brick building across the street. You'll see the signs. Can't miss it."

I bobbed my head in thanks. I turned to leave and heard his parting words just before I reached the stairs.

"Welcome to Embarrass, Cassidy Miller."

My new studio apartment was located above the town's Laundromat. The brick building was two stories with three apartments—A, B, and C—occupying the second floor. A short stairwell instead of an elevator led up to the apartments from a private alley entrance. There was another entrance through the Laundromat, but the landlady who owned the building and lived in apartment A kept that door locked to keep her customers from wandering upstairs.

The door to apartment C was swollen, requiring a little finesse to unlock the deadbolt to gain entrance. Only a few feet from the door were my packing boxes, piled in tidy stacks like adult-sized building blocks. Since I'd enlisted upon graduating high school, and between multiple tours in Afghanistan and bouncing from one military base to the next, I hadn't accumulated much more than what could fit into the saddlebags of my Harley. My civilian

31

wardrobe was similarly basic, having spent the majority of my adult life in a uniform.

The apartment came fully furnished, but the provided furniture was spartan. The layout was open with one of those folding screens to partition off the bedroom area from the rest of the apartment. The wood floors were scuffed and in need of a fresh sanding and layer of varnish. The windows were similarly old; white paint peeled up from the sills and the single panes of glass shuddered with every brisk gust of wind. It would probably feel like a greenhouse in the summer with the sun beating in through the southern exposure windows, and there was no air conditioner in sight. Three brick walls would make it nearly impossible to hang anything up—not that I had anything to hang.

The only drywall was in the kitchen area, which consisted of a single sink, refrigerator, oven, minimal counter space, and a small kitchen island with two stools that doubled as the dining room table. In the front foyer there was one narrow closet that would have to serve as storage for both my wardrobe and my belongings. I found the bathroom to be small, but functional: toilet, sink, and stand-up shower. There would be no more baths for me.

The living room was an easy chair and an old tube television propped on a milk crate. I dropped my duffle bag on the dark red chair. There was probably room for a grander living room or a proper dining room, but I had no talent for furniture arrangement or interior design.

I pulled out my phone and frowned at the "E" in the top left-hand corner—no internet—my apartment was a dead zone. Unless I foot the bill for my own hook-up, I'd have to go to the public library or the office to check my e-mail and search for porn.

I turned on the television and discovered it got all the local cable channels. I stopped flipping the channels when I found the Twins playing a double-header. At least I wouldn't be totally isolated up here.

Chapter Three

S ince I hadn't had time to go grocery shopping, and without reliable wireless service, I had to trust local word-of-mouth to find someplace for breakfast the next morning. The reed-thin, grey-haired man shuffling down Main Street walking his equally skinny dog assured me that everyone went to Stan's 24-hour diner. It was one of those old-fashioned drive-in joints with only a few tables; most people sat around the dozen and a half stools that hugged a huge, curved countertop. A flattop grill dominated the center of the restaurant where a man, who I assumed was Stan, made your food while you watched.

I settled down on a vacant stool situated between two older men. The man to my right had his eyes closed, and if not for the way the coarse hairs of his mustache fluttered with each exhale, I would have worried he had died in the middle of breakfast. The man on my left peeled a hardboiled egg with impressive dexterity as if he'd done it every morning of his life.

I ordered French toast and coffee from a waitress who stared at me like she was trying to look under my skin. It was obvious that people in Embarrass knew each other. I was a stranger, and I could see the curiosity and distrust in people's stares.

"You're not from around here."

I twisted on my stool to regard Mr. Hard-Boiled Egg. His light brown eyes squinted in contemplation.

"No, sir. I'm not."

"I'm Franklyn Walker," he said, grabbing my hand and giving it a hearty shake.

"Cassidy Miller," I returned. I eased my hand out of his tight grip. "I just got hired on with the police department."

"Police, eh?" He widened his toothy grin. "I used to be the Circuit Court judge, but now I'm one of those retirees. Last vestibule of royalty in society, I've always said. How many other people get called 'Your Honor?'"

"That's a good point, sir."

Franklyn Walker was one of those people who told you his life story within the first few minutes of meeting him. "I'm too old to have secrets anymore," he explained to me. He was small in build and easily excitable.

His wife, Deborah, perched beside him, was quiet and quick to roll her eyes. She seemed to balance out his over-exuberance. They'd been married for fifty years, and Franklyn wore that fact like a badge of honor.

When I asked if they had any kids, he said they did, but he claimed he didn't know how many. "I mostly saw them in the rearview mirror on family road trips," he told me. "That was back in the day before everyone flew everywhere. We had a station wagon with two back bench seats. I never could keep track of them all. Things have changed, but not always for the better," he continued on. "Now you get frisked every time you wanna get on an airplane."

"Frank," his wife scolded. "Leave the poor girl alone. She came here for breakfast, not to have her ear talked off."

"I like meeting new people," Franklyn defended himself. "Everyone I know is either buried in the Catholic cemetery or they've moved to Florida."

The bell above the diner door rang with the entrance of a new customer. I glanced briefly in the direction of the sound, and the French toast nearly fell out of my mouth.

It was her. The woman from the Minneapolis club.

"Coffee to go, please."

God, that voice.

Franklyn had fallen silent with the woman's entrance. He'd greeted everyone who walked in with a boisterous good morning and a comment about the weather or how good he thought the high school football team would be that season. But he said nothing to the raven-haired woman as she waited for her coffee.

I tried to stare as unobtrusively as possible. She was even more flawless in the light of day. Her grey trench coat was cinched at her small waist and obscured my view of most of her body. I let my gaze travel down the nylon stems of her legs to her black stilettos that probably cost more than my entire wardrobe.

My attention swept back up her body to her face, and I nearly choked when I realized she'd caught me staring. My throat constricted. Did she recognize me? Or had she forgotten about the clumsy girl who'd dumped multiple drinks on her dress?

She tucked a sweep of jet black hair behind an ear to reveal a pearl earring. Her caramel-colored eyes narrowed just slightly as if she was trying to make sense of my face. It was a look that said I was familiar, but she didn't know how. The club had been dark, and I was sure I looked different to her in daylight. She, however, looked just as beautiful, if not more so.

"Coffee's up." Stan set a lidded cardboard cup on the counter-top, breaking the woman's silent effort to figure out who I was. She placed a five-dollar bill on the counter and gave Stan a tight-lipped smile in thanks. She glanced once more in my direction before leaving. The bell over the diner entrance jangled with her exit.

I took one more sip from my coffee and pulled a ten-dollar bill out of my wallet. I tossed the money on the countertop and left my breakfast half-eaten and forgotten. I might not have been able to confront her in the diner, but that didn't mean I was going to let her walk away without a word. I didn't believe in coincidences.

After a quick goodbye to Franklyn and Deborah Walker, I left Stan's and paused on the concrete sidewalk out front. I looked left and then right. The city was starting to wake up; it was busier than when I'd shown up for breakfast, but I saw no sign of the dark-haired woman. I almost questioned if I'd imagined seeing her. Maybe my flashbacks had expanded beyond the desert war zone to include my most recent embarrassing moments.

My digital watch beeped with the new hour. I'd have to look for my mystery woman later; Chief Hart would be expecting me soon. I had her first name, but there was no way of knowing if the name she'd given me at the club was real. But it was a small town, and I was a good cop. I slipped on my aviators and smiled.

I stood in front of City Hall and looked up. The early morning sun was already high in the sky, and it backlit the cream-city brick building. City Hall was the tallest building in town, but at three stories, it didn't exactly dominate the skyline. My stomach was tight. Picking up the keys to my new apartment hadn't made me anxious, but reporting to City Hall for my first official day of work was different. It was close to the anxiety I'd felt when I'd been dropped off in the middle of the night with my recruit class at Parris Island for boot camp. This was real. This was really happening. I was going to do this thing.

I climbed the five concrete steps that led up to a set of glass double doors. The main entrance opened up to a high-ceilinged rotunda. Three skylights allowed natural light into the atrium. I absently rubbed at my bare arms, instantly regretting not bringing my leather jacket. City Hall was aggressively air conditioned even though the late spring weather outside remained unseasonably mild.

The second and third floors were visible through the carved out center of the building, and a dark wooden banister ran along the perimeter of the higher levels. People milled around, but the volume level was subdued. They talked in low tones and their shoes squeaked on the same white speckled laminate I'd seen the day before in the police department.

I inspected a sign that provided directions to the various offices housed in the building. Only the police department was located in the basement; the higher the floor, the higher the title and pay grade. On the top floor was the office of the Mayor, William J. Desjardin, and the county courtroom.

I took the center staircase down to the basement and police station. A woman about my mom's age sat at the desk where David Addams had been the previous day. Her desk phone rang just as I approached. She smiled at me and held up a finger for me to wait. "Good morning, Embarrass Police Department. This is Lori."

I rocked back and forth on my heels while I waited for her to finish her phone call.

Just beyond the departmental assistant's desk was a closed door with the word "Chief" stenciled onto its surface. As I stared, the door opened, and a large man rumbled out. I couldn't see beyond him as his massive frame took up the entire doorway.

His blond hair was thinner than I remembered and there were deep-set wrinkles between a pair of icy blue eyes. He wore a police uniform—brown shirt with golden yellow accents and tan pants. His large belly fell over his duty belt, and he wore nondescript black shoes that probably left scuffs on the laminate floor much to the custodian's chagrin. In the brown uniform he reminded me of a bear.

"Cassidy Miller!" Chief Laurence Hart had a booming voice—the kind that people in positions of authority always seemed to have. Two thick arms pulled me in for a back-cracking hug, and I found myself being lifted off my feet. The toes of my boots barely touched the ground.

Chief Hart and my dad had been best friends growing up together in St. Cloud. After high school, he had gotten his Associate's Degree in criminal justice at St. Cloud State and my dad had gone to work for the city, eschewing college altogether. Despite their different post-high school career paths, they'd kept in touch over the years. Chief Hart and his wife, Marilyn, had been a fixture at holiday get-togethers, but I hadn't seen the man since my high school graduation. I wondered what he made of me now.

He returned me to the floor and held me at arm's length. "Let me get a good look at you. I hardly recognized you. You're all grown up."

I ducked my head. "Yeah, it happens."

He smiled in a very paternal way. "I feel like the last time I saw you, you were running around your parents' backyard, grass stains on your knees, hair a mess, with a permanent Kool-aid mustache."

I ruffled my wild, blonde curls. "Well, the hair part hasn't changed much," I laughed.

"How's your old man?"

"He's good," I confirmed. "Enjoying retirement and driving my mom crazy."

"Hah!" The Chief let out a belly laugh. "Good for him."

Lori, the departmental secretary, hung up the phone. "Larry, that was Mayor Desjardin. He wants to see you when you have a minute."

Chief Hart bobbed his head. "Sure thing. Oh, Lori, this is

Cassidy. She's our new officer. Cassidy, this is Lori. It may say 'chief' on my office door, but she's the one who runs the place." He laughed again, loud and jolly.

Lori Stenson was a petite woman with short blonde curls tight against her scalp. She wore a white cardigan draped over her shoulders because of the highly refrigerated air. She looked a few years away from retirement, and had a warm, inviting smile like she'd just baked a homemade pie. I was sure her maternal presence had cooled down more than one hot-headed or disgruntled citizen —the police department's first line of defense.

"You met David yesterday," Chief Hart noted, "so that's pretty much everyone who works down here in the dungeon. We can go upstairs and I'll introduce you to a few more people you'll see around and be working with."

"Sounds good." A nervous stirring rumbled in my stomach. More new people.

"Oh! But before that." He pulled a set of keys from a corkboard on the wall. "Your keys and badge, Detective."

I pocketed the heavy ring of keys, but I paused to stare at my new Embarrass Police Department badge. The golden disk was nestled in a square leather holder attached to a silver beaded neck chain. "Detective?"

"Technically you're low woman on the totem pole beneath myself and Sergeant Addams, so I should be starting you out as an Officer. But the sad truth is we've got a minuscule budget. I was only able to convince the City Council that we needed a third officer if I promised them it wouldn't cost any money to the city. I was able to get some federal funding for your salary, but it's basically a living stipend so you can feed yourself. The Mayor's office is chipping in to pay for the apartment."

My mind spun with these new details. I hadn't even thought to ask about salary or benefits when I'd accepted the job. I'd just needed to get out of Minneapolis. That was benefit enough.

Chief Hart shook his head. "I'm sorry, Cassidy. I don't even have extra uniforms we could get refitted because you're ..." he gestured to my body, "and I'm ..." He waved his hands in front of his generous belly.

"And Detectives aren't uniformed police officers," I said, putting the pieces together.

He nodded. "On the bright side, you'll only have to share a squad car with one other person. You'll get your gun when you're officially on duty, and I'll see about getting you a duty belt that'll fit that tiny waist of yours," he chuckled. "Everything we've got would be like a hula hoop on you. Didn't they feed you in the military?"

I worried my lower lip. I could still remember the day I'd received my MARPAT digital camouflage. I had been nearly as excited as the day I'd earned my Eagle, Globe, and Anchor emblem at boot camp graduation. Not having a uniform shouldn't have bothered me. I'd spent enough of my life in uniform between the Marines and my time with the Minneapolis police. But I was an outsider in Embarrass, and without a proper uniform, I knew I'd continue to feel like a fish out of water.

"You'll be working third shift, 10:00 p.m. to 6:00 a.m.," Chief Hart continued. "You're really free to do what you want during those hours as long as you're available if a call comes in. We can set it up so calls to the station are forwarded to your cell phone during your shift."

"Who worked nights before me?" I asked.

"We had some kid fresh out of the academy for a bit, but he left to take a job elsewhere. Since then, David and I have been taking turns to cover third shift, but to be honest, it's a small town, Cassidy. Not a lot happens around here compared to the Twin Cities. You might get some calls from one of the bars about a patron who's been over-served or maybe some domestic calls after the Vikings lose," he chuckled, "but other than that, it's a glorified babysitting job." His tone was apologetic. "I hope you're still interested."

"I am," I cut him off before he could try to talk me out of it. "And I'm so very thankful for the opportunity, Chief."

He rubbed at the back of his freshly shaved neck. "Our families go back a long time, Cassidy. I'm just happy that I'm in a position to help you get through this."

My smile wavered. I hated feeling like a charity case or damaged goods. "I think I'll take a look around town and kind of get the lay of the land," I announced in a voice that sounded too cheerful. "You want me to come back at 10:00 p.m. tonight?"

"No, no. There's no rush. Take the night off, and we'll start fresh in the morning. I'll show you around a little more and then maybe have you do a ride along with Addams. Then, if you're feeling comfortable, we can start you on night shift for real on Wednesday or Thursday. Sound good?"

"That's perfect, Chief. Thank you."

"Great. I'll see you back here tomorrow afternoon. Enjoy your evening, Cassidy," he smiled. "It'll be your last night of freedom for a while."

I cracked open my second beer of the night and flopped down in the overstuffed chair in the living room. I patted at my distended stomach, feeling full and satisfied. The evidence of my unhealthy splurge was a greasy pizza box on the kitchen island. I promised myself to make a concerted effort to go to the grocery store the next day and buy something besides a six-pack of beer. For now, the Twins were on my television, and I had plans to watch the game and maybe get to bed early.

I looked away from the scoreless game when I heard a knock at my door. I set my open beer can on the floor and padded cautiously towards the sound. There wasn't a peephole, so I was forced to open the door without knowing who was on the other side. It was disorienting, like answering a landline with no Caller ID.

Standing in the hallway was the woman from the bar on my last night in Minneapolis—the same woman I'd seen at Stan's diner that morning.

My eyes widened in surprise.

"You and I have some unfinished business to attend to," she announced.

Strong, yet feminine hands fisted the material of my T-shirt and, despite me being taller, I found myself being walked backwards. She lunged forward and crushed her mouth against mine. I didn't have time to question the motives or reasons behind any of this. My brain knew enough not to over-think why there was a gorgeous woman pressing me against a brick wall and applying sweet pressure to my neck among hungry kisses.

Hands toyed with the bottom hem of my T-shirt before the top was yanked up and over my head and tossed to the floor.

The raven-haired woman separated long enough to sweep her eyes around the studio apartment. "Charming," she murmured.

Before I could muster a response, those painted lips were once again crushed against mine.

I fumbled only briefly with the small buttons at the front of her blouse. I popped the shirt open, one pearly white button at a time. When the last button had been freed, I tugged the bottom hem of the dress shirt out of her knee-length pencil skirt. The less-than-careful action drew a narrow-eyed look from her, which made me wonder if she'd ever been handled any less delicately than an expensive porcelain doll.

When I'd dealt with the last stubborn button and pushed her shirt off her shoulders, my reward was the flat plane of her stomach. I raked short nails down her pale, olive flesh. The black lacy bra, which had remained hidden beneath her white Oxford shirt, made my mouth go dry. It wasn't so much the bra that affected me, but the twin, perky breasts beneath the flimsy material. I palmed their slight weight in my hands and lightly squeezed the firm yet supple flesh. Her nipples hardened and pebbled, branding the center of my palms. But even the delicate layer of lace was too much distance between my hands and her unblemished skin. I slipped my hands beneath the underwire and bit back my own moan at the silken sensation of my hands against her skin.

A greedy feeling swept over me; I had to see all of this woman. *Now.* I had to feel all of her.

I abandoned her breasts to find the hidden zipper of the pencil skirt wrapped tightly around her narrow hips. She was a small woman, but not waifishly designed. I could tell she was fit, but it was an athleticism that came from yoga or Pilates or whatever exercises rich women did, not climbing up cargo nets or crawling under barbed wire in watery mud.

I lowered the zipper of her skirt and let gravity do the job as it fell to pool at her ankles. She stepped out of her high heels and out of the skirt, lowering herself in height by a few inches. I swept my eyes appreciatively across her near-naked form. She wore only her underwear and the sexiest garters I'd ever laid eyes on. I didn't think women actually wore those anymore, except in my fantasies. The grey sheer nylons stopped mid-thigh where they connected to the simple black garters. The flimsy French-cut panties were a little old fashioned for me, like a high-priced call girl from the 1980s, but on her they were magnificent.

With her now barefoot, we no longer saw eye-to-eye, but the unspoken challenge remained in her vibrant eyes and the knowing smirk never left her twisted mouth.

Her hands rested on the front of my jeans and she toyed with the metal button. She wasn't struggling to unfasten my pants; she was teasing me as if contemplating whether she wanted to unwrap a present or not. Her eyes never left mine. She gave a mighty tug and the unforgiving denim dug into me. My breath hitched, but I wasn't going to give her more than that. But I knew if she continued to dally, I'd be forced to take matters into my own hands.

She finally unbuttoned my jeans and slid the zipper down. I let her take her time as she peeled tight denim down my hips and thighs. It would have been faster and more efficient if I'd done it myself, but the pads of her fingers were exquisite on my skin as she worked those jeans down my legs.

Left only in my bra and underwear, I could have waited to see if she'd strip me of more, but I was too impatient to get my hands and mouth all over her. I felt like a racehorse in its corral, waiting for the starting bell.

With a simple movement, my hands were behind the crook of her knees, and I was lifting her off the ground. She made a surprised noise that I was able to carry her with limited effort, and her hands flew to the back of my neck and shoulders to stabilize herself as I carried her the few feet to the bed I'd only slept in once.

I was thankful I'd taken the time to wash my bedding before I'd packed it up. The sweet smell of laundry soap filled my nostrils as I laid her down on the bed and scrambled to hover over her. Soon it would be the scent of our conjoined arousal that perfumed the air.

I kissed along her rippled torso. I couldn't imagine the exercise and self-discipline required to achieve such perfection. My mouth found hers again, and my thigh came to rest between her legs. I ground against her and she moaned into my open mouth. She met each thrust of my muscled thigh with her own, and the noises coming out of her beautiful mouth and the sound of her labored breathing had me galloping toward my own release.

As painfully arousing as the sight of the garters were, I had no idea what to do with them. I reached between our bodies and slid her underwear to the side. She was shaved everywhere except for a closely cropped landing strip. I stroked my fingers over smooth, naked skin and through short, coarse hair while she arched into the touch.

Two fingers found their way inside of her, and I ground the heel of my palm into her clit. She released another delicious, throaty groan as I pushed deeper inside. It was about as intimate as a public restroom fuck with her still half-clothed and me more so, but I wasn't going to mount a protest.

Her palms slammed hard against my shoulder blades, and for a moment I thought she was going to make me stop. But those fingers curled around my shoulders, and she pulled me down tighter against her so our breasts crushed together.

Her hips kept jerking and bucking erratically, making it hard for me to find a rhythm. I pulled away, still on my knees on the mattress, and pressed my free hand flat against her lower abdomen while my other hand furiously pistoned in and out of her. Her mouth fell open and her eyes screwed shut. I could still feel the movements of her hips beneath me, but I was able to keep her pinned to the mattress.

Despite my physical fitness, my right bicep began to burn. Each hard thrust brought a grunt to my lips from exertion. Her cries had become more desperate and high-pitched, and she tightened around my fingers. Her hand shot out and she clutched my right arm, silently urging for just a little more. I wasn't sure I would outlast her orgasm, but I threw my own comfort to the side and focused on getting her off. I licked my thumb on the hand that had been holding her down and swiped it across her clit.

She jerked hard into me once more. "I'm cumming," she gasped.

It was the first time she'd spoken since the initial crush of lips unless you counted a heavy sigh or a slipped profanity or celestial praise.

She held tightly to my upper arms as she rode out her orgasm. I couldn't resist, so I swooped in for another kiss. Our tongues battled for dominance while her thighs quivered around my hand. I stayed inside of her until her legs stopped shaking. It was only then when I withdrew and collapsed beside her.

I was obviously hoping for some reciprocation, but I was too exhausted to say so. My lungs felt like I'd climbed a mountain, not just had furious sex with a beautiful woman. I was in shape, but I supposed that sex worked a different set of muscles than running did. I would just need more practice, I thought with a satisfied grin.

I rolled over at the same moment she rose from my bed.

"Where are you ..." The words got caught in my throat.

Her hair was slightly disheveled as she slid her blouse on and refastened the buttons.

"I have to go," she said simply.

My forehead furrowed. "Go?" The word made no sense to me.

"Yes," she sighed with growing impatience. She retrieved her skirt and zipped it back into place. "I have an early morning. I can't dally here."

I pulled myself to a seated position. All kinds of insecure questions came to mind: *Why can't you stay the night? Was I not any good? Will I see you again?*

I refused to allow myself to sound clingy and pathetic. I leaned over the edge of the bed and grabbed my T-shirt from the floor.

She sat at the bottom of the mattress. Her head was cocked to the side as she put her earrings back on. I hadn't noticed her taking them out. "I trust you'll be discrete?" Her caramel eyes regarded me.

"I just got into town," I said, slipping my T-shirt over my head. "Who would I tell?"

Her gaze flickered over me. "Mmm ... indeed."

She stepped into overpriced stilettos and left without another word.

I fell back onto my pillows and let out a deep breath as I stared at the ceiling and drummed my fingers against my abdomen. *What the hell was that?*

Leaving my bed, I grabbed my discarded jeans and made a face when I realized they were wet. Somewhere in our frantic scramble to rid each other of clothes, my beer had been knocked over. A puddle of carbonated alcohol pooled on the floor. I threw my pants in a corner of the room to deal with later. At least I wouldn't have to go far to the Laundromat.

There was another light knock at the door, and I launched into action, pulling on a pair of shorts and senses going on full alert. She'd come back. I felt a cocky grin slide into its usual place as I swung my apartment door open.

"Back for round ..." The words died in my mouth when I saw a pixie-haired woman standing in the hallway. "Sorry." I poked my head into the hallway and looked either way. The other woman was nowhere to be seen. "I thought you were someone else."

The second woman didn't appear fazed by my reaction. "Hi. I'm Grace Kelly Donovan. I live across the hallway." She jerked her thumb in the direction of Apartment B.

"Grace Kelly?" I repeated. "Like the actress?"

"Don't worry. We're not related," she said with a bright grin. "My parents are just obsessed with Old Hollywood."

"Oh." I leaned against the doorframe. "I'm Cassidy. Cassidy Miller," I returned. "My parents didn't name me after anyone."

"Welcome to the neighborhood, Cassidy Miller." She shoved a wicker basket into my arms.

"Wow. Thanks. This is really great." I sifted around in the basket, examining its contents. There were cookies and muffins and planted herbs and some other things I'd have to later explore more carefully. "You wanna crack into this thing?" I asked, pulling out a bottle of pinot noir.

"Oh, I-I really couldn't."

My smile returned, less cocky and more genuine. "You'd be doing me a big favor. Otherwise, I'll end up drinking the bottle all by myself. I've got terrible willpower for a cop."

Chapter Four

The weekly newspaper was on my welcome mat the next morning. I would have found this relatively unremarkable except for one detail—my picture was on the front page. I wasn't the main headline, but there was a story about me just under the middle fold. "Meet Our New Police Officer," the black bolded words announced, "Military Hero, Cassidy Miller."

"What the fuck?" I voiced aloud. I bent and picked up the paper to better assess the situation. I had no idea how a story about me had happened so quickly, or better yet, why it had happened at all, until I saw the byline. "That little weasel," I muttered.

Grace's apartment was steps away. I pounded on the front door. "Grace Kelly!" I yelled through the closed door. "I've got a bone to pick with you, Princess!"

The door down the hallway opened and Mrs. Graves, the owner of the building and the apartment's third occupant, peeked out into the hallway. I immediately stopped hitting the door.

"Is something wrong?" she asked.

"Uh, sorry." I tugged on my ponytail. "Do you know where I might find Grace?"

I doubted she'd tell me since she'd just caught me acting like a crazy person. She peered curiously at me, her newest tenant, over thick eyeglasses. "I imagine she's at work at the newspaper."

"Right." People had jobs. And they typically went to those jobs when the sun was up. "And where might I find that exactly?"

My anger had dissipated—mostly—by the time I made myself presentable enough to be seen in public and had driven my Harley to the other side of town in search of the *Embarrass Weekly* headquarters.

The newspaper office was one giant room filled with half a dozen uninhabited cubicles. An assortment of outdated computers and fax machines hummed in the background and telephones rang unanswered. I wondered if it was so busy because other people had also appeared in the newspaper without their permission.

An overweight black cat was sprawled over the top of a computer monitor. It cracked open one yellow eye to regard me, but apparently after deciding I wasn't a person of interest, it went back to its nap.

Grace walked out of a hidden back room.

"You mind explaining this to me?" I asked, tapping at my picture on the printed page.

"Hot off the press." She seemed unsurprised by the visit. "I thought the town might want to know a little more about its newest resident," she shrugged.

"I didn't realize I was *on the record* last night. And where the hell did you find this other stuff?" I demanded, feeling my anger building again. "I never told you the details of my time in Afghanistan."

"It's called the *Internet*. You're not that hard to find. It turns out they don't give out too many Navy Crosses—less than twenty for all of Operation Enduring Freedom if my research is correct."

She shook her head and a quirky grin appeared. "I don't know *why* you'd keep that a secret anyway. If it were me, that's what I'd lead with. 'Hi, I'm Grace Kelly Donovan, and I was awarded a medal of honor by the President of the United States. Could I get a coffee?'"

"It was the Secretary of the Navy, not the President," I corrected under my breath.

"See? It's a big frickin' deal," Grace insisted. "Why would you want to hide that?"

"I'm just ..." I rubbed at my arm. "I'm a private person. I didn't ask to be front page news."

"Well, you are now."

She smiled in such a playfully impish way that even though we'd only just met I found it hard to stay angry at her.

"Besides, in case you haven't noticed, Embarrass is a small town," she noted. "People would have eventually found out. Secrets don't stay secrets around here."

After my visit with Grace, I headed back to City Hall and the police department. Chief Hart showed me around the building and introduced me to a handful of people whose names and job titles I promptly forgot. In the afternoon, I met up with David Addams for a ride along to get the layout of town.

It didn't take long to make the rounds. Main Street was a four-mile long stretch with businesses lining either side of the road. The residential areas branched off from the central drag, and a school that housed preschool through high school was situated near the town's eastern border.

There were no stoplights in Embarrass. The two four-way stops at either side of the downtown strip were by far the busiest intersections within the city limits, forming a junction point for county highways.

"So what's your story, Miller?" David Addams asked as we crawled down Main Street.

"Not much to tell," I said.

"How does a Twin Cities cop end up taking a job up here in the boonies?"

"Just looking for a change."

I stared out the window of the police car. People stopped for pedestrians at crosswalks and they shared the road with bicycles. If I'd thought I'd stumbled into a time warp at the Embarrass Bed & Breakfast, it had expanded to the rest of the town as well.

"You okay over there?"

I turned my head away from the view beyond the window. "Yeah. Sure. Of course," I insisted.

"Sorry." David chuckled as we turned down a street that looked like every other residential street in town. "You just had this look on your face like you'd bitten off more than you could chew. I've seen that look before."

I stared out the side window again. "I'm fine."

I had to continually remind myself that this was what I wanted. I didn't want to sit behind a desk in Minneapolis; I wanted to be an active duty officer again. But driving around the largely vacant streets of Embarrass was making me realize that I might actually see more action behind a desk in Minneapolis than what I'd experience in a town so tiny I could probably chuck a rock from one border to the other.

I pulled myself out of discouraging thoughts. "Do you patrol town your entire shift?"

"A good portion of it," David confirmed. "I try to maintain a visible presence in town. I'm sure Chief told you, but we don't have a lot of crime around here. We're basically on call until the shit hits the fan. You can hang out at the station or drive around town; it's up to you. Just make sure you're available when your phone rings."

"How does that work? Who'll be calling me?"

"During regular business hours, Lori works the desk, so she fields all the non-emergency calls. Since you'll be working third shift, however, local calls to the station will be redirected to your cell phone. Most people know enough to call 911 if it's a real emergency, but sometimes, especially among the senior community, they'll call you directly, regardless."

"Who answers the emergency calls?" I asked.

"We've got a contract with the county dispatch center. When people call 911, the call goes there first. The dispatcher then determines what kind of assistance the caller needs: fire, ambulance, police, or a combination of those. If the police are needed, you'll hear about it on your police radio."

A grizzled old man who'd been walking along the side of the street crossed in front of the police car with no warning. I braced myself against the dashboard and slammed my right foot down on an imaginary break while David hit the real breaks just in time.

The man looked unfazed and continued to walk, swinging a green five-gallon bucket in one hand, as if he hadn't noticed he'd almost been run over.

"He's harmless," David said as if reading my thoughts.

I pushed hair out of my face that had fallen from my ponytail. "What's his deal?" My heart continued to pump with adrenaline.

"His name is Henry James. People in town call him Crazy Hank. "He collects cans and exchanges the scrap metal for beer down at Skip's place."

I wrinkled my nose. "That's awfully nice of them."

David grunted. "Yeah. He fought over in Vietnam and didn't come back the same." He turned the patrol car down another street. "Embarrass seems to be a haven for washed-up vets."

I bristled at David's words. I was sure Chief Hart wouldn't have said anything about my situation. I stared at David's profile and waited for him to continue or to at least clarify his latter statement.

"I was over in Afghanistan for a one-year tour in my early twenties," he said. He stroked his square jaw in thought. "I couldn't stay in that hell hole for longer than that though."

"Forward Operating Base Farah," I revealed with some trepidation. "Four years."

"No shit."

I nodded. "And Camp Leatherneck for four years after that."

"Fucking oohraah, Miller." He lightly slapped the steering wheel and laughed. "I didn't know you were one of Uncle Sam's Misguided Children, too." I could hear something new in his voice that had been absent before. Admiration. Respect. Camaraderie.

I laughed at the expression. "Didn't you read the newspaper today? Grace Donovan did a whole story on me."

David shook his head. "Glorified gossip rag," he opined. "I don't waste my time."

Something about the exchange helped me to relax as we continued to drive up and down the nearly deserted streets and the sun set in the west. I had suspected that David had been former military, but now that it was out in the open, I felt like I had another ally in this town.

Second shift didn't end until 10:00 p.m., but it was a quiet night, so David dropped me off in front of City Hall around 8:00 p.m. We agreed that I'd ride with him one more night before I officially took over third shift.

I leaned against the open driver's side window as he sat in the idling car. "Thanks for showing me the ropes, David."

"Sure thing," he waved. "See you tomorrow, Marine."

I shoved my hands in my pockets and watched the brown Crown Victoria drive away.

~

Embarrass was the type of town that had one of everything—not everything you necessarily needed—but what they had, there was only one of them: one gas station, one fast food restaurant, one school, one auto mechanic, one dentist, one hair salon, and one grocery store. I pushed my cart up and down the aisles in search of food to subsidize the leftover pizza and four beers currently residing in my refrigerator. The grocery store was clean and brightly lit, but it felt a little rundown like it hadn't been updated in several decades. The food selection was equally minimalist. If I had been the kind of person who only ate organic, non-fat, gluten-free, all natural food, I would have starved. Everything was full fat, layered in pesticides, and pumped full of steroids. And everything went into my cart. I probably could have eaten healthier if I stuck to Stan's diner for every meal, but at least eating at home provided the illusion of health.

"Cassidy Miller! Hey! Over here!" Grace Kelly Donovan waved at me from across the produce section. She maneuvered her grocery cart around a few other shoppers to make her way towards me near the deli counter.

I grimaced at the flailing woman. The attention gave me the same feeling as picking a cart with a squeaky wheel. I felt the eyes of every shopper on me.

"Hey, you!" she greeted again, parking her cart near mine. "It's good to see you. How was your day?"

I cast my eyes around the store, thankful that the onlookers had resumed their shopping. "It's kind of weird going grocery shopping and running into someone you recognize," I admitted.

"You've never lived in a small town before?"

"Not *this* small," I clarified. "I grew up in St. Cloud and then I was in Minneapolis. I saw my share of small villages in Afghanistan, but it's not like I went grocery shopping when I was deployed."

"This must be like living on a different planet compared to the life in the Army," Grace sympathized.

"Marines," I corrected.

She made a face. "Sorry. I probably just insulted you."

It was a reflex thing. I was proud to be a Marine, and I hated getting mistaken as a beetle cruncher or even a green beanie.

"No, it's okay. It's just a military thing. We don't like getting mistaken for the other guy, ya know?"

"Marines. Wow," she openly admired. "You can, like, kill a person with your bare hands, right?"

I forced a smile to my lips. If I had a dollar for every wild assumption people made when they found out I'd been in the Marine Corps.

"I'd be pretty handy on one of those reality shows where they drop you off on a deserted island," I confirmed, mindful of my words. I would have to be careful what I said around this woman so I didn't end up on the front page of the newspaper again. "But I feel like I missed out on a lot of things grown-ups are supposed to know how to do." My gaze slipped down to my grocery cart filled with easy-to-fix meals: frozen pizzas, macaroni and cheese boxes, and TV dinners.

Grace caught the source of my discomfort. "Oh, don't worry about that. Lots of people can't cook, and they don't have an excuse for it, unlike you."

"Well I guess I'd better figure it out, now that I don't have that excuse anymore."

"I love to cook, but I never have a reason to make food for anyone. Why don't you come over tomorrow night for dinner?"

"That's awfully kind, Grace," I said, fully intending to decline the offer.

"It's just Minnesota nice," she dismissed. "Plus, I feel kind of guilty for printing that story without giving you a heads up."

I frowned. "Yeah. That's another thing about small town life I'll have to get used to. People already think they know me."

"Is that such a bad thing?"

"I haven't decided yet," I shrugged.

"Let me know when you figure it out, eh?" she laughed pleasantly.

My eyes continued to roam rather than settling on the pretty face of the newspaper reporter. It was a learned habit from deployment, always scanning, investigating, and on the lookout for something suspicious or out of place. If it weren't for that habit I might have missed a familiar flash of dark hair and painted red lipstick across the produce section.

"Shit."

Grace's features clouded with concern. "What's wrong?"

The woman from the club, the same woman who had picked up coffee at Stan's diner and who had showed up at my apartment the previous night, stood in the center of the produce section. My first instinct was to duck behind Grace or her grocery cart. But I had no reason to hide; this wasn't a war zone, and I had nothing to be embarrassed about. I wasn't the one who'd shown up unannounced on someone's doorstep for sex.

"Nothing. Just remembering something."

She stuck out in the small-town grocery store where everyone else wore jeans and T-shirts with no one to impress. Her makeup was flawlessly applied with not a hair on her head out of place. Dark bangs swooped low over her forehead just above twin caramel-colored eyes framed in dark eyeliner and mascara. Her grey pants looked crisp and wrinkle-free, a dark blue top peeked out from the open collar of a short trench coat, and a neat string of pearls gleamed under the fluorescent lighting.

I watched her carefully inspect a pile of red delicious apples. She picked up each one individually, looking for bruises and other signs of imperfections. The rejected apples were returned to the pile, while those deemed good enough were bagged and placed in her cart. I wondered if given the chance to be under her scrutinizing eye again on which pile I'd end up.

"What's her story?"

Grace's head whipped around to follow the trajectory of my gaze. I hoped I wasn't being too obvious, especially in front of the town's newspaper reporter, but there was really no way to get the answers I wanted if I didn't ask the questions.

"Who? Julia?"

My lips curled up in a smile. So she *had* told me her real name.

"Yeah. Julia." I really liked how the name felt on my tongue. I recalled really liking the way Julia herself had felt on my tongue, too.

Grace seemed to shudder as she stood. "She scares me."

I wasn't expecting that response. "Her? Why?"

"She just ... has this aura about her. I mean, she's Julia frickin' Desjardin. She's the daughter of the richest family in town—the Mayor's daughter, in fact. Plus, she's smart as a whip being city attorney and all."

"City attorney?"

"Hence why she always looks like she just fell off the pages of a Banana Republic catalogue. But that's just Julia," Grace said with a shrug. "She's always been like that."

"So she grew up here?" I couldn't help licking my lips as I regarded the woman who continued to fill her grocery cart with fruits and vegetables, apparently unaware of the double set of eyes on her.

"Yeah. She went away for college, of course, but she came back maybe five or six years ago. Her dad used to be the district attorney, but when he became mayor, everyone moved up the ladder. The city attorney job opened up, and her family dragged her kicking and screaming from the Twin Cities to take the job. Or so the story goes."

"Is she married?" I was embarrassed the moment the words came out. I was sure Grace would be able to see through me.

"The Ice Queen?" Grace's face took on a comical look. "No man would be brave enough to even ask her on a date, let alone ask to marry her," she chuckled. "She, my friend, is untouchable."

My fingertips still burned with the memory of Julia's skin. Untouchable? Perhaps not.

Chapter Five

I met up with David Addams the next day at the start of second shift. It felt strange to me being a plainclothes police officer while David patrolled in his dark brown uniform, but I'd get used to it eventually.

My first impression of David had been unfair. He'd seemed like a misogynistic playboy, but the more time I spent with him, the more I liked him. He talked about Embarrass with true passion rather than the annoyance and resentment of someone who'd been unable to escape his hometown. He'd seen the world, and in the end, he'd chosen to come back to the only place he'd ever considered to be home. If pressed I would have probably called St. Cloud home. It was the town where I'd grown up and where my parents still lived, but I couldn't imagine ever moving back there for good. Maybe that meant I was still looking for home.

We patrolled up and down the city streets and just beyond the city border for the majority of the night. David treated me to dinner at Stan's, and we swapped a few innocent war stories about our time in Afghanistan. Like the day before, the evening had been uneventful with no calls to either the non-emergency number or the in-car radio.

The squad car idled in front of one of the biggest houses I'd seen in town. The two-story home was constructed of red brick with light blue wooden shutters that framed the large windows. The house was significantly longer than it was tall, and the landscaping looked professionally maintained.

I whistled under my breath. "That is one big ass house."

"It's the Mayor's house," David supplied. "Biggest house in town for the biggest man in town."

I stared out the window at the house, all lit up. "Does his daughter live with him?"

"Julia?" David sounded surprised that I knew the Mayor had a daughter, let alone knew her name. "No. She lives out in the country. It's just the Mayor and his wife in there."

"What do you think about the Desjardins?" I asked.

"They're rich. That's enough to know I'll never have anything in common with them. Julia and I went to the same school growing up, but we didn't have the same circle of friends. We still don't."

I had more questions about Julia Desjardin, but I couldn't ask them without sounding suspicious.

"Central to E-Two," a voice across the police radio squawked.

David picked up the in-car handset. "Go ahead, Central."

"E-Two, I've got a 10-16 at 182 North Spruce Street. Neighbors called in reporting yelling coming from inside the house."

"E-Two is en route, Central."

"E-Two," the dispatcher responded, "I see you en route at 17:42."

I shuffled through my brain to remember the police ten-codes for this particular town. Chief Hart had sent me the Embarrass Police Department manual a few weeks before I'd arrived. Each city had their own police ten-codes and it was important to know each department's specific codes. What was "Officer down" to one department could be "I'm taking a lunch break" to another.

"Domestic disturbance?"

David whipped the car around in an empty parking lot. "Yup. That'll probably be the majority of your calls on third shift. That and bartenders over-serving people."

"Or cutting them off," I noted.

It took only a few minutes to reach our destination. It was amazing to witness the size discrepancy between the Mayor's mansion and the trailer home we pulled up to. Even in a small town like Embarrass you had your Haves and your Have Nots.

David called in our arrival. "Central, E-Two and E-Three have arrived on scene."

The voice on the radio immediately responded. "E-Two and E-Three, I have you on scene at 17:46."

"Do you know who lives here?" I asked as I unbuckled my seatbelt and got out of the vehicle.

"John and Tricia Wagner and their son, Dennis."

The trailer home was parked in a gravel lot. The surrounding grass was sparse and mostly weeds. Cigarette butts littered the front yard. The three steps that led to the front door looked like they were under construction, so I hopped directly onto the front porch.

David came up behind me. "Hear anything?"

I shook my head. "Police," I called out. I knocked on the front door.

David reached for the doorknob and turned the handle. The door was unlocked.

"What are you doing?" I hissed when he opened the front door.

"Neighbors said they heard yelling," he said with a shrug. "There's my probable cause."

He stepped through the threshold, and I reluctantly followed.

The front door opened into a carpeted living room. The room was small and cramped, and it smelled like stale cigarettes.

I heard the screams coming from the back of the house. The exact words were muffled, but it sounded like a man yelling that someone was eating him. I took a step forward in the direction of the voice, but David put his arm in front of me.

"It's only your second day on the job."

I unfastened the leather strap that secured my gun in its holster. "Might as well start earning my keep then."

The yelling grew louder as we cautiously stalked down the narrow corridor. I gave a cursory glance into each room we passed —two bedrooms and the laundry room—to make sure they were empty.

David and I stood on either side of a closed door from where the loud noises originated. The yelling had largely subsided and had been replaced by a rhythmic smacking sound.

David and I made eye contact and he nodded once. I reached for the door handle, twisted hard, and pushed. The door swung free, unencumbered.

"Christ," David muttered under his breath.

A man stood alone in the bathroom, stripped down to cotton boxers. I quickly discovered what was causing the smacking noise. His palms were pressed flat against the bathroom wall, and he was hitting his head against the white subway tile. His blood was splattered on the walls and floor. He'd torn the sink clear from the wall, and water sprayed all over the bathroom, combining with blood to make a swirly pink mess on the floor.

The man turned toward us and howled. The animalistic sound made me flinch just enough that I wasn't prepared when he charged David. The man had no weapon—only his body—but he threw his arms around David's torso and tackled my partner to the ground.

I launched myself into the fray and, together, David and I

managed to wrestle the man to the ground and subdue him. I pulled my handcuffs out of their holder and cuffed him to restrain his arms behind his back.

David flipped the man over. "You gonna behave now, Dennis?"

The man—Dennis—nodded, momentarily mute.

I shouldn't have been surprised that David knew his attacker, but I'd never arrested someone I was on a first-name basis with.

David and I pulled Dennis to a seated position and propped him up against a wall. He squiggled in weak protest but appeared to have lost most of his fight.

"Gross." I tugged at the front of my wet shirt and separated it from my skin. My clothes were soaked with a mixture of water and blood from wrestling on the bathroom floor.

I took a moment to breathe out and survey the rest of the damage. Blood flowed freely from Dennis's forehead and dripped down his face, but without taking a closer look I couldn't be sure of the extent of his injury. Head wounds were notorious for looking worse than they actually were, so I wasn't going to panic that he would bleed out while we stood here.

The bathroom was demolished. The porcelain sink lay in fractured pieces, and the vanity mirror had been shattered. Large shards of mirrored glass were scattered on the ground. We'd been fortunate that none of us had rolled over the broken glass during our scuffle with Dennis.

David reached for the radio attached near his shoulder. He pressed down on the handset to call in the arrest, but lifted his thumb to first address me: "Watch out. He's a kicker."

"A what?"

I groaned when the man's foot connected between my legs. Even though I lacked the more sensitive genitalia of a male officer, it still stung and brought tears to my eyes.

"A kicker," David repeated. I would have smacked the shit-eating grin off of his face if I wasn't occupied with subduing my assailant.

I zip-tied Dennis's ankles together to keep him from lashing out again. I stood up and made sure I pushed off his body a little rougher than necessary. "How did you know that was going to happen?"

"It's not the first time I've had to arrest him." David wiped at his forehead. "I'm guessing he's back on animal tranquilizers."

"You're shittin' me. PCP?"

"It's a small, remote town. People get creative about their drugs."

"Dennis?" A woman's voice echoed down the hallway. I remembered we'd left the front door open.

"I got this." David stepped between the woman and the door to block her view of the destroyed bathroom and the bloodied man inside. "Mrs. Wagner, we received a call from a neighbor about a domestic disturbance. When Detective Miller and I investigated, we found your son in the bathroom, hurting himself. We've got him cuffed for his own protection."

"Oh, Dennis," the woman sighed. "What have you done now?"

"Ma'am, when we arrived on scene the bathroom sink had been torn from the wall," I spoke up. "Do you happen to know where your shut-off valves are?"

She eyeballed me for a moment before nodding. "It's in the laundry room. I'll go turn off the water."

"Was that his mom?" I asked when the woman left us.

"Yup. Her name's Tricia."

"What do we do with him now?" I asked, nodding in Dennis's direction. His head wound had stopped bleeding, but his face and bare chest were covered in dried blood. He looked like he'd come straight from a Satanic ritual.

"Let's hose him down in the shower so he doesn't get blood all over the back of the squad car, and then we can throw him in the drunk tank to sleep this off."

I wrinkled my nose. "Do I need to be here for the hosing off part?"

David chuckled. "Let's ask him." He towered over Dennis who was still sitting on the bathroom floor with his hands and legs bound. "Hey, Dennis. You gonna behave long enough so I can wash that blood off you? Or is Detective Miller here going to have to help?"

The man looked back and forth between David and me, blinking his blank eyes. With PCP rushing through his veins, I wondered how many heads he thought we had.

"I'll take care of Dennis if you'll go talk to Mrs. Wagner," David decided. "I'll need the water turned on again so I can at least rinse him off."

"Sure thing."

I went in search of Dennis's mother and found her sitting at the kitchen table, smoking a cigarette. She tapped ash into a glass tray that badly needed to be emptied.

"Mrs. Wagner?" I said, culling her attention.

She looked up at me with large blue eyes. "I don't know you. Do I?"

"No, ma'am. I'm Detective Cassidy Miller. I'm new."

In a town the size of Embarrass, everyone knew each other. I was an outsider. Police often witnessed people at their most vulnerable moments. It wouldn't be easy to get the townspeople to accept me as one of their own.

"Miller." She thought on my name before recognition lit up her eyes. "You're that girl from the newspaper."

I tried to smile, but it felt more like a grimace. Maybe I shouldn't have been so quick to forgive Grace. "Yes, ma'am."

"It's Tricia. No one's ever called me ma'am before."

"Sergeant Addams and I need to take your son to the jail to detox, ma'—" I cut myself off. After being in the Marines for so long, it had taken a while to drop the habit of sandwiching my sentences with formal titles. "But we'd like to rinse the blood off him first. And he'll probably appreciate a fresh set of clothes when he sobers up."

"Blood," she echoed.

"He, uh, he was hitting his head against the bathroom wall."

She sighed and her entire body sagged in the chair. "I just don't know what I'm going to do with that boy."

I took the opportunity to sit down in a vacant chair at the small kitchen table. I hadn't turned to abusing drugs and alcohol after returning to the States, but I knew a lot of guys who had.

"Maybe it's time for a little tough love," I gently offered. "If you keep bailing him out of trouble, he doesn't have incentive to grow up." It wasn't my place to be offering parenting advice, but I'd seen my share of Dennises when I'd been in the service. They'd finished high school and had no plan for afterwards.

"What would he do? Where would he even go?"

"How old is your son?"

"Thirty-five."

I nearly choked on her answer. With his face covered in blood I hadn't been able to decipher an age, but I hadn't expected that.

"Maybe it's time to cut the strings and let him struggle on his own for a little while."

She didn't reply to that, but her body language showed extreme fatigue. Coming home from work to find the police in her house had to be exhausting. She lit another cigarette and took a long, cathartic drag.

"You ready to motor, partner?" David popped his head into the kitchen.

"How's Dennis?" I asked.

"Freshly showered and ready to sleep things off at the county jail."

I stood up from the kitchen table. Tricia Wagner continued to smoke. She stared blankly ahead and pinched her cigarette between her thumb and forefinger.

"Will you be alright, ma'am?" I asked, rearranging my duty belt.

She nodded, looking emotionally drained.

"We'll call when Dennis is ready to be released on bail," David said.

David's words brought a sharp look to Mrs. Wagner's face. "That won't be necessary. Dennis can wait in jail for his trial."

I felt a small surge of satisfaction, but David tittered beside me. "Are you sure? It's gonna be a few days for the judge to get around to his case—maybe even a week."

I recognized the doubt that flashed over her features as she second-guessed herself. "Oh, well maybe you should call me."

David and I carted a sluggish Dennis Wagner outside and into the backseat of the squad car. His feet moved steadily, but his upper body was about as responsive as a cooked noodle.

I was annoyed that David had weakened Tricia Wagner's resolve. She didn't need a person in a position of authority like a police officer to question her judgment. David should have supported her decision to let her troubled son deal with the consequences of his poor decision making. But it was only my second day on the job and therefore not my place to call him out.

David drummed his hands on the top of the squad car. "You hungry?"

I could always eat, but I was eager to change my clothes. My jeans were damp and my T-shirt was saturated with water and blood. I tugged at the front of my shirt. "Sure, but mind swinging by my apartment first so I can get out of these rags?"

David held up his hands. "Woah, Miller, you could at least treat me to dinner first before you bring me back to your place. I don't know who you've been talking to, but I don't move that fast."

I tugged open the passenger side door and slid into the front seat. "Real cute."

My surroundings may have changed, but the one constant was the routine razzing I received as a female in a male-dominated environment. David Addams wasn't necessarily a jerk. Being in a high-pressure, stressful job like the military or police made that kind of teasing camaraderie a necessity. The ability to joke around just moments after grappling with a junky was as much of a job skill as hitting a target at a firing range.

David pulled the car into drive, and I watched as the Wagner homestead got smaller and smaller in the side mirror. Chief Hart had promised a glorified babysitting job, but my second night on duty suggested something else.

Chapter Six

The floor plan of Grace Kelly's apartment was the mirror image of mine across the hallway, but she'd done far more to the interior to make it feel like a home instead of an oversized dorm room. The natural light made the studio apartment similarly bright and inviting, but it was the positioning of furniture and the charming, attentive details that set it apart from the minimalistic way I'd been living. Pictures of my hostess with friends or family, smiles broad and arms wrapped around each other, filled the walls and spare shelf space.

One picture stood out: Grace with two other similarly aged and appearing women.

"You're a triplet?" I called to her in the kitchen.

"Yeah. But technically I'm the middle child."

"Do they live in Embarrass?"

"No. They're out of state with their families. I'm the only one who stayed."

"Are your parents still around?" I asked.

"Yup. See them every week at church," Grace chuckled. "We

go to brunch at Stan's afterwards. Been doing it for as long as I can remember."

I put the picture frame back on its shelf and scanned over the books on Grace's bookshelves. "Hey, is this your yearbook?" I asked.

I heard her laugh from the kitchen. "Oh, yeah. I can't believe I still have that thing after all these years. I'm such a hoarder."

My fingers flexed with the urge to pluck the thin hardcover book from its place on the shelf and look for the name "Desjardin, Julia" in the index. Instead, I forced my hand to fall limply at my side.

"Dinner's ready," Grace beamed. She pulled a glass casserole dish from the oven, her hands protected by oven gloves. "I hope you brought your appetite."

"Smells good," I remarked, shoving my hands into the back pockets of my jeans.

Grace set the casserole pan on a pot holder in the center of the kitchen island and wiped her hands on the front of her apron. Like my apartment, she had no formal dining room, but since it was just the two of us, there was plenty of space at the island.

"How are you settling in?" she asked. She used a metal spatula to serve me a square of lasagna. I practically drooled at the meat and cheese filling that spilled all over my plate.

"It's been going well. Chief Hart and David Addams have been doing a really nice job of easing me into the job," I said. I held up my plate so she could spoon green beans next to the steaming lasagna. "Monday I met some people who work at City Hall, and the past two nights I've been patrolling with David."

Grace unfolded her napkin and placed it on her lap. "See any action yet?"

My fork hovered in front of my mouth. *Action?* Was that a question about Julia Desjardin or Dennis Wagner, I wondered. I assumed she was asking about the latter, but I knew enough not to talk about work with a reporter. "It's been pretty routine so far. But tonight's my first shift on my own, so who knows."

Grace lifted her glass of milk to toast. "Here's to catching all the bad guys."

I raised my water glass in return and clinked our cups together. "Here's to seeing some action." I wiggled my eyebrows.

"God, don't I wish," Grace giggled. "I can't remember the last time I went on a date."

"You don't have to go on a date to get laid." I was living proof of that.

Her eyelashes fluttered, and she ducked her head. I saw the telltale blush creep onto her cheeks.

"Sorry. Was that too much?" I could be crass sometimes when it came to talking about sex. I'd lived with soldiers for the past eight years.

"No. You're fine. We're all adults." She cut into her lasagna and blew on the first mouthful to cool it. "I guess I'm just a little old fashioned when it comes to these things."

"So why aren't you dating?" I started to dissect my food as well. I hadn't had a home-cooked meal like this in months—probably not since the last time I'd visited my parents.

"Right. Because the choice of suitors here is endless," she said, shaking her head.

"What about David Addams?"

She quirked an eyebrow. "Cowboy?"

"Cowboy?" I chuckled. I'd have to remember to ask about that nickname the next time I saw him. "Sure. He's an attractive guy. And he's got a steady job."

"What more could a girl hope for, huh?" Grace laughed without humor. "I've known Cowboy since preschool. I taught him how to tie his shoes in kindergarten. No great romance there."

"And that's what you're looking for? Romance?"

Grace pushed the food around on her plate with her fork. "It's silly, I know. At my age I should be married with at least three kids."

I held up my hands. "Hey, no judgment from me. I haven't had a serious relationship in, like, my entire life."

"I'm sure you're exaggerating."

"I've dated, but no one significant."

"Why not?"

I shrugged and continued to shovel more of the flavorful food into my mouth. "Never found someone I liked enough to commit to, I guess."

The food was delicious and Grace made for a charming dinner companion. I was glad I hadn't done something idiotic when she'd written that story about me that might have stifled a potential friendship. I had a lot of male friends because I was able to talk about sports and cars, but I usually had little in common with straight women, so it was nice to be able to hang out so effortlessly with Grace.

I'd have to get her to teach me how to cook. Maybe I could teach her how to shoot a gun in return.

The night sky was clear, and with the sun having set hours ago, I could see my breath with every exhale. A nervous energy knotted at my stomach as I slid into the driver's seat of the old Crown Vic. My jeans caught on the leather causing my backside to skid along its surface. It brought me back to an instructor's words at the police academy: if you don't feel nervous before the start of your shift, you're going to get yourself hurt. The moment the job becomes routine is the moment you let your guard down.

I curled my fingers around the steering wheel and breathed in. The scent of the leather was familiar and comfortable. Police cars, regardless if you lived in the Twin Cities or Embarrass, Minnesota, all smelled the same. I started up the car and let it sit in park until the engine heated up and warm air began to blast out of the vents. The squad car had seen better days, but it was infinitely better than riding desk for the rest of my working years. If I had wanted to sit behind a desk all day, I would have gotten a degree in business.

It was strange being in the squad car by myself. When I'd been in Afghanistan, you obviously never went anywhere by yourself, and I hadn't been on the Minneapolis force long enough to warrant my own car. But patrolling alone did have its benefits. For one, it was actually safer than working with a partner. It forced you to slow down and be more cautious when you knew you were your own backup.

I drove around town for the first few hours, getting used to the vehicle and how it pulled slightly to the left. At this late hour, I saw no one on the road, but perhaps with tomorrow being Friday, I would see more action then.

I flicked my eyes to the rearview mirror and followed a silver pickup truck as it drove past me. It was the first vehicle I'd seen all night. I squinted my eyes when I noticed only one red taillight was illuminated. The other one had been smashed out.

I turned the squad car around and flipped on my overhead bubble lights, just a few red and blue flashes to alert the driver. The truck responded immediately and its driver veered the vehicle onto the shoulder of the road.

I pulled directly behind the extended cab pickup and parked my car.

I reached for the in-car radio. "Central, this is E-Three."

"Go ahead, E-Three."

"I need you to run a plate for me. Minnesota plate five, seven, eight, Echo, Adam, Victor." It was technically a routine traffic stop, but the academy had drilled into me that there was nothing routine about police work.

The dispatcher repeated the plate back to me. "That car is registered to Cyrus Tabor who lives at 356 East Maple in Embarrass, Minnesota."

A local. "Anything else I should know about?"

"You're clear."

I climbed out of the car, leaving it running, and walked to the passenger side of the stopped vehicle even though the street was empty and there was only the driver visible in the cab of the truck.

I waited for the driver to roll down the window.

"Yes, Officer?"

I flashed my Maglite inside the cab. The interior of the truck looked new—bucket seats instead of a single bench, heated leather seats, and a multi-disc changer in the dashboard. "License and registration, please."

The driver leaned over the center console and reached for the glove compartment.

I flinched at the abrupt movement. "Slowly, please."

"Was I speeding?" He fished around the glove compartment, and I kept the heel of my palm on my holstered gun.

"You've got a taillight out."

"Oh, yeah," he chuckled. "Backed the damn thing into a tree last month when I was hauling stuff off to the city dump. You should have heard the wife yell when I brought the truck home. Just got it a few months ago and here I was breaking it already. But I told her better me than anyone else putting the first dent in it."

He talked to me like we were old acquaintances. No one spoke to me like that when I was in uniform in Minneapolis, not even when they were drunk. People usually got spooked being pulled over. *Small town, Minnesota*, I sighed to myself.

"Sir, can I see your driver's license?"

"Sorry, Officer. I must've left my wallet in my good jeans."

I sighed even more loudly. "Your good jeans?"

"The ones without the holes."

"Of course." I resisted rolling my eyes. "Do you have any form of identification on you, Mister..."

"Tabor. Cyrus Tabor. I own the hardware store. And no, like I told you, I left my wallet in my good jeans."

I closed my ticket book. "Mr. Tabor, I'm letting you off with a verbal warning. Please get that taillight fixed as soon as possible; it's a danger to you and to other drivers. And in the future, don't leave your wallet at home in your good pants."

He bobbed his head. "Will do, lady cop."

When I got back to the car, I called central dispatch to let them know I was still alive. Cyrus Tabor gingerly eased his truck back onto the road, and I watched as his single taillight disappeared into the night.

I pressed my forehead against the leather steering column. What was I doing here?

~

Afghanistan, 2012

We've received intelligence and a new directive. We're to be deployed to a village in the south—a Taliban stronghold. No one says the name because he might as well be the Loch Ness Monster or Bigfoot. None of us ever expects to find Bin Laden in this godforsaken country. He could be hiding anywhere—Afghanistan, Pakistan, Iran. Hell, he could be hanging out in West Hollywood selling maps to the stars' homes or farming corn in Des Moines, Iowa. The best we can hope for is to capture someone much farther down the chain of command.

I climb into the back of the Medium Tactical Vehicle Replacement. The six tires on the MTVR are almost as tall as me. There's a palpable excitement and tension in our group. It's our first convoy in who knows how long. We've been getting cabin fever—

days filled with nothing but ping-pong, beer, and porn. There's been nothing brave or valiant to write home about.

You let your guard down when you're on base. You're surrounded by reminders of your life in the States and the comforts of a far more civilized existence. It's easier to think you're safe in those moments, especially when you've just done ten hours of patrolling the streets of Kabul in an armored car. But the truth is, you're never far from danger—from a surprise attack that leaves you and your buddies broken, banged up, or even dead.

We aren't Military Police who patrol almost daily, sometimes on foot, sometimes in a vehicle, so sitting assholes to elbows inside the MTVR doesn't come natural to me. My commander touches the radio at his ear. "We are Oscar Mike," he tells the three-vehicle convoy.

We haven't been on the road for even an hour when I see the enormous explosion of smoke, debris, and chunks of concrete. Then comes the loud boom. The smoke climbs higher and higher into the sky.

"Push through, driver! Push through!" my LT yells. Our driver hesitates and I know what she's thinking; leave no man behind. But it's also her job to keep moving so the third vehicle in the convoy can get out of the kill zone in case there's additional IEDs. Our vehicle lurches forward again until we're clear of the debris.

The door opens and when I rush outside with the rest of my unit I get a front-row view of the damage. The lead vehicle has been hit, mostly on the passenger side. The seven-ton vehicle looks helpless, little more than a beat-up tin can. Its passengers yell for assistance. Orders are barked into my ear and as the soldiers from the third vehicle set up a perimeter around the disabled MTVR, the Marines from my group are assisting the wounded.

I reach one of the injured men. He's so new to the unit, I don't know his name yet. He's been hit, and it looks pretty bad. His uniform is charred, torn, and bloody on the right side, and his leg has been shredded up from shrapnel. I yank a tourniquet out of my kit—Velcro straps on a plastic stick—and wrap it around his thigh.

"Oh, God!" he squeals when I apply pressure to the wound. "I don't want to die! I don't want to die!"

"Shut up!" I yell back. "You're not going to die!"

I'm supposed to be the signal officer, but I'm more concerned right now with stopping the blood and saving this Marine's life.

I'm tugged backwards by the convoy commander. "Get on the horn and call in some help!" he yells at me.

My training rather than my instincts finally kicks in, and I get on the foxtrot. "Medevac! Medevac!" I yell into the radio. "God damn it, I need a medevac!"

The sound of rotor blades above is like angels singing.

Sunlight pierced the flimsy drapes that covered my apartment windows. I squinted into the late morning sun. Beyond the single pane windows, I could hear the sounds of a city taking its lunch break. I'd only gone to bed a few hours earlier, but it would take some time to acclimate to my new schedule of working at night while trying to sleep during the day. But more than the difficulties of getting used to working third shift, I typically avoided losing myself to too much sleep. It was safer that way.

I rolled over in bed and retrieved my phone from an end table. After the past few nights I was due a friendly, yet annoying voice.

Rich answered after the first ring. "Shit, girl. I thought you were dead. People disappear up there, you know."

"You busy?"

"Nope. Having lunch at Mickey's."

"Damn it. Don't rub it in," I grumbled. I had been impressed by Stan's diner, but nothing could compete with Mickey's.

"You hear that?" The phone filled with loud crunching noises.

"That's the sound of me devouring a BLT, onion rings, and a strawberry shake."

My body gurgled at the suggestion, and I pressed my hand to my stomach. "You're a real asshole."

He continued to chew in my ear. "What's up?"

I ran my fingers through my tangled hair. "Just checking in. It's been a while."

"You're breaking my heart, Miller. I didn't figure you for the sentimental type."

I grunted unintelligently.

He laughed. "Small Town, USA not everything you imagined it would be?"

"It's fine. The people here are really nice and accommodating."

"But ..."

"There's no 'but.' Things are good. It's what I need right now."

"That's real good to hear, Cass."

"So what's new?" I pressed. "I've gotta live vicariously through you."

Rich pushed out a deep breath. "All jokes aside, I'm actually working on a case that'll turn your stomach."

I sat up in bed with renewed interest in our conversation. Rich was a detective, but he was assigned to Internal Affairs. He always seemed in the thick of it.

"Illinois highway patrol stops a car with a burned out taillight. The plates check out, but the driver doesn't have ID on him. They run his prints and discover the car belongs to his brother, who hasn't yet discovered his car has been stolen, and his wife is dead in the trunk from carbon monoxide poisoning."

The details were disturbing, but I didn't understand why he was telling me this story. "If Illinois troopers pulled him over, why are you working the case?"

Rich sighed heavily in my ear. "One of our guys pulled him

over hours earlier for the same broken taillight. He wrote the driver a ticket for not having his license on him, but didn't bother to run his prints through the mobile scanner."

"Oh no," I sighed.

Rich was silent on the other end before he found his voice again. "If our guy had swiped his prints the first time, we could have stopped him before he got to Illinois; but more importantly, his wife would probably still be alive."

"God, Rich. That's horrible."

I thought about Cyrus Tabor who owned the hardware store and his broken taillight. Without identification, I'd had to take him at his word that he was who he'd said he was.

"I know. Our guy's a wreck. He's been suspended with pay, but I don't know if he'll be able to bounce back from this. I don't suppose you've got any advice for me?"

"Make him take the maximum time off, but don't leave him out there on an island. Being alone with his thoughts and his regrets is gonna eat him up."

"Yeah. Thanks, Rookie. That's good stuff. Keep doing your thing up there, eh? I'll let the gang know you're kicking ass as usual."

Kicking ass in Embarrass? Not exactly.

Lori was on the phone when I visited the police station a few hours later.

"Is he in there?" I quietly asked, nodding towards Chief Hart's office door. It was slightly ajar.

She nodded and continued with her call.

Inside his office, Chief Hart slowly pecked at his computer's keyboard. A half-eaten sandwich that I assumed his wife had packed for him was on his desk.

"Hey, Chief."

Chief Hart looked away from his computer screen and took off his readers. "Cassidy—what are you doing here? Didn't you just get off duty a few hours ago?"

I flopped down in the chair across from his desk. "Yeah, but I had a question I wanted to ask you."

"Go ahead."

"Does the department have mobile fingerprint readers?"

His eyebrows knit together. "I'm guessing no since I've never heard of this thing before."

"Oh." I sat up straighter in the chair. "Well, it's this device that attaches to your smart phone. If you pull someone over and they don't have identification, you can swipe their fingerprints and the mobile reader checks it against AFIS."

The Automated Fingerprint Identification System, or AFIS, was the state's fingerprint database. The FBI managed the national database.

"David and I know everyone in town. You'll learn everyone's names soon enough, too."

"But what about people from out of town?" I pointed out.

"This gadget sounds like it costs money, Cassidy. And if you've got eyes, you'll notice we don't have a lot of that around here."

He nodded in the direction of a blue plastic bucket in the corner of his office which was catching water dripping from an exposed pipe.

"Oh, speaking of money," he said, "don't forget to fill out your I9s and W2s so you get paid."

"Who do I need to see about that?" I asked.

"Wendy Clark. She's the city clerk, which means she's basically in charge of the city's bank accounts. I'd recommend talking to her right away. Your stipend came from a federal grant, but we should probably follow up to make sure the money doesn't get earmarked for something else."

I immediately stood up. "I'll go talk to her right now." I wasn't about to let my meager living allowance get used for a park bench.

Wendy Clark's office was on the first floor. When I'd entered the Office of the City Clerk, an assistant had informed me that Mrs. Clark was busy in a meeting and that I'd have to wait. I stood in the atrium of City Hall, hands shoved in the pockets of my leather jacket, as I waited for the City Clerk to wrap up her meeting.

Concept art for future buildings and other city projects hung on the walls in the atrium. I stood in front of blueprints and inspected the concept art for a proposed city park. In addition to a castle-like jungle gym there was also a splash pad—a miniature water park.

"Can I help you with something?"

I looked away from the blueprints in the direction from where the voice had come.

A man who looked to be in his mid-forties stood outside of his office with his hands shoved into the pockets of his flat-front dress pants. He was the first person I'd seen in town wearing a tie.

"I'm just waiting for Mrs. Clark to finish her meeting."

"Is there something I can help you with?"

"Not unless you're in charge of payroll."

He laughed and held his hands up. "Nothing so important as that."

I spotted the nameplate on his office door. "Peter Lacroix. City Architect," I read aloud. "Nope. Not important at all."

Peter Lacroix was a tall, thin, mustached man who looked like he'd played Division II basketball in his college years, but now had to settle for pick-up games during lunch hour with other city employees.

"Did you draw all of these?" I asked, nodding to the concept art displayed on the hallway walls.

Peter slipped beside me. "Most of them. I did the plan for the City Hall upgrades that were completed last fall, and the face-lift to Veteran's Park."

"It looks like there's been a lot of improvements to the city recently," I observed. "You guys must be doing something right."

"Well, the Veteran's Park renovations never happened, unfortunately," he said, tapping the drawings I'd so recently admired. "We applied for a grant to get the work done, but it didn't get chosen. Do you have kids?"

"Me? No." The answer came out a little too adamantly. "You?"

Peter nodded. "A boy and a girl. They were really excited about the park when I was working on the plans at home." He pointed to the drawing. "My youngest one, Amelia, she even suggested the miniature lighthouse that sprayed water from its lantern."

"That's cute," I mused. "Maybe the park redesign will still happen someday."

Peter looked thoughtfully at the framed plans. "Yeah. Maybe."

High heels clicked down the hallway, and somehow I instinctually knew that Julia Desjardin wasn't far behind. I hadn't seen her in town since the grocery store on Tuesday evening. I had wanted to reach out to her after that, but I hadn't wanted to seem like a stalker. Her steps faltered only slightly when she spotted me with the city architect.

Peter sucked in a deep breath as if readying himself. "Hi, Julia," he greeted.

"Hello, Peter." Her eyes landed briefly on me. "Detective Miller."

"Madam Prosecutor," I returned evenly, schooling my reaction. I was surprised she knew my title and last name, but she'd managed to hunt down my apartment, so I shouldn't have been too shocked.

"Miller!" Peter Lacroix's face lit up in recognition. "That's why you looked so familiar. From the newspaper."

I rubbed at the back of my neck. "Yeah, a regular old celebrity. That's me."

Julia snorted and continued on her way to the single elevator in the center of the city building. Unforgiving heels clicked down the corridor.

"It was nice meeting you, Peter," I said absently. I found myself unwontedly staring at the elegant woman who waited for the lift. "Good luck with that park. I hope Amelia gets her lighthouse."

Peter nodded his thanks and slipped back into his office.

The purpose of my first floor visit momentarily forgotten, I sidled up next to Julia.

"Where are you headed to?"

She stared straight ahead at the elevator that refused to arrive. "I'm going to trial. Some of us actually work, Miss Miller."

"I'm off-duty. You can call me Cassidy."

Julia mashed a manicured finger into the elevator button again as if to hasten its arrival. "I'd rather not."

"Why don't you take the stairs?"

"Because, Detective, the courtroom is on the third floor and these are new shoes," she said with an annoyed sigh. "I'd rather not have to be on my feet all day while I'm defending the city, distracted by the blisters on my ankles."

"Have you been avoiding me?"

"I'm talking to you right now, aren't I?"

I struggled for a witty retort, but before one came to mind, the elevator doors swished open. Julia stepped inside without another glance.

The doors closed in front of my face.

Chapter Seven

The national weather alert warned of flash flooding and hail the size of golf balls, but instead of being curled up in my apartment, I was on duty. As the daylight hours turned to night, the storm had only intensified. The lightning came so frequently, it was like strobe lights outside the police car windows. I tried to ignore the flashing lights, knowing they could trigger unpleasant memories, and read a book by flashlight.

The guys on base used to play war-simulation video games between assignments. I never understood it. I got enough of that on a daily basis without spending my free time engaged in gunfire, too. To pass the time I read books, fiction mostly. I wasn't a great reader in high school, but the stories became my escape from the desert—like something straight out of *Reading Rainbow*.

A female dispatcher's voice came over the radio. "E-Three, this is Central. What's your twenty?"

"Central, this is E-Three," I responded. I peered through the darkness for street signs at the closest intersection. "My twenty is First and Main."

"E-Three, I've got a disabled vehicle near Jefferson and Cook. Code 1."

"10-4, Central. Be advised E-Three is en-route."

I bent the top corner of the page I had been reading and tossed my book into the glove compartment.

The streets were wet with an inch or so of standing water, and the water level rose the closer I drove to my destination. I slowed the patrol car to a slow crawl when I came upon a dark luxury vehicle parked on the side of the road. The headlights were on and the wipers swished back and forth.

I pulled my vehicle off to the opposite side of the street where the standing water was less deep. "Of all the crumby nights," I grumbled to myself as I unfastened my seatbelt.

I made the call to dispatch to let them know I'd reached the disabled vehicle. I hopped out of the squad car and, burying my head into the lapel of my jacket, I rushed over to the passenger side window of the black Mercedes. When I reached the car, I realized I knew the driver. Intimately.

"What the hell are you doing out here?"

The woman sitting inside the car pressed her lips together, but she didn't respond.

"I'd suggest finding a different place to park, Madam Prosecutor," I yelled through the closed window. "I don't trust that river if the rain keeps this up."

The window lowered. "I'm not parked here on purpose, Detective," Julia snapped. "I certainly know better than to park my car by a swollen river."

"Oh." My hair was now plastered to my face. "Then what are you doing out here?" I yelled over the rain.

Julia leaned closer to the open window. "I was on my way home ..." She trailed off and frowned. "Detective, get in the car."

"Why?"

"Because in case you haven't noticed, dear, we're in the middle of a monsoon."

I heard the power locks pop open. Normally I would have insisted I was fine where I was, but the rain continued to fall down in thick, unending sheets. Self-preservation won over my stubborn pride. I yanked the front passenger door open and slid inside, slamming the door closed behind me.

"Mind the leather," Julia sniffed, no doubt regretting inviting my soggy body into her luxury vehicle.

"So you were just about to tell me why on earth you're out this late, and why you're parked on the side of the road."

"I don't have the luxury of working banker hours, Detective. I was in court for most of the day, and I still had work to do afterwards. I was just driving home when I drove through what I *thought* was a mud puddle; it turned out to be a lake," she said sourly. "I didn't get very far until my engine died."

"My car works. I'll drive you home."

"You really expect me to get out of my car in this weather?" Julia said dully. She gripped the steering wheel tighter and continued to stare straight ahead. The inside of the windshield was starting to fog up.

"It's just *rain*. I don't imagine you'll melt."

Julia continued to sit, immobile in her vehicle, petulant like a pouting child.

I made an audibly frustrated noise. I became all arms and elbows as I tried to peel off my damp jacket. The task was made more difficult in the confines of the car.

"What are you doing?" Julia sounded annoyed and put-off.

I pushed open the passenger side door and launched back into the rain.

"Detective Miller!" Julia yelled crossly as the mist of the storm came through the open door.

I slammed the door shut and shuffled around the front of the vehicle as the unrelenting storm pelted me with a fresh assault of water. Hardly waterproof, I held my jacket over the driver's side door like a shield.

Julia remained firmly planted in her car for another moment longer. The weather had taken such a nasty turn, I could practically see my breath in the air.

Through the windshield I saw Julia's mouth moving in a silent curse. She reached into the backseat and grabbed her leather briefcase. She turned up the collar of her grey trench coat even though the extra inches of fabric would do little to protect her from the deluge.

When she finally opened up the driver's side door, I hopped backwards to get out of the door's trajectory before returning to my place, using my jacket as a makeshift umbrella for her.

Julia tucked her head deeper into her upturned jacket lapel and shuffled along in her high heels while I did my best to usher her to the police car while keeping my jacket above us both. Julia got the majority of the now-soggy coat, and the left side of my body became saturated from the rain.

Julia jerked open the passenger side door of the Embarrass squad car. I was thankful I hadn't routinely locked the vehicle when I'd gone to investigate the disabled car. I could only imagine her annoyance if she'd found the door to be locked and she'd had to stand outside in the rain for even a moment longer.

With Julia secured in the front seat, I scrambled in front of the hood to reach the driver's side. I felt like a drowned rat by the time I was back behind the driver's wheel.

"Mind the leather," I echoed her earlier command.

The squad car had seen far worse than raindrops, but Julia didn't comment. She fluffed at her wilted locks and ran a finger under each eye to check for runny mascara.

I started up the car. It made a small whine in protest before the engine thankfully turned over. "Where am I taking you?"

"To my house, obviously."

"I don't know where that is," I admitted.

Julia rolled her eyes at what I was sure she interpreted to be my complete incompetency. "Down this road, take a right at the four-way stop."

I shifted the car out of park and began to drive in the direction Julia had provided. We were the only car on the deserted county road. I grabbed the in-car radio handset. "Central, this is E-Three."

"Go ahead, E-Three."

"Be advised on the disabled car. I'll be driving the citizen home now."

"10-4, E-Three. I see you en route at 1:13."

"The citizen?" Julia repeated when I'd returned the handset to its holster.

"Do you want all the little old ladies in Embarrass to know I'm driving you home? I thought you liked it when I was discreet." I couldn't hide the bite in my tone.

"Fine," she snapped.

We drove without talking for another five miles with only the occasional squawk of the police radio interrupting the quiet.

"You really live all the way out here?" I asked, breaking what I thought had become a stifling silence.

"It's hardly a strenuous commute," Julia sniffed.

The wipers worked furiously, and I leaned towards the windshield to better see the black road. The inside of the windshield had started to fog up and the defroster wasn't blasting out any air. I wiped away at a patch of fog. The night was inky black and a thick cloud cover obscured the stars and most of the moon. Even without the torrential downpour, it would have been hard to see.

"Is this vehicle even safe to drive?" Julia asked tightly.

"Hey, at least the engine works," I shot back, defensive about the squad car even though I'd been on the police force less than a week.

With Julia's exasperated help, I eventually pulled up in front of a regal-looking red brick home. Two white columns framed either side of a blue front door.

"You really didn't have an umbrella in your car or briefcase?" I lamented, looking out my car window. The rain refused to let up.

"No, Detective Miller. No umbrella. What about you?"

"I think there's a plastic rain poncho in the emergency kit in the trunk."

"I'll risk the rain," came her disgruntled response. Julia pushed open her door and was out in the rain before I could turn off the car. Her designer heels clacked on concrete as she stalked up the walkway that led to the front entrance.

The city prosecutor's home was nicer than any of the houses people owned back in St. Cloud. It was also significantly grander than any of the residences in Embarrass, including the Mayor's home. The front foyer was massive, complete with vaulted ceilings, a crystal chandelier, and a grand staircase that reminded me a little bit of *Gone With the Wind*. The floor was white marble with an elaborate medallion inlay design directly beneath the overhead chandelier. I knew I had to be gaping.

"Shoes."

I hopped on one foot as I struggled to pull off my knee-high leather boots. They were a tight fit even without being soaked through and clinging to my jeans. When I had succeeded, I carefully lined them up on a welcome mat next to a pair of rain boots and muddy running shoes.

Julia disappeared through the first door on the right. I didn't know if I should follow. I peered up the imposing staircase. "You live in this great big house all by yourself?" I called out. I wasn't surprised that my voice echoed in the caverns of Julia's home.

"Last time I checked."

I turned my gaze away from the staircase, surprised to see Julia standing in the doorway from whence she'd originally entered. She leaned against the doorjamb. My eyes traveled down the meticulously tailored suit which had been hidden beneath her grey trench coat, and down to her stillettoed feet.

The suit was magnificent, just like the woman who wore it. I couldn't help wondering if she chose undergarments with the same kind of care as she did the rest of her wardrobe. Suits had the potential to be boxy and masculine, clinging to the wrong body parts while hiding others that should have been on display. But Julia wore her clothes; they didn't wear her. The fitted black suit jacket cinched at her waistline. The dramatic lapel was ribbed with a thin white pinstripe. A single strand of white pearls lay against her collarbone. Under the open jacket was a white blouse that fit like a second skin. I hated button-up shirts on myself. My body wasn't proportioned the right way, and the front buttons always left unsightly gaps that made me feel sloppy, unfinished, and exposed. But there were no gaps in Julia's shirt despite the way the material stretched across her chest.

The blouse was tucked into straight-legged dress pants, the material matching the black of her jacket. At her waist was a black leather belt of medium thickness with a shiny silver buckle in a dramatic geometric shape. Black stiletto heels with a vaguely reptilian texture spiked out at the bottom of her pants. Everything about the outfit screamed money, professionalism, and refinement.

I felt underdressed in my signature Henley top, skinny jeans, and now without my knee-high brown leather boots. I had never cared much for fashion or the proper fit of clothes. My wardrobe was classic and comfortable without looking sloppy, and personally I liked the way my trim but muscled biceps looked in the long-sleeved cotton tops.

"Hi." I felt a little shy. "I like your house."

"It was my grandparent's," Julia explained. "But when my grandmother passed, it went to me."

"But this is a mansion."

"I'm well aware of that. But as you've probably experienced firsthand, real estate in this town is hard to come by."

Julia disappeared into the room once again and this time, I followed.

A great fire burned in a massive fireplace in the den. I crossed the room to inspect the fire, drawn to its heat like a moth to a flame. It was real, not one of those push-button gas fireplaces that flickered around fake wood and did little more than provide atmosphere. The heat of the flames felt good on my face.

Julia pulled two crystal tumblers from an ornate, built-in cabinet. Partitioned lead glass parted to display a collection of light pink Depression glass and other expensive-looking glassware. She pulled a decanter of amber liquid from a hutch. "Have a drink, Detective?"

I turned from the fire. "No. I shouldn't. I'm on duty."

"Neat or on the rocks?" Julia ignored my statement and poured the liquid into both glasses, two fingers of bourbon in each.

"Neither. Still on duty," I resisted.

Julia continued to disregard my words. "You seem like a woman who takes her bourbon neat." She handed me one of the glasses.

Despite my earlier refusal, I took the proffered glass. *I don't have to drink it,* I told myself. *I'll just hold it to be polite.*

Julia lifted her drink to her lips and watched me over the rim of her glass. When she set her beverage back down on the hutch, her red lipstick remained on the rim.

"If you won't have a drink, at least stay long enough for your clothes to dry," she said. "My conscience wouldn't be able to handle the guilt if you got sick on account of saving me."

I fingered my damp leather jacket, limp in my arms.

"Hang it by the fire, Detective," Julia instructed, her voice bordering on the ridiculous. "That's how these things work."

I shrugged and slung the coat over the top of a high-backed easy chair. Julia picked it up and hung it with more care so it could more efficiently dry.

The overhead lights flickered and then went out.

Julia sighed loudly. "As if this night could get any worse."

I clutched the drink tighter in my hands. "Where are you going?"

"To check on the fuse box, although I suspect that's not the culprit."

"Now *you* sound like the detective," I tried to joke.

Julia made a humming noise and walked out of the room, leaving me alone with my drink and the crackling fire.

The rain continued to pound against the grand windows of the den. I brushed a thick curtain out of the way to peer outside. Without the aid of the front porch lights, the night had swallowed up everything outside. I couldn't even see my patrol car, but I hoped it was still parked outside and hadn't floated away.

Julia returned with a lighted candle. "Well, it's not the fuse box; I imagine town is without power because of the storm."

"I should probably get back to the station then."

"Why? Are you an electrician?" Julia posed.

"No. But if someone needs to get a hold of me—"

"They'll call your cell phone or central dispatch. The landline at the police station won't be working with the power outage."

"Oh. Right."

Julia smiled mildly. "Detective, if I didn't know better, I'd say you were eager to leave me."

"I'm on duty," I excused myself. "I shouldn't be wasting taxpayer money sitting with you, having a cocktail."

"How very noble."

Julia fished the crystal glass out of my cupped hands. She

drained the contents of my untouched drink. "Thank you for your assistance tonight. I'm sorry I've kept you from doing your job."

"You didn't ..." I ran my fingers though still damp blonde tendrils. I was the one feeling guilty now.

Julia left the den, leaving me to scramble for my jacket and find my way back to the front entryway. I silently pulled my leather boots back on under the careful watch of the city prosecutor.

The front door opened. "Have a nice night, Miss Miller," Julia stated curtly. Her long, elegant fingers curled around the outer edge of the ornately carved front door. "Do stay safe."

I turned off the county highway and back into town. The rain had lightened up significantly, and downtown was lit up like a Christmas tree. Upon further investigation, I discovered a fallen tree branch had severed a power line. I called in the downed line to the electric company, but a sleepy, disgruntled voice informed me that nothing could be done about it for a few days. Apparently Minnesota nice didn't extend to the electric company.

The return drive to Julia's house came with little thought until I was standing on her front stoop. Was I just doing my job or was I looking for an excuse to see the city prosecutor again? Without electricity, I couldn't have called Julia's landline to give her an update, and I didn't have her cell phone number either. All of these realizations put me moderately at ease about my decision to be knocking on her door at this hour.

I could just make out the sound of footsteps on the other side of the front door before it opened. My eyes practically bulged at the expensive silk robe that barely reached the top of Julia's kneecaps. She pulled the sash tighter around her lithe waist when she saw me. Her face was unreadable, but she looked unaffected by my presence or that she was in her pajamas. "Two house calls in one night? To what do I owe this surprise?"

I took a step backwards. "I just wanted to let you know that I found a downed power line a few miles from here. Town has power, but you don't. I called it in to the electric company, but they won't get to it for a few days."

Julia ran the tip of her tongue over still painted lips. Even though she'd changed out of her work clothes, her makeup remained in place, like her armor or a mask. "Thank you."

I shoved my hands into my jacket pockets and my hands curled around my key ring in one pocket and my cell phone in the other. "I, uh, I also took the liberty of calling the city garage about your car. They're not open until the morning, obviously, but I left a voicemail telling them where to find your car so they can tow and fix it."

At the admission, Julia's carefully sculpted eyebrows rose on her unlined forehead. "You're very thorough, aren't you?"

"Just, uh, doing my job." It was cold outside and despite my jacket, I shivered. My clothes were still damp from earlier. I wondered how Julia could stand the night chill in silk negligee.

"Would you like to come in, Detective?"

"I really shouldn't." I technically had another three hours on duty until Chief Hart came to relieve me.

"At least let me thank you properly for this second trip out here. I promise it won't be more alcohol."

My eyes traveled the perimeter of the doorway with the same kind of practiced scrutiny as I would have done in Afghanistan. The surrounding environments couldn't have been more different, but the heightened anxiety was similar.

Julia stood in the open threshold, holding court and smirking. My gaze was drawn to her waist when she tightened the robe's sash again. I had a pretty good idea what would happen if I accepted her invitation. I glanced once at the watch at my wrist. After all, what else did two people do at 3:00 a.m.?

"Come inside, Detective." Julia stepped back inside and back into the darkness. "I won't bite."

The inside of Julia's home looked different cloaked by night and the absence of electricity. Thin lines of moonlight cast across the marble floor in the entryway, filtered through the narrow windows on either side of the solid front door. I stood motionless in the grand foyer while I waited for my eyes to adjust to the lack of light and for my orientation to return. I only knew the den to the immediate right. The rest of the house was a mystery.

"This way, Detective." Julia's voice came from behind me. I felt the gentle swipe of fingers graze my lower back and circle around to my side as she strode past me. That hand came to curl around my wrist and she tugged me deeper into her home.

With no electricity and the sounds of a sleeping city miles away, the house was silent. Julia was barefoot with no heels to clack against the marble tiles. The chunky heels of my own boots sounded hollow in the entranceway.

"Shoes?" I paused. It wasn't a comment about Julia's footwear, but rather a question about what to do with my own.

"I had no idea you'd be so trainable, Miss Miller." I could practically hear the amused smile in her words. "You may leave them on," she permitted.

I allowed Julia to guide me down a long hallway, darker than the rest of the home as there were no windows in the corridor. The hallway opened up to an open kitchen, massive in size with high, vaulted ceilings. The entire back wall seemed to be constructed of glass, giving an unobstructed view of a private backyard illuminated by the pale yellow of the fat moon that hung in the midnight black sky.

Julia dropped my wrist and walked around a large L-shaped island. "Are you hungry?" she asked.

I stood awkwardly now without her guidance. I shoved my hands into the tight front pockets of my jeans. "I can always eat," I routinely said.

She opened the double doors of a stainless-steel refrigerator. The insides remained dark without the aid of internal lighting. "I'm afraid I'm a little short on cheeseburgers and snack cakes. I don't normally keep that kind of food in my house."

I narrowed my eyes. "What makes you think I eat garbage like that?" I did, but there was no reason why she should have known that. I'd been so worried about her thinking that *I* was a stalker, it hadn't occurred to me that maybe she was watching me in return.

"I saw your cart at the grocery store."

"Oh." I thought I'd gone unnoticed.

She moved to a cabinet drawer and, upon pulling it out, produced two spoons. She went to the refrigerator next, bent at the waist, and pulled free the freezer drawer beneath. I should have removed my stare from the way Julia's short robe crawled up her naked thighs, but I'd already exhibited an unparalleled amount of self-control for one day.

When Julia righted herself, she held a cardboard cylinder container in one hand.

"Ice cream?" I wondered aloud when I saw the packaging.

She pushed a lock of hair out of her eyes. "Butter pecan." She set the container on the island and pried the top open. "If I'm to be without electricity for the next few days, I might as well take care of this so it doesn't go to waste."

It seemed to me that Julia was trying to justify the indulgence, but I kept my observation to myself.

I reached across the island and snagged one of the spoons. "No chocolate?"

She shrugged and dipped her spoon into the new container.

"This is about as indulgent as I allow." I watched the creamy mixture at the end of Julia's spoon with unrivaled jealousy. The tip of the spoon disappeared between parted lips and re-emerged clean. "Food-wise."

"Do you have any vices, Madam Prosecutor?"

Julia gave me a predatory stare. "A few."

I dug less delicately into the container than my compatriot. Butter pecan ice cream overflowed on my spoon, and I shoved the utensil into my mouth before it could fall off.

Julia's steady gaze regarded me as she took another modest spoonful. "Such enthusiasm," she murmured.

I wiped at my mouth with the back of my hand. I knew my table manners were lacking, but I had no pressing desire to eat ice cream straight out of the container with raised pinkies.

"So this was your grandparent's house?"

I wasn't an expert at making small talk, but I found it a necessity around her. I was quickly learning that if I didn't control the conversation topic with this woman, she found a way to make me uncomfortable. It wasn't purely physical, and there was a class element to be sure, but I mostly didn't want the city attorney asking too many questions about my own life. I was loathe to hand over my past to be judged and studied.

"It was." Julia swirled the tip of her spoon in the ice cream and dragged the caramel ribbon across its surface. "I have many fond memories of playing here as a child."

"They let you play in here? It feels more like a museum," I said.

Julia stood up straight, no longer leaning into the island. "This house was a lot different when filled with family and love," she defended. "If it feels like a mausoleum now, then I'm the only one to blame."

"I didn't mean anything by it."

"No. I know you didn't." She stabbed her spoon into the ice

cream as though planting a flag into the ground. "You should probably leave, Miss Miller. I know you have work to get back to."

Julia scooped up the barely touched ice cream. She tossed her spoon into the sink where it clattered noisily before throwing the entire ice cream container into the garbage.

"Julia, I really didn't mean to offend you," I frowned. Guilt washed over me at how quickly her manner had chilled. One minute we'd been sharing ice cream, and the next moment it was melting at the bottom of a garbage bag.

She didn't respond to my most recent plea. Instead, she walked out of the kitchen, leaving me behind.

Feeling a little shell-shocked, I licked the last remnants of caramel and vanilla ice cream from my spoon before carefully setting it down on the kitchen island. I gathered my thoughts and emotions around me like battle armor and left the kitchen as well.

When I found Julia, she was standing at the front door, which was now open and awaiting my departure. I didn't need to be asked to leave again. I stomped past her, feeling a combination of embarrassment and indignation. I was thankful I was already wearing my boots as pulling them back on would have only prolonged my visit.

"Miss Miller."

I hesitated in my dramatic exit at the name. When I turned to regard Julia, I found myself pinned by dark eyes.

"Thank you again for your assistance tonight."

Before I could muster an indifferent reply, soft lips were pressing against mine. Julia tasted faintly of sweetened caramel and roasted pecans. But just as quickly as I had come to the realization that she was kissing me, those painted lips were gone and the front door was closing, shutting me outside on the front stoop.

My fingertips went to my lips as I walked backwards and stumbled on one of the concrete steps. I looked up at the dark manor and licked at my lips, still feeling and tasting Julia on them.

Chapter Eight

The bell over the door at Stan's diner rang with the arrival of another breakfast customer. I was sitting on a stool next to my breakfast buddy, Franklyn Walker, with my back facing the front entrance, so I didn't see the newcomer. I leaned over my plate and continued to slice into my western omelet.

"Coffee, please," came a familiar, throaty rasp. "To go." The voice was closer than I would have expected, nearly vibrating off my right ear.

I slowly turned on my stool. Julia was hovering so close that my knees nearly knocked into her when I did the about-face.

"Good morning, Detective," she greeted with a subtle bob of her beautiful head.

"Madam Prosecutor," I returned.

She slipped fitted black leather gloves off her hands and set them on the diner's counter. "I trust the rest of your night went well?"

"Yeah. It did, thanks."

Julia looked perfect as usual, no signs of a pre-dawn visitor or a morning without modern conveniences like hot water for a shower. She leaned against the counter as she waited for her coffee order. "This is starting to become a habit, running into you. Do you eat every meal here?"

I lifted my shoulders helplessly. "Stan makes a great omelet," I defended myself and my lack of culinary acumen.

"I wonder how it would compare to one of mine?" she mused. I watched the tip of her pink tongue touch against a small scar at the top edge of her lipsticked mouth. I hadn't noticed the thin white line before under the pulsing neon lights of a Minneapolis club; or in the crush of mouths during hurried, one-sided sex; or even by the light of the fire in her cozy den. I wanted to know the story behind the scar. I wanted to know all of Julia's stories. I wanted to see all of her scars.

I licked my own lips at the memory of our last, albeit brief, kiss. Julia had tasted delicious. Her lips had been soft, and she had tasted like caramel and butter pecan. If I were braver, more brazen, I knew just the words to rattle the unflappable lawyer: *Is that an invitation?*

But the moment passed, and Stan brought Julia her coffee while I returned my attention to my plate of cooling food. She left without another word, the door slamming and bell jingling with her exit.

I stabbed viciously at my eggs and side of hash browns. Heroes were supposed to be brave. But all that woman had ever made me feel was afraid.

The position of mayor of a small town generally came with few responsibilities; it was a formality, a person who represented the town, waving in the Fourth of July Parade at the citizens sitting on lawn chairs and curbs as the fire trucks rolled by. But in Embarrass, Mayor William J. Desjardin was more than a simple figure-head. Not only was he was head of the City Council and an honorary member of other similar city commissions, but he had an office in City Hall where he oversaw the day-to-day operations of the town—a job that normally would have gone to the City Manager.

Mayor Desjardin's office occupied a corner slot on the third floor of City Hall, across the hallway from the courtroom. I wouldn't have had a reason to go to his office if we'd had a bigger police department or if he'd been a typical town mayor instead of a city manager. We had a modest department, but that didn't mean we had to use outdated technology. Chief Hart and David Addams might have known everyone in town, but until I had a better grasp on the city's residents, a mobile fingerprint reader was necessary.

The Mayor was an imposing figure. His pale blue eyes scruti-nized me when I knocked on his office door. His blond hair had turned silver and his pallid skin looked as though he hadn't seen the sun in decades. It struck me that he looked nothing like his daughter.

"Cassidy Miller," I said, shaking the man's hand.

"Miller." He let the name roll over his tongue. "You're the new police officer we've hired, correct?"

"Yes, sir." I straightened my shoulders, well aware that this man was ultimately my boss, but also the father of the woman on whom I had a desperate crush. It was a little surreal.

"Please have a seat." He motioned to the open chair across from his black lacquered desk. He folded his hands on his desk and steepled his long, pale fingers. "How can I help you?"

I shifted in the chair and my belt squeaked against the leather upholstery. "I wanted to see you about new equipment for the police department. I talked to Chief Hart about it, but he suggested I talk to you instead." He hadn't done any such thing, but I didn't need to let the Mayor know that I was going over my superior's head for this.

"What kind of equipment are we talking about, Miss Miller?"

"It's called a mobile fingerprint reader. Too often when we make a traffic stop, many drivers don't have any form of identification on them," I began. "The fingerprint reader is connected to AFIS—the automated fingerprint identification system, which is the state-wide database of fingerprints. With a simple scan of a driver's prints, we can verify who they are, but more importantly, be alerted if there's a warrant out on them."

The Mayor frowned. "I'm sure you can appreciate that budgets are tight these days—"

"I promise it's not some fancy, unnecessary gadget, sir," I interrupted. "It was an incredibly helpful tool when I worked in Minneapolis."

He made a humming noise. "I'll take a look into it, Officer Miller."

"Detective."

"Excuse me?" He had the eyebrow arch like his daughter, and I suddenly saw the resemblance. I self-consciously squirmed in my chair. "Sorry. It's just that I'm *Detective* Miller, not Officer."

William Desjardin's features were unreadable. "I'll remember that for the future."

He stood from his desk and I took that as my signal that it was time to leave. I found the Desjardins' hospitality lacking, but I kept that observation to myself.

The sun had set hours ago and the street lamps were all lit along Main Street. Behind City Hall, the employee parking lot was empty except for a few city-owned trucks and one beat-up compact car. My key ring jingled as I looked for the key to the police car. I jerked my head away from my task when I heard heels click solidly on the pavement.

"Good evening, Madam Prosecutor," I greeted when I saw her. "Another late night?" She seemed to keep even stranger work hours than me.

Julia stalked up to the blue compact car and shoved a key in the lock on the driver's side door. "So it would seem." She jiggled the key, but the locking mechanism refused to turn.

I looped my thumbs into the front of my duty belt. "You're not trying to hijack that car right in front of a police officer, are you?"

She growled and tossed her briefcase on the dented hood and refocused on the stubborn lock. "It's a rental from the auto shop."

"Because your Mercedes blew up," I said, remembering. "Wow. They really hooked you up," I chuckled. The compact car made my old Crown Vic look high-end.

A scowl marred her beautiful face. "I prosecuted one of the co-owners of the auto shop for public drunkenness a few years ago; apparently he's still upset about that." She blew out a deep breath that disrupted her side-swept hair. She continued to struggle with the lock for a moment longer until she threw her hands up in disgust. "I give up. I'm walking home."

"Not in those heels you're not," I remarked. "Here, let me try."

"Unless you're the car whisperer," she huffed, jamming her key ring into my hands, "I fail to see how you—"

I wiggled the key in the keyhole until I felt it catch. It turned without further protest.

Julia blinked at me. "How did you ..."

I gave a nonchalant shrug, although I was personally surprised I'd succeeded where she'd failed. "Sometimes these stubborn things just need a little coaxing and a gentle touch."

She arched an eyebrow, looking a mixture of amused and perplexed. "Indeed. Either way, thank you for your assistance. You've seemed to save me twice in as many days."

"I'm no superhero."

"Aren't you?" she challenged. "Defending the citizens of Embarrass from unknown terrors while they sleep?"

I grinned and leaned my hip against the side of the police car. It was still warm from David's shift. "You make me sound like Batman or something."

"Mmm ... not enough tricks in your utility belt, I'm afraid."

I tugged at my duty belt. "Oh, I'd show you some tricks if given the chance."

A ghost of a smile played at Julia's red, painted mouth. "I believe I've seen your tricks before, Detective."

"That was just a preview." I pushed off the police car to stand erect. This was comfortable. This was familiar. I could do banter. "How long are you stuck with this beater?"

"Hopefully not for too much longer."

I nodded. "Well, if you need help popping that lock again, I'm only a phone call away."

Her intoxicating mouth twisted into a knowing smile. "I'm sure you'd love the opportunity to pop my lock again."

"I ... that wasn't what I-I didn't mean . . ." I sputtered. She narrowed the distance between us, and my backside bumped the side panel of the police car. Maybe this *wasn't* comfortable.

Julia had me pinned to the car, and a presumptuous hand rested on my hip. "That's a fancy necklace, Detective. Did you get that out of a Cracker Jack box?"

I touched the badge that hung around my neck. "It's how detectives wear their badges."

She slipped the metal beaded chain off me, pulling it past my ears and hair. "Detectives, perhaps. But it's not how *heroes* wear them." Her fingers ghosted against my skin.

"No?" I felt frozen under her brazen attentions.

Julia separated the badge from its leather pouch. "No, dear. For you ... something different."

105

I held my breath when her hand came to rest on my hip. She hooked her thumb under the heavy gun belt around my waist and tugged as she slid the badge's back fastening between leather and dark denim. The badge rested snug and secure against my hipbone.

"Much better, I think," she practically purred in my ear. Her mouth sought the stretch of my neck, and I groaned when I felt her mouth, soft and wet against my skin.

"I-I should probably be getting to work," I announced.

She seemed to sigh into me. "Yes. I suppose it is that time." She bit down, hard.

"Damn it!" I pulled back angrily. My hand went to the tender spot, fingers touching over the space where Julia's teeth had just been. I was sure to have a mark there in the morning.

"Have a nice night, Detective," Julia smiled smugly. She climbed into the driver's seat of her replacement car. "Do be safe."

I laid on top of the covers on my bed, stripped down to underwear and a black tank top, as I watched the lazy circles of the ceiling fan overhead. It was damnably hot. I'd opened all the windows to coax in a cool breeze, but no air would circulate through the studio apartment. Whoever had designed the building hadn't thought about the need for cross-breezes. The windows were in the wrong places. It was frustrating; it was still cold enough outside to warrant wearing a jacket, and yet the humidity of my apartment was like a suffocating blanket.

My clothes from the previous day hung over the easy chair in the corner of the apartment. My eyes fell to a flash of gold among the cotton blends. My badge was still secured to my leather belt, and the badge holder Chief Hart had given me was empty on the floor. Aside from my interaction with Julia at the start of my shift, work had been uneventful. I'd gone on a call about a noise complaint which turned out to be a barking dog, and I'd written a ticket to someone for speeding down Main Street, but I'd seen no one else the rest of my shift.

I scratched at a mosquito bite on my upper arm. My face felt like it was covered in a fine layer of grease even though I'd showered when I'd gotten home from work just a few hours earlier. My back was on fire simply from having contact with the bed beneath me. I was never going to fall asleep.

I considered my options. I could wander around the freezer section at the grocery store or spend the day at the air-conditioned public library, but I wouldn't get to sleep at either place. City Hall would be temperature controlled, and I remembered seeing a cot in a back room in the police station. It would have to do for now, or at least until I had time to order an air conditioner online.

I dragged myself out of bed and trudged the few steps to the bathroom to make myself presentable enough to be seen in public. It wouldn't take much. I ran a wide-toothed comb through my stubborn curls and began to brush my teeth.

I pulled my hair out of the way, twisting it over one shoulder. I leaned down and spit out the wasted toothpaste. When I righted myself, I gaped at my mirrored reflection.

"Fucking, eh," I grumbled. I leaned closer to the vanity mirror and squinted my eyes. A giant, purple and red bruise stared back at me near the space where my neck met my shoulder. I touched my fingers to the tender flesh.

"Fucking Julia." I flung my long hair back over my shoulder, hiding the fresh bite. Twenty-eight years old with a hickie. Awesome.

When I left the bathroom, I heard a soft knock at my door. I didn't feel like company, but maybe Grace Kelly had made more baked goods. I pulled on my jeans from the previous night and refastened the belt. Another knock, this time louder, rattled the door.

"Coming!" I yelled.

I jerked open the door and nearly gasped at the woman standing in the hallway.

"Julia."

She was dressed for work, her grey trench coat over another immaculate outfit. She seemed to have a penchant for crisply pressed Oxford shirts, unbuttoned to the third button. Her dress pants hugged at slight curves, although I would have described her as more straight than curvy.

"Hello, Detective," she greeted in that low rasp that made my knees wobble every time. "I hope this isn't a bad time. I didn't want to visit too early in case you were still sleeping."

"N-no," I stuttered. "It's fine."

I felt her gaze sweep over me, and her eyes lingered at the gold badge at my hipbone. "I'm glad to see my words didn't fall on deaf ears." Her lips pursed knowingly.

Deaf, no. Burning, yes. I could feel the embarrassed redness enflame my pale cheeks and creep up to the tips of my ears. "I was just too tired to change it back this morning."

"Mmhm," she hummed.

"What, um, can I help you? Do you need help with something?"

"Surprisingly, no. I simply thought it was about time I welcomed the newest member of the Embarrass police force to town."

I noticed the potted plant in her arms for the first time. She shifted its weight from one hip to the other.

"I thought you'd already welcomed me."

Her red, painted lips thinned, but she didn't take the bait. "Then consider it a housewarming present." She shoved the plant into my waiting arms.

I hefted the ceramic pot and inspected its contents. A plant with long, yellow-green leaves shot out of the fresh dirt. "I'm not very good with these things."

"I suspected as much. Luckily, spider plants are resilient. I doubt even you could kill this plant, Detective."

Not waiting for an invite, Julia pushed past me.

"You can call me, Cassidy, you know."

"I like to keep things professional."

I wondered at that. How professional was it for a police officer and the city prosecutor to hook up? I didn't think I had an anti-fraternizing clause in my contract like we had in the Marines, but to be honest, I hadn't really read my new contract all that carefully.

"Do you always push people away?"

Julia's mouth opened and closed. I wondered if anyone had ever called her on her shit before.

"Yes. It's what I do best."

"Maybe second best," I said, grinning mischievously.

Her eyes narrowed. I imagined her as an annoyed cat, long tail flicking back and forth in agitation.

"What do I feed this thing?" I set the plant on the kitchen island. It looked like a cross between something out of a Dr. Seuss book and a horror film, like it might crawl out of its container at any moment and suffocate me. I poked at the long, spiked leaves with uncertainty.

She carefully removed her black leather gloves, but she kept on her long trench coat. "Water."

"That's it?"

"I can assure you that it requires no blood sacrifice."

"What about sunlight?"

"Yes, it's probably better if you left it near a window and not hide it away in a closet."

I continued to stare at the green stalks of the plant. The last time I'd been entrusted with a living thing had been a goldfish in the fourth grade. It hadn't lasted the night.

"It's a plant, Miss Miller, not my first born. If you somehow manage to kill it, I won't be angry with you."

It wasn't the plant that was making me nervous; it was her.

"Don't bite your nails, dear."

I jerked my hand away from my mouth. I hadn't even realized I'd been doing that. "I can't help it."

"Sure you can. You just need to give your mouth something else to do."

"Are you offering?" I flashed a cheeky grin. The first and only time she'd been in my apartment, our mouths had been occupied, but it hadn't exactly been in conversation.

Julia wrinkled her nose. "Hardly. I was going to suggest chewing gum."

"Can I get you something to eat or drink?" I stumbled the few steps to the refrigerator and opened the door. It was embarrassingly bare. I had little to offer other than half a gallon of skim milk and a ketchup bottle.

"No, thank you. I can't stay. I have to prepare for court later this afternoon. I just wanted to drop off the plant."

"Oh. Uh, thanks."

"It's nothing."

I chewed on my lower lip. "You're different in this town. Different than the woman I met in Minneapolis."

"I'm sure I don't know what you mean," Julia coolly replied.

"You're harder, I guess. More guarded."

"Have you ever considered that I just don't like you, Detective?"

I leaned my hip against the kitchen island. "I don't know why not."

"Perhaps I don't take kindly to being drowned."

I furrowed my eyebrows. "When did I..." I blinked in confusion until I realized to what she was referring. "Spilling my drink on you is hardly *drowning* you."

"*Four* drinks," she reminded me. "I'm half a mind to send you the bill for my dry cleaning."

"What were you doing in the Twin Cities?"

"Why do you want to know?" Julia countered. "Is it part of an on-going investigation?"

"Let's say it is."

"It was a reunion of sorts. I was meeting up with some friends from college."

"You have friends?" I teased.

Julia's expression was unreadable. "Shocking. I know."

I instantly regretted the jab. I didn't know this woman well enough to be teasing her. Yes, we'd shared a bed once, but that didn't mean we were on friendly terms.

Julia's dark eyes regarded me. "Why are you in this town?" she asked. The question seemed as if it had been weighing on her mind for some time. "Certainly a war hero like yourself has more job prospects than working the nightshift in a town where nothing happens?"

"Chief Hart is an old family friend. It's ... it's a favor."

Julia seemed to let my words roll around in her head as if deciding if it was an adequate answer. "How very charitable of you."

I didn't bother to correct her.

Chapter Nine

The back room in the police station wasn't much larger than a generous closet. It doubled as the evidence locker and the ammunitions storage. The crackle of the police radio was like white noise, and I let out an exhausted breath as I settled onto the canvas cot. It wasn't any more comfortable than the bed in my apartment, but the room benefitted from its basement location and central air. Surrounded by boxes of rifle shells and incandescent light bulbs, I was finally able to fall asleep.

Afghanistan, 2012

He says his name is Amir, and I have no sympathy for him. He complains of thirst, but we're all suffering from lack of the basic human necessities. Because of him, my friends are dead and Pensacola might as well be. He's not the mark. I don't even know if he's going to be of any use to the mission. But whatever information he can share certainly won't be worth the loss of lives.

I pretend I don't speak his language, so he tries again in very broken English. Still, I ignore him. Why the hell should I care if he has to take a piss? He should consider himself lucky that I haven't stuck the dangerous end of my M16 into his complaining mouth.

I've never killed anyone—not directly by my own hand, at least —but it doesn't really matter. I'm a part of the war machine. People die all the time in battle—terrible people, but also good people.

I bet his stripped flesh would dry up in this heat just like jerky. I've already cannibalized my foxtrot to get a signal to call for help. What's one more act of cannibalism?

I woke up to the sound of a muffled conversation. I recognized Chief Hart's voice right away, but the other voice was less familiar. The backroom was completely dark, and it took me a moment to remember where I was.

"I'm giving you a direct order to drop this," the second male voice declared.

I fixed my ponytail, which had worked its way loose while I slept. I tentatively pushed open the door and I winced into the light that crept through the doorway.

Chief Hart stood by himself outside of his office door, looking over notes on a yellow legal pad. I looked around the station for the owner of the second voice, but he had disappeared. I scratched my head. Maybe I'd imagined it all.

"Morning, Chief." My voice sounded like a bullfrog's croak. I cleared the sludge from my throat with a cough.

Chief Hart visibly flinched. "Jesus, Cassidy! What were you doing back there?"

"Taking a nap," I yawned. "It was too hot to sleep in my apartment."

"I should tell the Mayor he doesn't have to spend money on an apartment for you; you can just live in the back room," he chuckled.

"Speaking of the Mayor, has he talked to you about those mobile fingerprint readers?" I asked.

Chief Hart frowned and shook his head. "I told you we don't have the budget for that."

"I know. But I told the Mayor it would be really beneficial if we had them."

"You talked to William Desjardin?"

"Uh, yeah." I realized how bad it looked that I'd gone over his head to continue to pursue this.

Chief Hart folded his arms across his broad chest. "No. He hasn't talked to me about it. But I suppose if he changes his mind, he'll talk directly to you, since I'm just taking up space."

I held up my hands. "Chief, no, I ... I." I didn't know what to say. He'd been so generous in offering me this position, and how had I repaid him? My stomach turned in disappointment at myself.

"I'm going to be late for court," Chief Hart grumbled. "David's getting sued. We can talk about this later."

"Wait. He's what?"

"Being sued by one of the local business owners. It's really nothing to worry about; it's more of an annoyance than anything." Chief Hart looked distracted. "The city prosecutor is a real ball buster, but you'll be happy to have her on your side if you ever need her."

"Julia Desjardin, right?" For some reason, saying her name out loud felt taboo.

Chief Hart nodded. "She represents the city, but also the police force if we're ever sued as a department, or like in David's case, as individuals."

"Can, uh, is anyone allowed to go to the trial?" I asked.

"Yes, but I don't know why you'd waste your time."

"I'd like to go to support David." That much was true, but it would be a lie if I didn't admit that I was curious to see the city prosecutor in action.

~

On the third floor of City Hall, the county courtroom served as a catchall for every phase of criminal justice from arraignment to the trial to sentencing. I thought the courtroom was impressive in size with about ten rows of seats for observers on either side of the central aisle. The juror box on the right hand side of the courtroom was currently empty as the presiding judge, not a panel of peers, would decide David's fate. I hadn't realized it, having been a police officer for less than a year, but getting sued wasn't that unusual, and it was even more frequent in small towns where police officers and civilians were on a first-name basis.

I almost didn't recognize David out of uniform. He sat by himself at a long wooden table at the front of the courtroom. He'd gotten a haircut since I'd last seen him, and his light brown hair was buzzed even shorter than I was used to. Instead of the brown and yellow police uniform, he wore a dark suit and a light blue tie that matched the color of his eyes. The boyish smile that was a regular fixture on his face was missing that day.

The plaintiff, Gregory Espinosa, was the owner of a local bar that served food on the side. I hadn't yet patronized the establishment, but its reputation preceded itself. If the stories I'd heard from both David and Grace Kelly were true, it was a miracle the place hadn't been shut down by the liquor commission or the health department. Espinosa claimed that David had unfairly targeted his bar and had been harassing him, his employees, and his patrons while on duty. It was Julia's job to prove that the plaintiff was full of shit.

Instead of the details of the civil court case, I found myself distracted by the back slit of Julia's pencil skirt which revealed perfectly toned calves, hugged today by shin-high boots. She was masterful and clearly in her element. I couldn't take my eyes off her as she stalked around the courtroom, and it was clear the local judge was having the same problem. It wasn't just that she looked like perfection in a power suit tailored to the lean lines of her figure. Her body language seemed to dare the plaintiff to continue making his accusations against David.

A small man, whom I assumed to be Greg Espinosa, sat in the witness box. His shoulders were slumped forward and the pencil-thin mustache stretched across his upper lip twitched in agitation. He waved a pointed finger in David's direction. "That man has been harassing my business and my customers since he got hired by Chief Hart," he bellowed.

"By 'harassment,' would that be in reference to the over ten citations your bar and bartenders have received for serving minors?" Julia posed.

"I fire everyone who serves alcohol to teens," the man defended himself. "But I can't watch my staff every moment. I can't be held responsible if they break the law."

"Actually, Mr. Espinosa, you can," Julia sternly returned. "That is precisely the language used on the stipulation in your liquor license and is therefore terms for the revocation of said license."

"How do you expect me to run a bar and grill with no alcohol?" the man sputtered. "That would put me out of business!"

"Then I suggest you find a new business, since you clearly aren't very good at your current job," she snapped.

"Counselor." The overseeing judge's tone was a warning. "Will you approach the bench, please?"

Julia inclined her head. "Of course, your Honor."

The two conversed at the front of the courtroom, but their

voices were too low for me to decipher a word shared between them. When Julia stepped away and returned to her side of the courtroom, her face was unreadable.

"I've heard all that I care to," the judge announced. "Mr. Addams, I'm dismissing the charges against you. I have been presented with no evidence that you were doing anything but your job." He struck the gavel block when the room filled with voices. "Mr. Espinosa, I'm temporarily suspending your liquor license. It's not in my power to revoke it entirely; that's what City Council is for. It is my recommendation, however, that there be a hearing at the next City Council meeting to decide the fate of your business." He swung his gavel twice more. "Court is adjourned."

David leapt to his feet at the clearing of his name. He grabbed one of Julia's hands with both of his and gave it a vigorous shake. "Julia, I can't thank you enough."

Julia smoothly pulled her hand away and pushed a stray lock off her forehead. "You're very welcome, Sergeant Addams." She began to gather her notes and put them inside her leather brief-case. "But I was merely doing my job, much like yourself."

David loosened his tie as though too much time with it properly around his neck was suffocating. "Still, I feel like I owe you. Let me take you out for a celebratory dinner tonight." He gave what I thought was a particularly charming smile.

I felt my heart seize inside my chest. David Addams was an attractive man. I didn't know the direction of Julia's sexuality—if it steered to both men and women—but I dreaded her response.

"That won't be necessary," Julia coolly dismissed. Her eyes met mine briefly, face still emotionless, before she resuming packing her things.

"Hey, congratulations," I said, standing awkwardly at the front of the courtroom. I schooled my features, hoping the horror I'd previously felt as I'd witnessed David asking out my Dream Woman wasn't written on my face.

David jerked his thumb in Julia's direction as she walked out of the courtroom, looking as if she wanted to avoid further conversations. "That one's a pitbull," he chuckled, "but I'm sure as shit glad she's *our* pitbull."

I bobbed my head, not sure what else to say. "I'll see you later, man. And congrats again."

I rushed out of the courtroom and into the hallway where I spotted the city prosecutor. She stalked across the atrium, one high-heeled foot in front of the other. She walked like she was on a catwalk, not on her way to the elevator.

"Julia!" I called out.

She pulled up short. "Yes, Detective?" she sighed with impatience.

"You were amazing in there." I quickened my step to keep up with the prosecutor's long strides.

"I was adequate."

"You won," I needlessly pointed out.

"Gregory Espinosa had no case against Sergeant Addams. He was breaking the law, and David was doing his job. He'd given Gregory plenty of warnings—too many if you ask me—to turn his business around. I'd have him thrown in jail for serving minors, but apparently no one else seems to care that much for the law."

I swallowed hard, summoning my courage. "I thought maybe you'd like to have dinner with me tonight to celebrate your victory." I didn't want to be obvious that I'd overheard David's invitation. His forwardness was making me feel uncharacteristically brave.

"No." The refusal came without hesitation.

"But you have to eat, right?" I tried again. "It doesn't have to be a big deal." I could tell I was floundering, reaching. "What if we just happened to show up at Stan's tonight at the same time and ate at the same table?"

The elevator doors opened with an echoing ding. Julia stepped inside the lift. "Again, Miss Miller, no. Unlike yourself I do not ply myself with grease and trans fats."

I could do nothing as the elevator doors closed in my face for a second time.

It was another stormy night. The rain was light, but it pelted the windshield of the squad car with each brisk gust of wind. I sat in my patrol car, watching the lights turn on and off on the second floor of Julia's mansion. I imagined the city prosecutor moving from one room to the next as she readied herself for bed. I thought about her from earlier that day, stalking around the courtroom like she controlled it and everyone inside of it. Watching Julia Desjardin was quickly becoming one of my favorite pastimes.

I couldn't help but think back to our one and only sexual encounter. We'd had plenty of charged interactions since then, which told me I wasn't just a one-time thing, but I continued to feel intimidated by her commanding presence to make a forward move. If I were braver or bolder we would have had sex again, I was sure of it. But instead of knocking on her front door and inviting myself in for a cocktail, I continued to sit in my patrol car outside of her palatial home like I was on a stakeout. But Julia was no criminal, unless you counted the sinful way she wore sensible pantsuits.

I wondered what she'd be wearing if I were to knock on her front door at this hour. I typically cared little for fashion, but when it came to Julia I noticed every refined detail. She was impeccable, which naturally made me want to smudge her perfectly applied lipstick or rake my fingers through her carefully styled hair. I wanted to rumple and crease dry-clean only blouses and unfasten the hidden buttons of tailor-fitted pants and slip my fingers beneath the expensive lace undergarment I was sure to find there.

119

Lost to waking dreams, I didn't notice that the lights to the mansion had begun to burn a little brighter because of movement at the front of the house. A knock on the passenger side window of the patrol car had me jolting out of inappropriate thoughts.

I hastily rolled down the window, and Julia leaned through the door.

"Car problems, Detective?"

"No, I uh ..."

The front passenger door opened, and I was greeted with a blast of night air as Julia slipped inside the car. "I hope you're not stalking me."

"S-stalking?" I stumbled on the word. "Of course not." She was wearing the same lavender short robe from the night I'd driven her home, and it took all my willpower to tear my eyes away from her naked thighs.

"Then I wonder what could be the reason for this unexpected late-night visit."

"I'm just patrolling," I insisted.

Julia hummed. "I wonder if you're as thorough with other things are you are with police work." She wet her dark, stained lips and toyed with the collar of my jacket. Her fingers moved up and tickled the shell of my ear.

I released an uneasy breath. "J-Julia." My voice wavered on her name.

"Come on, Detective." She ran a blunt fingernail down the column of my pale throat, no doubt leaving a pink line on my fair skin in her wake. "Tell me this isn't what you had in mind when you decided to park in front of my house."

"I wasn't thinking about anything," I weakly protested.

"And perhaps, my dear, that is precisely why we do this."

Julia lifted her backside off the leather passenger seat. Her hands slipped beneath her robe, causing the silk material to part and exposing even more olive-toned thigh. My eyes bulged, and I jerked my head to stare purposefully forward rather than at the woman currently wiggling out of her underwear.

"I think there's just enough room," she said, thinking aloud.

Leather creaked and noised its protest, but I could not do the same as Julia crawled over the center console to settle on my lap, one knee on either side of my thighs. She rested her arms on my shoulders and idly played with the wavy curls at the nape of my neck.

"Well, Detective?" Her tone was low, but taunting, challenging me to make the next move.

If this was a game of seduction chicken, I was sure to lose. Of their own fruition, my eyes fell to my lap where Julia sat. I found myself breathing heavier than usual as I drank in the parted thighs and the flimsy robe material, the only thing that separated me from what I remembered as being a glorious view.

There was little else we could do in the front seat of a squad car, especially with all the radio equipment crowding the center console area. I didn't think Julia was the type for a quick fuck in the backseat of a police car, the backs of her naked thighs sticking to the leather seats and a seatbelt digging into her tailbone. Yet, here she was, straddling me in the front seat, leaning back against the steering wheel.

I slipped a hand between our bodies. I tugged at the sash around her slim waist, causing the sides of her robe to fall open. Beneath the robe I discovered a dark violet shift that matched the underwear she had so expertly cast off. My hands ignored the warning signs flashing inside my head as I cupped her breasts through the delicate material and felt her nipples immediately respond.

I let my fingers trail down the center of her chest, feeling the fine bones of her collarbone and then her ribcage beneath my fingers, down to the soft skin of a flat stomach. I dallied with the bottom hem of her lingerie top, indecisive.

"I'm starting to sense that voyeurism is your thing," she husked.

I slid both hands beneath the soft material, letting it bunch up at my wrists as I inched the short sleep dress farther up Julia's thighs until I was rewarded with a view of her shaved folds.

I wet my bottom lip and circled my thumb against Julia's clit briefly before sliding solidly into her with two fingers. She released a soft cry and her head fell back. Her back bumped into the steering wheel, pressing long enough to sound the horn. But we were isolated out in the country with no one to hear our activities. I watched in fascination of the view of my fingers piercing Julia's swollen sex, illuminated only by the full moon.

If she'd taken the time to pop the button on my jeans and work her way beneath my underwear, she would have discovered me hot and wet and ready for her fingers. But her hands never strayed from the lapel of my jacket. She bucked against my fingers while my seatbelt remained fastened and my clothing undisturbed.

"Harder, Detective," Julia demanded. "Make me feel it."

I wrapped my free arm around her waist, only so happy to oblige. Every time I thrust into her, her body lurched backwards and she bumped into the car horn. I was thankful she didn't have neighbors in earshot who might call the non-emergency line to report someone continually beeping their horn.

Julia's head fell forward so her lips were brushing against my ear. I closed my eyes and focused on the texture of her soft lips against the shell of my ear and her ragged intake of air every time I bottomed out. I clumsily rubbed the pad of my thumb against her clit, bumping into her with each solid thrust. Her breathing became more shallow and she rolled her hips as she bounced faster and harder against my fingers. It was all I could do to keep up with her frenetic pace.

"So close." Her words spurred me on. "So fucking close, Cassidy."

I gripped her tight around her torso so I could better control the pace and angle of my fingers. I curled my middle and index fingers, and she made a strangled noise.

"Kiss me," I commanded. It was probably the boldest thing I'd done since meeting her. I curled my fingers a second time.

Her hands left the lapel of my jacket and moved instead to cradle my face. I gasped from the simple intimacy of the gesture. Her mouth was soft and careful, a far cry from the bruising pace she demanded from me elsewhere.

She swabbed her tongue against my lower lip and along my straight teeth. I quietly groaned against her lipsticked mouth. The kiss was filled with such tender emotion that I nearly forgot what my right hand was supposed to be doing. I curled my fingers again and her body stiffened against me. Her eyes snapped shut, and she held onto my ears and breathed a gasp into my open mouth.

"Cum for me, Julia," I coaxed. I corkscrewed my fingers inside her.

I held her close as her orgasm struck her like hundreds of tiny electric shocks. When her body sagged against me, I gently eased saturated fingers out of her and wrapped both arms around her waist. She was still breathing hard with our foreheads pressed together. I stroked my hands in the small of her back.

"Thank you, Detective," she clipped in her most city prosecutor-like voice. "You were very thorough as expected."

I frowned at the formality. What had happened to the breathy murmur of Cassidy just moments before?

Julia extricated herself from my lap and returned to the passenger seat. She flipped the sun visor down and wiped at the smudged lipstick at the corners of her mouth and raked her fingers through slightly mussed black hair.

I blinked in wonder at the woman who had just come undone only seconds before by my own hands as she calmly collected herself. Julia remained silent, and without another look in my

123

direction, she opened the passenger side door and slid out into the night.

I watched after her as she strode up the concrete walkway, pulling the sash of her robe more tightly around her waist. Sensing movement, the front lights came on more brightly, and she disappeared inside the house without looking back.

I stayed parked outside for only a moment later, wondering at what had just happened. But when it was clear that the city prosecutor would not be making another appearance that night, I pulled the vehicle out of park and drove away.

The next day I stayed at home instead of wandering around City Hall until just before my shift was supposed to start. Lately I had spent too much of my free time roaming City Hall on the off-chance that I might bump into the city attorney. After what had happened the previous night, however, I thought it best to avoid the municipal building until I was scheduled to work.

I heard the jangle of David's duty belt before I actually saw him. He seemed to have more swagger to his step than usual, which I attributed to his civil court case being dismissed.

He strode up to Lori's desk and dropped a pair of dark purple underwear in front of me. "Lose something?" he grinned.

"Jesus." I snatched the lace garment off the desk and shoved it into my jacket pocket. "Laundry day. Yeah," I stumbled. "It must've fallen out of the hamper."

He looked at me with renewed interest as if the lace undergarment had reminded him of my gender. "You wanna get something to eat before work someday?"

"That's nice of you to offer, but I like to keep things professional."

"Sure. Yeah. I get it. Anyway," he cleared his throat. "I wanted to show you something. Besides your underwear," he said with a chuckle. He produced a piece of paper and slid it across the desk.

I glanced at the photocopied page. "What am I looking at?"

"It's a purchase order for police radios."

"And?" Nothing at first-glance looked amiss.

"And look at the numbers."

I scanned over the receipt. My face scrunched, not understanding, until my eyes fell on the number purchased and their total ticket price. "Forty radios?" I read aloud. "What would Embarrass need with forty police radios?"

"My question exactly. Last time I checked, there were only three of us. Hell, I don't even think there's forty city employees in this entire building."

I continued to inspect the receipt. "Maybe we ordered them for the neighboring counties? Like, there was a group discount?"

David shrugged. "Maybe," he conceded. "But I think this deserves another look. Money like that," he said, tapping at the six-figure price tag at the bottom of the receipt, "isn't something to ignore."

Chapter Ten

I thought about keeping the underwear as a souvenir, but a bigger part of me wanted to see the reaction on Julia's face when confronted with evidence of our late-night rendezvous. For once, I'd have the upper hand.

I drove my Harley out to her house after work and a few hours of sleep. I knocked on the front door, but after a few moments of waiting, I went to look elsewhere. Julia's Mercedes was parked in the long circular driveway out front, so I knew she had to be around somewhere. I left the front stoop to continue to search for the homeowner. When I made my way to the side yard, I heard the soft sounds of music filtering from the rear of the house. Turning another corner, I found Julia in the backyard, on her knees in the lawn, her head tilted down in concentration. In front of her were impressive rosebushes that she was diligently cutting back.

I had no green thumb, but if I gardened, I imagined I'd wear old jeans and a T-shirt. Not so for Julia Desjardin. Her hair was down, but pulled back from her face with a headscarf and over-sized sunglasses. It made her look a little like Jackie Kennedy

Onassis. Her lips were painted a familiar red shade. Her sleeveless navy shell with the gold buttons looked straight out of a Banana Republic catalog. I couldn't quite make out the shape or style of her pants since she was on her knees, but they certainly weren't tattered blue jeans. I wondered if Julia even *owned* a pair of jeans.

She was impossibly elegant. *How can she look so perfect, even when she's gardening?* I wondered. It was truly maddening.

I shoved the underwear back into my jacket pocket when I saw that she wasn't alone. Julia smiled fondly at the woman beside her. She was older, maybe in her sixties or even seventies, and delicately built in the way older women tend to be. Her dark hair was streaked with white, pulled back into a tight bun that reminded me of the hairstyle we'd been required to wear in the Marines. A red cardigan covered her narrow shoulders and a double string of pearls adorned her neck. Despite her advanced age, she wielded the pruning tools with familiarity.

"Hi."

Julia snapped to attention at the sound of my voice. Her caramel eyes were hidden by the oversized sunglasses, so I couldn't be sure of her reaction to my uninvited appearance.

"Cassidy, would you be a dear and grab that bag of mulch from the back shed?"

She had used my first name to address me—not Detective or Miss Miller. I couldn't recall if or when that had ever happened outside of our more intimate encounters. I nodded dumbly and obeyed the request. Nothing seemed to rattle the unflappable city prosecutor—not even the unexpected arrival of a member of the local police force in her backyard.

Near the back of Julia's lawn was a small wooden storage shed, painted red and white like a miniature barn. The doors were open and inside I found the typical things one might have in a shed: lawn mower, snow blower, weed whacker, and a wall of tools. I wondered if Julia paid someone to take care of her yard. I couldn't imagine the city attorney snow-blowing her driveway in the dead of winter. The mental image of Julia, resplendent in high heels and a snowsuit, bordered on the ridiculous.

The bag of mulch wasn't heavy, maybe forty pounds or so, and it smelled like chocolate. I set it down near Julia who rewarded the effort with a soft, melting smile.

"Anything else?" I asked.

"If you'd like to make yourself useful, you could put a layer of mulch over the roses' root systems. They'll need a good two or three inches to protect them until the weather warms up."

Happy to have something to do, I dutifully took to the task and troweled shovelfuls of the cocoa-smelling mulch over the flowerbeds. Between my efforts, I glanced in the direction of Julia and the older woman. Julia hadn't bothered to introduce me to her, and the other woman hadn't seemed to notice my presence, but I tried not to feel insulted. The two women chatted back and forth. I didn't mean to eavesdrop, but none of their conversation made sense to me, which made it even harder to ignore.

"Ms. Desjardin?" A woman in salmon-colored scrubs stood in the backyard. I had been so focused on mulch and eavesdropping that I hadn't noticed her arrival.

"Yes?" Both Julia and the older woman responded simultaneously.

The woman, whom I assumed to be a nurse by the way she was dressed, smiled kindly. "I'm ready to take her back."

Julia stood and brushed away at the dirt that had collected at her knees. "Come now, dear," she urged. She helped the other woman stand up, treating her as though she were made of glass.

The nurse gingerly took the woman by the elbow and led her around the side of the house. "Is Jonathan coming home?" I heard the elderly woman ask her caretaker.

The nurse looked perplexed, as if not knowing how to answer

the question. "Maybe, Mrs. Desjardin. We should get back and get you cleaned up just in case."

"Oh, that would be lovely," the dark-haired woman smiled. "I hope he comes home soon."

I stood up from the flowerbed and brushed away the grass, dirt, and mulch that stuck to front of my jeans. "Is that your mother?"

Julia stared after the two women and watched the nurse carefully assist her patient ease into the passenger side of a maroon Cadillac. "Yes."

"You look like her."

Julia turned away from the car and retrained her focus on the rosebushes. "I think that's how these things usually work, dear."

I fiddled with the metal snips that Julia's mother had left behind. They looked dangerous, like they could sever a finger if I wasn't careful. "The mulch is done. Can I ... do you still need help with the flowers?"

"I've got a little more pruning to do. You can help, if you'd like."

"I don't know the first thing about flowers," I said, feeling useless. Chalk it up to another thing grown-ups were supposed to be knowledgeable about.

"I'll talk you through it. You might not know much about flowers and plants, but I know you're proficient at taking my directions."

A faint heat slid up my chest as I squirmed beneath her stare. I cleared my throat and averted my eyes.

"You're going to start at the bottom of the plant and work your way up." Julia could switch gears faster than I could keep up. "We're going to cut away all the winter damage—any old wood that might be broken, damaged, or diseased. The goal is to open up the plant to air and sunlight; even though we're cutting away at the plant, it will make it healthier and stronger."

"Okay."

"So find an area that you think you might want to cut away," she instructed.

I opened the snips and closed them around a branch. I applied minimal pressure, but stopped just short of cutting off the twig. "What if I cut off something that should have stayed?"

"Don't worry; you can't kill the plant by pruning too much. Just, you know, don't cut it off entirely at the bottom."

"Give me a little credit," I snorted even though the clippers were foreign in my palm.

"Cut it at a forty-five degree angle. And when you make the cut, be decisive about it. You want the cut to be sharp, not ragged."

I held my breath and cut off a tiny branch. The dead wood silently fell to the mulch. It wasn't much, but I hadn't been brave enough to cut away more. I positioned the blades around a second branch and began again. The more I clipped away, the more confident I became. I felt Julia hovering just behind me.

"Very nice. Just like that," she approved. "I knew you'd be a quick study."

I turned to look at her; Julia's caramel eyes danced, and I experienced a rush of adrenalin, privately pleased at the praise. I had an urge to kiss her, but I retrained my attention on the thorny rosebush.

"So you have to this every year or something?"

She nodded and returned to her own plant. "Around this time of year to get rid of any winter damage and again after they bloom to keep their shape."

"That seems like a lot of work."

"If anything is worth doing," she said, "it's worth doing well. I don't mind a little sweat and blood if the results are to my liking."

"Ouch." I shook out my stinging hand.

My jerky motions didn't go unnoticed. "What's wrong?"

"Your roses bit me," I found myself pouting.

"Let me see."

I shoved my finger into my mouth and sucked.

Julia's features darkened. "Stop being such a child. I need to see how serious your cut is."

"It's just a little scratch," I insisted.

Julia stood up. "Come on," she sighed. "You need to wash it out. It could get infected."

"It's *fine*, Julia. I've had much worse." I had the scars to prove it.

She rolled her eyes. "Rose thorn cuts can cause *sporothrix schenckii*. There's a fungus on the thorns. Do you want to keep your fingers?"

I might have been imagining it, but I thought I saw her cheeks tint at the mention of my fingers. Normally I wouldn't have let such an opportunity pass and would have made a smart comment about how Julia was probably more concerned about me keeping my fingers than I was myself, but I was a little spooked by this rose thorn mushroom disease. I happened to like all of my body parts where they were.

Julia didn't bother waiting on me to make a decision. She strode through the lawn to the backdoor of her house, and I silently followed.

The rear entrance led into the kitchen. I wanted to pause to take in the gourmet room with its high-end upgrades, seeing it for the first time in the daylight, but not wanting to get lost in the mansion, I kept close behind Julia who continued to move swiftly through the house.

The powder room on the first floor was just large enough for a toilet and sink. Julia pulled a small basket of first-aid supplies from the cabinet beneath the sink.

"Give me your hand," she commanded.

"Which one?"

Julia rolled her eyes. "The one with the cut, Detective."

"Oh. Right."

I stuck out my right hand and tried not to flinch at her touch. Julia wet a cotton swab in peroxide and dabbed at the cut on my finger. I shoved down my protest as the stinging liquid cleaned out the wound. Pain was weakness leaving the body.

The silence in the small room was palpable. Julia's voice was quiet as though speaking any louder was forbidden. "I know you have questions."

"I do," I confirmed. "But it isn't any of my business."

"It's okay to ask."

"Is your mother ... is she not well? I'm sorry," I forced out. "You don't have to answer that."

"She has dementia." Julia cut a square of gauze and wrapped it around my finger. "Her mind started to go about five years ago. That woman who came to pick her up is my mother's live-in nurse. Taking care of her is a full-time job."

"Your father doesn't do that?"

"My father is the Mayor. He can't be bothered to look after his sick wife."

"Tell me how you really feel."

Julia's mouth quirked into a tired frown, knowing her raw emotions had been momentarily exposed. She tugged the bandana from her head and ran a hand through her hair.

"I would have her live with me—this is her childhood home, after all—but I'm at City Hall all day and night, much like my father, and it's too far of a drive into town if something were to happen to her."

"You're not on trial, Julia. I'm not here to pass judgment on you or your family."

"People talk," she said stiffly. "I know they think I'm heartless, letting my own mother be taken care of by strangers."

"Let them think what they want," I shrugged. "They're just bored with their own lives so they need to scrutinize others to bring a little excitement into an otherwise dull existence."

Julia exhaled deeply. "The perks of small-town life."

"Why stay?"

"In Embarrass?"

"Yeah. You're a really good lawyer. Your talents are being wasted on prosecuting bike thieves and drunken property damagers. You should be the District Attorney or at least the city prosecutor in a bigger city."

She scoffed and flipped her short, raven hair. "Whatever for? It's not like I need the money or the notoriety. I have them both here."

"But don't you ever want, I don't know...*more*?"

"Once," she said darkly. "But it didn't get me very far." She unwrapped a Band-Aid and dressed the small wound with the gauze and sticky bandage. "There. All done."

I flexed my finger and inspected her work. "Not bad."

Before I could dig more deeply into what I was sure was a sensitive topic, Julia was changing the subject and smiling too brightly. "Would you like to stay for dinner?"

I quirked an eyebrow. "I feel like this is a trick question."

"How could that ever be construed as a trick question?" Julia let out with building annoyance.

"You ask me if I'd like to stay for dinner. I say 'yes,' and you say, 'too bad.'"

Julia shook her head at the overly-cautious approach. "I can guarantee I'll do no such thing. So?"

"So what?"

Julia rolled her eyes. "Dinner, Miss Miller. Are you staying or not?"

I smiled serenely. "I thought you'd never ask."

$\sim$

Dinner was an Italian wedding meatball soup with red kale and crusts of still-warm sourdough bread. I had two bowls, not caring if Julia judged me for having an appetite. The soup was too good not to ask for seconds.

Julia watched me with amused, dark eyes as I devoured the food in front of me seemingly without taking a breath. Meals were for survival, not savoring. I ate, hungry, tense, on the edge of my chair with my feet cemented to the floor, and legs bent at a forty-five degree angle. My left hand, the one not used to mechanically move food to my mouth, remained flat on my knee.

"If you've left anything in the Dutch oven, I can package it up so you'll have leftovers," Julia offered, taking a sip of her red wine.

I slowed the movement of my spoon. "It's really good," I said, defending my appetite.

"Thank you, dear." Julia spared me additional embarrassment even though it would have been easy. Too easy.

I used the cloth napkin to wipe my mouth. A grandfather clock chimed the late hour from somewhere in the cavernous house.

"You should probably get going, Miss Miller. I know you have to work tonight, and I wouldn't want you to overstay your welcome."

I stood on Julia's front stoop with a Tupperware container filled with leftover soup tucked under my arm.

"Go on a date with me?" I blurted out.

"A date?" Julia said the word as if it held no meaning. "I don't *date*, Miss Miller."

"You just have illicit affairs?"

"I'd hardly call this an affair," she scoffed.

"Well, I don't know what to call it." I flapped my free arm at my side. "I'm kinda new to all this."

"Your tongue would indicate otherwise, dear."

"Relationships, I mean," I said, feeling the blush on my cheeks. "I-I've never had a proper girlfriend."

She folded her arms across her chest. "Why ever not?"

"I've only been out of the Marine Corps for a year."

Her features furrowed. "But wasn't Don't Ask, Don't Tell repealed before then?"

"Yeah, but that didn't mean I was ready for my own Coming Out parade."

Julia made a humming noise. "I can't give you any more." She hugged herself when a brisk wind fluttered her hair. "This is all I have to offer. Is it enough?"

"I'm not sure."

I was halfway home before I remembered the purple lace underwear still in my pocket. I'd have to give them back another time, I thought with a wry smile. It gave me a reason to see the city prosecutor outside of office hours again, soon.

When I returned to my apartment, I stashed the leftovers in the refrigerator and slipped into clean clothes, not that it really mattered what I wore on duty.

A brisk knock at my front door made my heart to flutter. Maybe I wouldn't have to wait very long to see Julia again after all.

I unlocked the deadbolt and threw open the door.

The person standing in the hallway frowned deeply. "You don't write. You don't call. Are we breaking up?"

I leaned my head against my forearm and barked out a laugh. "It's nice to see you too, Rich."

Chapter Eleven

When I came out of the bathroom, Rich was mid-mouthful in the soup Julia had packaged up for me to take home. "Hey! Way to make yourself at home," I complained.

He smiled around the spoonful and swallowed it down. "This stuff's dreamy, Miller," he hummed in approval. "When did you learn to cook?"

I ran my fingers roughly through blonde locks before pulling them back in a ponytail. "I didn't. A friend made it."

Rich continued shoveling the soup into his mouth. "I want your friend to be my friend."

"Not that I don't appreciate the surprise, but what are you doing here?"

"I was out on the bike today and decided to keep driving," he shrugged.

"That's a pretty long impromptu road trip." The drive from the Twin Cities to Embarrass on a motorcycle was at least three and a half hours, maybe even four. "Is everything okay?"

"Yeah. I just needed a break from the city."

I frowned. "How is that guy doing? The one cop you told me about?"

Rich ran his hand over his shaved bald head. "We had to let him go. The family of the woman who died was going to sue the department for gross negligence if we kept him on the payroll."

"Shit."

"I know. I really wanted to help the guy out, but it was just too much of a fuck up to come back from."

Another knock interrupted our conversation. I stomped over to the door. "God, I'm feeling popular today," I grumbled.

Grace Kelly looked startled by the force with which I opened the door.

"Hey," I greeted with a grunt. "Join the party," I waved her inside.

Grace poked her head through the doorway, looking uncertain. "Uh, is this a bad time?"

I flopped down on the easy chair and began pulling my leather boots on over my jeans. "Nope. Just getting ready for work. Come on in."

Grace took a step forward. When she saw Rich standing over the kitchen sink, finishing off Julia's soup, she hesitated in the doorway. "Are you sure I'm not interrupting anything?"

"Rich, meet my neighbor, Grace Kelly Donovan. Grace, this is Detective Richard Gammon. We used to work together in Minneapolis."

Rich wiped his mouth with the back of his hand and then wiped his palm clean on his jeans. "Nice to meet you."

Grace looked skeptically at Rich's outstretched arm as though it carried disease. "It's nice to meet you, too, Detective," she said as they shook hands.

"Is this your friend, Cass?" Rich asked.

"No."

Grace's eyebrows shot up.

"No! I mean she's *a* friend," I quickly recovered. "She's just not *the* friend—the soup friend."

Grace looked more confused than ever. "Soup friend?"

"Nothing. Not important. So what's up?" I asked, finishing zipping up my boots.

"Oh." Grace blinked a few times as if she'd forgotten the reason for her visit. "I wanted to invite you to the Summer Solstice festival tomorrow. It's to celebrate the longest day of the year. The town has a little festival on Main Street. It's fun."

"Will there be beer?" Rich asked.

"Yes."

"And will *you* be there?"

Grace's eyelashes fluttered. "Uh huh."

"Then I'm in," he beamed. "What time should we pick you up?"

"We'll try to make it, Grace," I pumped on the breaks. I didn't like the way Rich was ogling my pretty neighbor. "Thanks for the invite."

Grace continued to look between Rich and myself. I could tell her inner reporter was filing away questions to interrogate me with later. "We should do dinner again soon, Cass."

"Yeah, that would be great." I ushered Grace towards the door with my hand in the small of her back. The longer she stuck around, the more opportunity Rich had to spill my secrets.

"Okay, well, I hope you can make it tomorrow!" she chirped as I practically pushed her out of the apartment.

"See you later, Grace!" Rich called after her.

I shut the door and released a long sigh.

"So ... is Grace seeing anyone?" Rich stroked the scruff on his chin.

I spun on my heel to regard my friend. "You stay away from her, you wolf."

He held up his hands, surrendering.

"She's too sweet for you, Rich."

"I like sweet," Rich said contemplatively. "I can do sweet."

I shook my head. "I've gotta get to work."

The night had been longer than usual. I didn't know if it was because I knew my friend was sitting alone in my apartment with Grace Kelly just across the hallway, or if the Summer Solstice had kicked in early.

When I finally got off work around 6:00 a.m., Rich was sitting upright on the easy chair, snoring like a downshifting semi-truck. I fell into my own bed and closed my eyes. Luckily, I was used to sleeping through similarly loud noises after living in a war zone.

I woke up a few hours later, not to Rich snoring, but to the sound of an ice cream truck playing its song. I stayed in bed and listened as the truck drove up and down the surrounding residential streets. I could hear its jangled song grow stronger and fade again. Children's voices carried through my open apartment windows.

"Are we under attack?" Rich's voice called out to me.

I stood on top of my bed so I could peer out the high windows. A gaggle of children swarmed the ice cream truck like zombies after brains.

"It would appear so."

Rich was at the kitchen island shoveling Cap'n Crunch cereal into this mouth when I left my bedroom area. "Good morning, sunshine," he greeted in a far too cheerful tone. "What's on the agenda for today?"

"You eat all my food, *and* you expect me to entertain you?"

"I drove all this way. It's the least you could do."

I sighed deeply, letting my body sag with its weight. "Let me grab a quick shower, and I can give you the grand tour of town."

Rich's spoon clanked in the empty cereal bowl. "What are we going to do once those five minutes are up?"

"Fair enough," I laughed. "I guess we could check out that Summer Solstice thing."

"Oh yeah," Rich said, remembering. "And we can check out your cute neighbor, too."

"Leave Grace alone," I warned.

Rich gave me a cunning smile. "Don't tell me you've got a crush on that cute little thing."

Grace was attractive, but she was also very straight and not my type at all. Even without my massive crush on Julia, she was a too sweet and domestic for my tastes. I was drawn to women a little more dark and dangerous and far more unattainable.

I considered telling Rich about Julia, but I myself didn't know how to explain what was going on between us without bringing anyone else into our complicated relationship.

My apartment tended to run uncomfortably warm, which was a stark contrast to the weather outside. It was officially the first day of summer, but it was rainy, foggy, and barely sixty degrees Fahrenheit. The unseasonably cool weather hadn't appeared to dampen anyone's interest in the Summer Solstice celebration, however.

The streets surrounding my apartment were closed to traffic for the city-wide festival. Local businesses had dragged their wares onto the sidewalks in front of their storefronts, and others peddled handmade crafts from portable booths. Carnival games were scattered throughout the few city blocks, and tents selling sweets like cotton candy, lemonade, and funnel cakes beckoned to festival-goers.

Rich and I grabbed coffee from Stan's and began to walk from one end of town to the other. I saw a lot of familiar faces, and it felt good to have so many locals acknowledge me with a friendly wave.

"You didn't tell me you were a celebrity, Miller," Rich remarked after my breakfast buddy Franklyn Walker stopped me to say hello.

I took a sip of my coffee and grinned. "And just think," I said, linking an arm through Rich's, "people probably think you're my boyfriend, visiting from out of town. You're famous by association."

Rich laughed. "You could do a lot worse."

"Not by much, I'm afraid," I teased back.

I missed this—the easy banter and familiarity I had with friends like Rich. I was becoming more comfortable in this town, but in my years of traveling the globe I'd found deep, enduring friendships like I had with Rich to be rare. Julia and I bantered, but there was always barbs or orgasms attached to our conversations. It was a rollercoaster with that woman.

"Cassidy!" Grace Kelly Donovan flagged us down.

I grabbed Rich's bicep and squeezed. "Behave yourself, Detective," I warned under my breath.

He looked at me with mock injury. "I'm offended, Cassidy. I'm always a perfect gentleman."

Grace was all smiles and eager energy when she walked up to us. "You made it!" she beamed.

"Well, you made the Summer Solstice festival sound so exciting, I told Cass that there was no way I'd miss it." Rich's tone matched Grace's enthusiasm, and I instantly bristled. My friend was up to no good.

Grace fell into step with us as we continued our promenade down Main Street. "What do you think of our little town, Detective Gammon?"

"Please, call me Rich." His smile was disarming. "I haven't

been here too long, but what I've seen," he made a big show of looking Grace up and down, "is completely charming."

An attractive blush colored Grace's pale cheeks. Great.

"I should be getting back to the church booth," she murmured. "I just wanted to say hi."

Rich's eye contact was unrelenting. He pulled off his knit cap. "It was nice to see you again, Grace. I hope you enjoy the rest of your day."

Grace ducked her head and regarded my over-the-top friend from beneath her heavy eyelashes. "You wouldn't be interested in some corn on the cob, would you? We sell the best in town at our booth."

"I happen to have a weakness for sweet corn," Rich grinned. "Lead the way."

Grace flashed a look in my direction. "Do you want some too, Cassidy?" I was honestly surprised she remembered I was still standing there.

I waved a hand. "No, you two have fun. I'll be fine on my own."

Needing no more prompting form me, the two skipped away in the direction of corn on the cob.

Left on my own, I continued to stroll along Main Street to check out the sights, sounds, and smells of the block party. A high school garage band was setting up its gear on a small, covered stage, and with nothing else to do, I stopped to watch them tune their instruments while I finished my lukewarm drink.

I was finishing the dregs of my coffee when Rich found me. "Some party, huh?" he grinned.

"I see you got your corn."

Rich bit aggressively into the corncob. "It's good," he mumbled around the overly large bite.

I glanced over at my friend and smirked. "Rich," I laughed, "you're a total mess."

Rich's face, normally ruggedly attractive, was covered in butter and salt. I wiped his chin with a napkin, beginning to erase the excess.

"Seriously, have you never eaten corn on the cob before? You're like a two year old with a birthday cake."

"Hey, I've had corn before," he protested as he let me clean his face. "It just usually comes in cans or in frozen baggies. Hey, isn't that..." Rich trailed off. "Jesus, Miller. Isn't that your girlfriend from the club?"

"What?" I whipped my head around to see who he was pointing at.

Julia stood near a craft booth that was selling homemade quilts. She wore a long black jacket and her lipstick was a vibrant red. Standing next to her was a man I didn't recognize. He said something to her, and she laughed. I stared at him and his dark hair, dark eyes, and brilliant white smile that seemed to dazzle even on this overcast day.

I hated the smile that seemed to come so effortlessly to her lips when I had to stand on my head to be rewarded with even a smirk. I hated the way she touched his arm, a familiar and easy gesture. I didn't know this man, but I knew I hated him if he was able to produce such a reaction from her without even trying.

"She's not my girlfriend," I grit out. She wouldn't even let me take her on a date.

"Did you know she would be here?" Rich questioned.

"She lives in Embarrass if that's what you're asking."

"But I'm guessing you didn't expect her to be arm-in-arm with Captain America over there."

My silence was answer enough.

"C'mon, Miller." Rich threw a bulky arm over my shoulder. "Let's get you good and drunk."

∾

I sat at my kitchen island, nursing a beer and my fragile ego. It was my only drink of the evening as I still had my shift that night.

"I don't know what it is about her," I sighed. I tipped my beer to the side until the amber liquid threatened to spill out.

"She's beautiful," Rich noted from his seat in the easy chair. He'd seemed to commandeer it as his spot in the apartment.

I nodded. "Can't argue with you there." I worried the beer bottle between my hands. "At work is when it's the worst. I find myself looking for excuses to talk to her, to even just walk past her open office door. I just want to be *near* her."

Rich whistled. "That's some crush."

"Yeah, but the damn thing is, I *know* she likes me back. She just, I don't know, won't let herself."

"Get someone to cover for you," he said, draining the last of his third beer. "We'll get to the bottom of this Julia case before the night is over."

"I can't. There *is* no one else to take my shift," I protested sullenly.

It was about 7:00 a.m. by the time I finally dragged myself home. The Summer Solstice festival had shut down when the sun had set, but the locals had simply moved their festivities to the bars. It had been a busier shift than usual and I'd stayed at the station an extra hour to get a head start on the paperwork.

I unlocked my apartment door and reached for the light toggle. The overhead light went on, accompanied by a surprised gasp.

Grace Kelly fell off the easy chair. Her backside connected hard with the wooden floor. I only saw enough to realize that her shirt was also on the floor.

My hands flew to cover my eyes. "Holy shit!"

The sounds of fumbling, quiet grunting, and frenetic scurrying filled my ears.

"My eyes! My eyes!" I complained.

"Knock much, Miller?" Rich growled.

I kept my hands fisted over my eyes. "Put a sock on the door-knob much?" I countered.

Grace's voice was surprisingly composed. "You can look now."

"I don't want to," I stubbornly protested.

"Grow up, Rookie."

Only reluctantly did I remove my hands from my face.

Grace's shirt was back on, and her cheeks were tinted pink. Rich looked similarly embarrassed, but I imagined he had more experience with this kind of thing.

"I brought breakfast," Grace announced. A six pack of muffins sat untouched on the kitchen island next to a half-finished bottle of red wine—the breakfast of champions.

I held up my hands to stop the apologies and excuses. "You're both adults. Just don't have sex on my bed and we're cool."

Grace hopped to her feet. "I'll just be going now. I need to get to work anyway."

I held up a hand to stop Rich's verbal diarrhea of excuses. "I'm exhausted. You can explain yourself after I've had a few hours sleep."

His lips pressed together and he nodded.

I flopped onto my bed, not bothering to change out of my clothes from work. I slept with no fear of dreaming.

I woke up a few hours later. I wasn't ready to get out of bed, but I knew Rich had to get back to the Twin Cities. I found him sitting at the kitchen island with a magazine open in front of him. He looked up and smiled when he heard me shuffle into the room.

"Hey, I'm sorry about that thing with your friend, Miller." Rich rubbed his hand over his shaved scalp, something I noticed that he did when he was uncomfortable. "It just kind of happened."

"Let me guess; you slipped and your mouth just fell on hers, huh?"

A lopsided grin came to Rich's chiseled features. "Yeah."

"I'd appreciate it that when you leave this morning, you don't leave a trail of trampled hearts behind. I'm the one who has to pick up after you," I said sternly.

"I like Grace," he admitted. "She's easy to talk to."

"And she's also adorable."

"Yeah, that helps, too."

I walked Rich down to his waiting motorcycle which was parked in the alley behind the Laundromat.

"Thanks for the visit, man," I said, clapping him on the shoulder. "It's nice knowing you guys haven't forgotten about me."

Rich grinned broadly and slipped his helmet over his shaved head. "You've kind of hard to forget, Rookie." His motorcycle roared to life.

"Call before you make another road trip, okay? I'll see about switching shifts or something."

"You got it."

I watched the road until Rich's silhouette disappeared in the distance. I thought about what to do next with my day. I could try to go back to sleep, or I could finish up the paperwork from my busy night. Neither option sounded all that appealing, but only one of them didn't scare me.

Chapter Twelve

"Hold the elevator, please!" a voice called out. Not thinking, I threw my arm between the two closing doors. The metal seized on my forearm before the doors shuddered back open on the first floor of City Hall.

Julia slipped into the elevator, looking uncharacteristically flustered. "Thank you," she said, not bothering to look in my direction. She stared at her cell phone and chewed on her lower lip.

"Good morning, Madam Prosecutor," I greeted, not able to hide the ice in my tone. After being traumatized from walking in on Rich and Grace that morning, I'd nearly forgotten the blow to my ego that seeing Julia on someone else's arm at Summer Solstice had caused. Seeing her again reopened the hurt.

Julia looked up from her phone at the sound of my voice. "Oh, good morning," she returned. "Thank you for holding the elevator."

"No problem. New shoes?" I bit out.

"No. But my legs are a little sore from the weekend."

"From pruning your roses or from something less innocent?"

147

Julia's manicured eyebrows pinched together. "I'm sure I don't know what you mean, Detective."

We both stared straight ahead as the elevator ascended to the second floor. I worked the muscles in my jaw. This woman was impossible. She ran hot at night, but icy cold in the daytime. I could feel my anger rising along with the elevator. I'd just about made up my mind to stop playing this game with her.

Julia punched a button, and the elevator wrenched to a stop. A shrill alarm sounded.

"What the hell are you doing?" I blustered.

Julia folded her arms. "Tell me, Miss Miller. Have I done something to incur your wrath this morning?"

"I'm fine," I snapped.

"So you say, but the barbs in your words would indicate otherwise."

"Why do you even care?"

Julia's lips pressed together in a straight line. "I thought you and I had an understanding. An ... arrangement, if you will."

"You mean how you let me fuck you, insist you don't date, but then the very next day you're cozied up to some hunk of a man?"

Her features furrowed. "Hunk of a man?" she echoed.

"I saw you at Summer Solstice."

Her face continued to display her confusion and barely veiled anger until she unexpectedly laughed.

I crossed my arms over my chest. "I fail to see the humor in this."

"Reggie, my *cousin*, was in town yesterday. My parents practically raised him, so he's like a brother to me. He visits now and again and looks me up when he does. He'll be pleased to know you think so highly of his looks."

"Oh." I blinked. "Good genes, I guess."

Julia punched the emergency stop button and the lift lurched back to life. "I'm glad we've resolved your idiocracy at least for one day."

I stared at my shoes, feeling like a fool. I didn't want to wear my emotions on my sleeve.

I felt the faintest pressure against the side of my hand. I looked over to see Julia's hand barely grazing my own. A feminine pinkie finger reached out, tickling the side of my hand. I licked my lips and stared straight ahead rather than acknowledge what she was doing. This was all too confusing.

The elevator came to a stop and the doors slid open on the second floor.

"Have a nice day, Detective," Julia clipped, sashaying out of the elevator.

I stared after her retreating form, heels clicking on the marble floor that led to her office. I was sure she walked with an exaggerated swish of her hips, and I privately smiled that the show was all for me.

A single streetlight illuminated the house at the end of the residential street. The ranch-style home was covered in grey vinyl siding, and a single metal pipe from a wood-burning stove stuck out of the flat roof like an antennae. The yard was tidy; boxwood bushes lined the front of the house, and flowerboxes overflowing with petunias framed the front door. All the interior lights were out in Chief Hart's house, which wasn't unusual considering it was just after midnight.

I peered out into the thick night. "What are we doing out here?"

"It's called a stakeout, Miller." David slumped down in the drivers' seat of the squad car.

"And why are we staking-out Chief Hart's house?"

"Because someone wants us to think we spent nearly a quarter of a million dollars on police radios."

"And what? You think Chief Hart is a radio hoarder?"

David slapped the steering wheel. "No. Of course not. But what if he pocketed the money that the invoice said went to police radios?"

I squinted at a small, shadowy figure squatting on the front stoop. "Is that a lawn gnome?"

"Yeah. It gets stolen at least once a month," David dismissed. "It's like a rite of passage for high school kids around here."

"I take it you stole it at one point in time."

David chuckled darkly. "I plead the fifth."

I let out a deep breath. "A man with a lawn gnome doesn't exactly scream 'money embezzler.'"

"It's always the person you least expect." David's eyes never strayed from the police chief's darkened home.

"And what exactly is the Chief spending his money on, Addams? Replacement lawn ornaments?"

David's fingers wrapped tightly around the steering wheel. "There's something going on, Miller. I can feel it. I just don't know what it is yet."

"I don't think we're gonna figure it out tonight." I clapped David on the shoulder. "How about some pie at Stan's, huh? I'll even buy."

David stared out the windshield. "Okay. Fine." He shifted the parked car into drive. "But this isn't over."

I knocked on the wooden door with the words "City Prosecutor" stenciled on the outside.

"Yes?"

I poked my head through the doorway. Julia didn't look up

from the stack of papers on her desk. She wore reading glasses perched near the end of her nose. Instead of looking matronly, the glasses only added to her appeal. No surprise there.

"Peace offering for being an idiot yesterday?"

Julia's head snapped up, and she removed her glasses in one smooth movement at the sound of my voice.

"I thought you might like some lunch."

"And what grease-laden product have you brought with you today, Detective?"

"Cheeseburger and fries." I produced a carryout bag from Stan's. The grease spots were already visible through the white bag.

Julia laid her hands on her desk. "You know I don't eat that," she said sternly.

"It's for me," I beamed. "I brought you a chicken Caesar salad."

Julia's mouth twitched. "What kind of chicken?"

"Grilled. Not fried. No breading."

"Come in."

I burst through the office door before she could change her mind and revoke the invitation. I put the bag with Julia's salad in front of her on the desk and sat down in an opposite chair with my own food on my lap.

"So I guess I found the magic words. Or food."

"You just caught me in a moment of weakness," Julia brushed off. "I've been elbow deep in contracts today, and I lost track of time."

"Your weakness is my gain," I said as I unwrapped my cheeseburger. Stan put the melted cheese underneath the ground beef patty, and it made all the difference. It was one of the best burgers I'd ever had.

"And you're awfully persistent." Julia pulled the plastic container that held her salad out of the takeout bag.

"Only because you're so stubborn."

"So if I had said yes the first time you asked me to dinner, you would have lost interest in me by now?"

"Why don't you keep saying yes, and we'll both find out?" I challenged between mouthfuls of burger.

Julia delicately stabbed her salad with the plastic fork she'd found included in the bag. "Clever, Detective."

"Hey, I'm not just a pretty face attached to a smoking hot body," I shrugged. I fished a fistful of fries out of the bottom of the bag and shoved them in my mouth.

"I don't see how a steady diet of Twinkies and beer could possibly help your physique."

I lifted the bottom of my Henley top, revealing my defined abdomen. "If it works, why question it?"

I saw Julia's eyes fall first to my tightened torso before she returned her gaze to her salad container. "Do you ever sleep, Detective?"

I tugged my shirt back into place. "Pardon?"

"I know for a fact that you work hellish night hours, and yet I see you at City Hall during the day. Do you ever sleep?" she repeated the question.

The seemingly harmless inquiry caused me to squirm in my chair like she'd caught me in a lie. I shoved my half-eaten burger back into the carryout bag. "I'm sorry. I'll go. I know you're busy." With a quick look around to make sure I hadn't forgotten anything, I awkwardly stood up.

"Cassidy, I didn't mean for you to leave." Julia's refined features furrowed.

"No. I—you're right. I should go."

I hustled out of the room leaving behind the lingering scent of fried foods.

I stumbled out of Julia's office feeling like a fool. My shoes squeaked on the tile floor, and I rushed down the second floor stairs to escape outside even though I harbored no fantasies that Julia might come after me.

I'd been able to get the woman alone, close to being civil, close to the woman with the dancing eyes that I remembered from the first night we'd met. But I'd let an innocent question about my sleep patterns rip that moment away.

I flinched when a file folder was slapped down in front of me. A large hand pinned the papers to the spare desk in the police department.

"What's this?" I asked. I opened the file and inspected its contents. I shuffled through the papers inside.

"I went online to the State's grant allocation portal," David said. "They've got a list of every grant they've awarded to each county in the state." He took the folder back and flipped through the papers until he found the printout he wanted. He slid it across the desk.

I picked it up and read. "Embarrass was awarded three and a half million dollars from the State?"

"And that's just been in the past five years." David was practically salivating with energy. "They don't have older information online, but I'm going to write and get the ten previous years."

I picked up the full file again. "Where did that kind of money go to?"

"I'm still working on that. But if it's more car radios, we have to do something about this."

I picked through the printouts. "I'm guessing you'd like some help."

David's grin was both boyish and charming.

"What do you need me to do?" I sighed, giving in.

"Yes!" He punched his fist in the air. "Okay, so here's the

deal," he said, his voice lowering and his face taking on a serious look. "Every purchase order goes through the City Treasurer's office. No money goes in or out of City Hall without those ladies knowing. I'll track down that end of the paperwork if you can take care of the grant money side of things—how much money was awarded, for what, and who wrote the grant. Then we can compare notes."

"And you want to do all this without the Chief knowing?" I guessed with a frown.

David nodded. "Until we know for sure, this has to stay between you and me."

"I've known Larry Hart all my life, David. He and my dad were best friends growing up. I just don't see him being the mastermind in some money fraud scheme."

"I'm just asking for a little discretion right now. Who knows? Maybe that three and a half million dollars is legit and was spent fixing up the town. But maybe it's just the tip of the iceberg, and this place has been crumbling down around its ears for no reason." The lines of David's face were hard and drawn. "This is my home, Miller. I just want to do right by it."

I stood up and struck the bargain. "Then let's figure this thing out, Addams."

Chapter Thirteen

I sat at my kitchen island with papers spread across its surface. My hair was back in a loose braid, tossed over my shoulder, to keep it from getting in the way. When I'd volunteered to help David investigate the allocation of state grant money, I'd underestimated the time it would take to chart out each individual grant proposal and application status.

The authorship of each grant was hard to decipher as well. Grant cover letters seemed to originate from the department who would most benefit from the award, but all were signed and addressed by the Mayor who served as grant administrator. Because these weren't the original grant applications, it was unclear if the signature was the Mayor's own or a rubber stamp, so there was no way to know if he'd ever seen the files.

I let out an exhausted sigh. David had wanted to keep this between us, but I was no great brain. I needed help.

∼

Julia was seated behind her office desk. She had removed her suit jacket and was down to a dark blue blouse whose rich color made her raven hair practically iridescent.

When I knocked on the doorjamb, she looked up sharply over a stack of papers. "Yes?"

"Can I ask you something?"

"No, I will not make out with you." Her red lips curled up.

"Did you just try to make a joke, Madam Prosecutor?" I smirked.

She removed her glasses and let them hang around her neck from their chain. My eyes were drawn to where they rested against her breasts. "What can I help you with, Detective?"

I waved a thick stack of papers in the air. "I need your help deciphering some city construction contracts."

Julia motioned for me to come in, and she returned her reading glasses to their perch on her nose. "I read too much as a child," she explained even though I had made no comment about the glasses. "I had bifocals by the time I was in fourth grade."

"I would love to see your school portraits."

"Never going to happen, Miss Miller. Now, what specifically do you have questions about?"

She made no mention of the awkward nature in which I had ended our last interaction. I couldn't tell if the question was at the tip of her tongue or if she'd dismissed the way I had bolted from lunch as just another of my idiosyncrasies.

I tried to focus on the real reason I'd come to see Julia. Flirting would have to be shelved for now.

"What if a capital project, let's say a public park," I hypothesized, "applies for a grant. Is there ever a scenario where the park could win funding, but no one ever tells the City Council they'd been awarded the grant and then someone pockets all that grant money instead of building a park?"

"No."

"Just that easy?" I asked. "No?"

"Even though the phrasing of your question was rather convoluted, Miss Miller. It's a fairly straightforward answer." Julia folded her hands on her desk. "Think of grants as reimbursements. An actual park would have to be built, and the city would have spent actual money to build the park. The grant money comes in *after* the park has already been built in the form of a reimbursement."

"Okay." Dead end number one. "So no fake parks. How about, is there any way to cross-reference building contracts with how much a project *should* have cost?"

Her features furrowed. "I'm not entirely sure what you're asking."

"Like, the new public library downtown," I proposed. "The work was done, that much is obvious; I've driven by the building a hundred times. But is there any way to find out if the work they did actually cost that much?"

"City contracts are awarded to the most attractive bidder," she said. "Outside contractors tell whomever is in charge of the project—in the case of the library, the Director of the Downtown District Authority—how much the job will cost. The contract doesn't necessarily go to the lowest bidder, especially when there's available money involved instead of raising the millage. But the bid generally goes to the best combination of price, efficiency, and quality of work. Does that answer your question?"

"Not really." My brow crinkled, making ridges on my forehead. "So there's no real way for me to figure out how much, for example," I glanced once at the building contract, "a library roof installation should cost?"

"This isn't the grocery store, Miss Miller. There's no price check on Aisle Five. You could probably procure the paperwork on the failed bids and compare and contrast the cost of the same job for each builder, but there are no fixed prices in the construction world. It's called the Open Market for a reason."

I flipped through the paperwork, sure I'd missed some important fact or piece of information that would help me out.

"Care to tell me why you're so interested in how much money it takes to build a library?"

I shook my head. "No."

Julia's eyes narrowed at the response. She was obviously a woman who wasn't used to that word. "Then I guess our business is done, Detective."

Her head bent back toward the documents she had been previously inspecting. I took that as a sign that I was being dismissed. I gathered up my own paperwork and left her office without another word.

The biggest and most recent capital project I had come across was the new public library, but I couldn't find a connection to any grant applications that indicated they'd been awarded outside money for the project. I decided to go see the new building myself.

The head librarian, Meg Peterson, met me at the front entrance.

"Good afternoon, Detective Miller," she greeted. "I saw you walking up so I thought I'd welcome you myself." Her light green eyes crinkled at the corners when she smiled. Her long hair was a mess of dyed red curls, and her grey roots openly defied her chemical attempts to tame them. She wore a cardigan and high-waisted khaki shorts. It was very Minnesota Mom as though she'd spent the day making hot dish or lemon squares.

We shook hands and she gave me a tour of the facilities. The public library was an impressive building for such a small town like Embarrass. In addition to the large rooms filled with works of fiction and non-fiction, there was a designated wing just for children's books and a computer lab filled with updated electronics. The carpet and paint throughout the building still smelled fresh.

I thought it was surprisingly busy for a weekday, but I really didn't go to libraries often, so I had nothing on which to base my observations. The last time I'd been to a library had been for a wedding in St. Paul. One of the guys I'd worked with in the police department had had his reception at the St. Paul public library. It had been a pretty fancy affair—marble columns and a vaulted rotunda and all that. Rich and I had gone together as fake dates, and he'd flirted with bridesmaids all night while I'd taken advantage of the open bar.

Meg Peterson and I stood in the center atrium. "How did Embarrass afford such a massive project like a new library?" I hadn't been able to find any city levies or grants attached to the multi-million dollar sticker price.

"The Community Foundation."

"What's that?"

"It's basically a private citizen's group," she told me. "They do fundraisers and provide grants for things like town improvements and college scholarships."

"And they funded the construction of this *entire* building?"

Meg smiled proudly. "And the books inside. Quite the accomplishment for a little town, right?"

"What else can you tell me about the Community Fund?"

"What would you like to know?" she asked.

"Basic stuff," I shrugged. "It's history? How and why it got started?"

She nodded and crossed her arms in front of her chest. "About four or five years ago a few of us moms were having a chat about how we could get more involved in the community. We have PTA, naturally, but that only really affects our kids' schools. There's also church volunteer organizations, but those are divided among the denominations, and the same could be said about groups like the Lions Club or the Kiwanis. We wanted to create something town-wide that everyone in Embarrass could come together under. We started out with small projects," she continued. "We had a pretty healthy endowment fund thanks to a generous donation from Target, and we used the accrued interest money on college scholarships for local kids."

"What about the library? I saw the ticket price for that—that can't be from bank interest."

"The library construction was mostly private donations. The City had applied for a number of state and federal grants with no success and the tax levy failed to pass, so when no external agencies would help, the Community Foundation took over the project and made it happen."

"And everyone in the group decided that the new library should be the Community Fund's responsibility?" I asked.

"It was always the intention of the group to at least partially fund the new building. The library needed to grow its collections, but there wasn't room in the old building, and we needed a space with more reliable temperature controls to keep the books safe."

She ushered me towards a free standing wall that was covered with a large copper plate. Individual names were engraved into the metal. "We thought this would be a nice thank you to recognize everyone who made a donation to the Community Fund for the project," she said.

I gave a cursory scan of the names, impressed with myself that I recognized quite a few.

"These levels, they indicate how much a person donated, right?"

"That's right," she nodded. "Most people gave a gift of about fifty or one hundred dollars, but others were able to be far more generous."

At the very top of the wall, under the label of Founder's Club, were two names. I recognized them both. One was the local dentist whose office was next door to City Hall and the second was Mayor William J. Desjardin.

I tapped on their names. "How much did you have to donate to be in the Founder's Club level?"

Meg's face scrunched up in thought. "I think that was half a million dollars."

"Jesus," I sputtered. "Who has that kind of money to just give away?"

"Apparently Dr. Mercury and the Mayor," she grinned.

I whistled under my breath. I should have been a politician or a dentist apparently.

Meg turned on her heel. "Let's set you up with a library card."

I hadn't planned on getting a card, but I figured it was the polite thing to do. Minnesota nice, even. "Sounds great."

My trip to the public library had not brought me closer to finding a lead on this case, but I now had a newly laminated library card in my wallet thanks to the visit.

Lori was the only one in the department when I returned from my field trip. The Chief was out on a complaint and David wouldn't be in for a few hours. I thought about going upstairs to see if the city prosecutor was in, but I didn't want to be slapped with a restraining order. I really needed to get a hobby.

Back at my apartment, I wasted time watching television and picking at an unappealing frozen dinner until my shift began. My phone rang as I dumped the plastic tray into the garbage can stored in a cupboard beneath the kitchen sink. I didn't recognize the phone number, but I answered my cell anyway.

"Miller here."

"Cass?"

I picked the last of my dinner out of my teeth. "Yeah?"

"It's Pensacola."

Shit. The breath forcefully left my lungs like I'd been sucker punched. I had to sit down on the closest surface, which happened to be my bed.

"I got your number from your mom," he explained before I could form the question. "She said you took a job up north."

"Yeah. Little town called Embarrass."

"Last time we talked you were working in the Twin Cities."

There was an implicit question in his observation. "I needed a change of pace," I explained. "It got a little too big for me."

"I hear that."

"So, what about you? How's things?" I glanced at my alarm clock. I had no excuse to cut this call short. I had hours until I was due at work. I stood from the bed and paced the few steps to the kitchen and opened the refrigerator, not out of hunger, but routine. A six-pack of beer beckoned to me. I shut the refrigerator door instead.

He laughed out roughly. "Trying not to go stir crazy."

"How's Claire?" I almost didn't want to ask in case I was stepping into a bear trap. The phone rattled with a giant exhale, and I sucked in my own breath.

"She's pregnant."

"Holy shit, man!"

"Yeah, I know." He chuckled at my reaction. "And we recently found out we're having a boy."

"That's awesome, Pense. Congratulations."

"Thanks. Anyway." He fell silent. "I just wanted to call. They tell me it's good for me."

"I'm glad you did," I said. "It was good to hear your voice."

"Yours too, Cass."

"Give my love to Claire."

"Sure thing, buddy."

I ended the call and hung my head.

Afghanistan, 2012

My mouth is dry and dirty. I can never drink enough water to sate my thirst, and my lips are perpetually cracked from the blistering sun. You don't get tan out here—you get dirty sand lines—residue caked on your skin that penetrates your exposed pores so deeply it takes multiple showers to wash away the final traces of desert. If you thought beach sand got wedged in all the worst spots, you haven't experienced anything.

The sun is hot on my face—too hot. There's been no reprieve from this unforgiving, unrelenting heat for days. I don't know how long we've been here; I've lost track of the time.

I have to sleep on my stomach because my back is on fire. My deodorant stopped working weeks ago, but I've gotten used to my own stench. It's nothing compared to the rancid perfume of rotting flesh. I stare at the sky and the unmoving clouds until I'm forced to blink. Small birds jet across the sky, and the sounds of real jets echo off in the distance, taunting me. Even if they flew directly over us, they'd never hear our cries for help.

Pensacola has shrapnel in his gut, and his leg has been torn apart by a dirty bomb. It could have been worse though; everyone else in the unit is FUBAR. I periodically squeeze his injured leg even though I know it's going to hurt like hell. His screams confirm he's still alive.

"When's the bird getting here?" he asks.

"The foxtrot is out. We'll have to wait and pray."

I touch the just-in-case-letter folded in my chest pocket just beneath my flack jacket. I decided to write it after experiencing my first death of a Marine during my first tour, and since then I've carried it around kind of as a good luck charm. The tone in the letter is light, joking almost. In it I tell my dad to use the life insurance money to buy that boat he's always wanted.

I don't cry. Crying means I've given up on myself.

My phone jangled loudly, shaking me from my dream.

"Hello?" I hoped that it wasn't obvious from my voice that I'd been sleeping on duty. "Embarrass Police," I remembered to add.

"Cassidy?"

It took me a moment to recognize the voice. It was Julia, but she sounded upset.

"What's wrong?"

"It's my mother. She's wandered off. My father can't find her."

"Where are you?" I asked.

"At their house."

"I'll be right there." I hung up without waiting for her response. I turned the key in the ignition, and the police car roared to life.

All the lights were on at Mayor Desjardin's house when I arrived. Julia's black Mercedes was parked out front. The house was situated on a little hill with a steep set of concrete stairs carved into the earth. I bounded up the stairs and rang the doorbell. Julia answered the door, not her father.

She looked like she'd been roused from sleep as I had. I couldn't help but give her a visual once over. Instead of her usual power suit she wore black capri yoga pants and a half-zip running jacket. It was the least formal I'd ever seen her. Even her underwear was fancier than her current outfit. It made me want to draw her in for a hug. I wanted to whisper into her hair that I'd find her mom—that everything was going to be okay. I could see her wrestling with her own impulses as well, and it made me feel a little better.

She took a step backwards. "Please come in, Detective."

Mayor Desjardin's home was far less lavish than Julia's, but compared to the majority of houses I'd been in, it was still a mansion. She brought me through a formal sitting room and into a dining area where the Mayor was sitting. A glass decanter of an amber liquid was on the polished wood table, and he clutched a well glass in one hand.

He lifted his head when we walked in. "Detective Miller," he greeted. "Thank you for coming so soon."

I nodded in response although I was privately pleased that he'd remembered my rank.

It was a little surreal to be standing in a room with both Julia and her father. I'd never had a proper girlfriend before, so I'd never met anyone's parents under that context. Julia wasn't my girlfriend though, and the circumstances for this meeting were completely professional.

"When did you notice your wife was missing, sir?" I jumped right into the reason I was there for. It would do no good wasting time, exchanging pleasantries.

"I woke up around 1:00 a.m. to use the bathroom. When I came back to bed, I noticed she was gone. I don't know if she left when I was in the restroom or if it happened earlier in the night and I hadn't noticed."

It was nearly 3:00 a.m.

"I called for her, but when she didn't respond, I searched the house. That's when I noticed the front door was open."

"Are any vehicles missing?" I asked.

"No." He shook his head. "The cars are all here, thank God."

I nodded, taking in all this information. The timetable was vague, but as long as she'd remained on foot, our radius where she could have gone was minimal.

"I'll call Sergeant Addams, and we'll do a sweep of the immediate area and then work our way out until we find her."

"Is that really necessary?" Mr. Desjardin asked.

"Do you want to find your wife?" My voice came out a little too sharply.

"Of course, Detective," he snapped back. "I just don't know if it's necessary to call Sergeant Addams at this hour."

I ignored the Mayor and pulled up David's number on my phone. He picked up after three long rings.

"David, it's Cassidy. Mrs. Desjardin ..." I covered the phone with my hand. "What's your mother's first name?"

Julia blinked once. I could tell this was surreal to her as well. "Olivia."

I returned to the phone call. "Olivia Desjardin is missing."

David's response was appropriately eloquent: "Shit."

"Yeah. She's on foot, but she's been gone about two hours, so the perimeter's getting wider by the minute."

"I'll take town north of the river and you take south?" he proposed.

"Sounds good. Call me if you find anything."

"Will do."

I hung up the phone. "David and I will split up town," I addressed Julia and her father. "I'll call when we find something."

"I want to come with," Julia asserted.

I hesitated. It probably wasn't a good idea, especially with our shared background. But I knew she wouldn't take no for an answer.

"Sure. You can ride with me," I reluctantly agreed. "Four eyes are better than two."

The Mayor looked uneasy. "Should I ride with Sergeant Addams?"

"No. You should stay here incase your wife returns," I directed. "Someone should be here just in case."

He nodded his acquiescence.

"Stay close to the phone, Mr. Desjardin. Call the non-emergency number direct if your wife comes home. We'll let you know as soon as we've got something on our end."

I drove slowly down the residential areas surrounding the Desjardin house and used the high beams to cut through the black night. Julia was understandably silent in the car. Only the occasional crackle of the in-car police radio penetrated our silence.

"Has this ever happened before?" I asked. I wasn't filling an uncomfortable silence I told myself. I was doing my job.

"No. Not that my father's told me, at least."

"Why didn't he call the police right away?" Too much time had passed between him noticing his wife's absence and me receiving Julia's call. The longer we waited, the less likely it was that we'd find Mrs. Desjardin.

"He thought he could find her on his own. He's arrogant and proud." She frowned. "It runs in the family."

I didn't say anything in response.

We continued to drive. I thought I'd found something a few times, but each turned out to be a stay cat or a raccoon.

"Are you close with your parents?" she asked me as we continued to slowly drive up and down the streets of Embarrass.

"As close as a person who spent a decade abroad can be," I shrugged. "I don't see much of them, but I try to call whenever I remember to."

"What do they do?"

"They're both retired now, but my mom was a piano teacher and my dad was a utility man for my hometown."

"No cops?"

"Nope."

"Somehow I pictured you coming from a long line of police officers."

"I kind of chose it as default," I admitted. "I didn't know what else to do with my life after the military. I figured I was a pretty good shot, so I might as well try out the police academy." I turned the question on her. "Did you always want to be a city prosecutor?"

"It's not really the kind of occupation little girls dream about," she replied.

"I imagine not too many little girls dream about being a cop either."

Julia raked her fingers through her hair. She didn't look at me; she continued to stare out the passenger side window. "I started off majoring in Classical Studies. I loved Greek and Roman mythology. But my father told me the shortest book ever written was Job Opportunities for Classical Studies Majors, so I switched to Law."

I squinted beyond the illumination of my headlights. I didn't want her to think I'd grown bored with our conversation, but a black pickup truck with oversized wheels was parked on the side of the road. Even in the dark I could see the red, orange, and yellow flames on the hood and doors. The words "Cowboy Up" had been painted on the tailgate.

"What is that monstrosity?" I wondered aloud.

"I believe that would belong to your partner in crime," Julia said.

"David?"

The man in question climbed out of the vehicle and jogged in my direction. I rolled down the driver's side window of the squad car.

"Hey," he said, sounding a little out of breath.

"Dude, what's up with your truck?" I couldn't help asking.

He looked back at the vehicle and beamed with visible pride. "She's a beauty, isn't she?"

"She's something alright," I mumbled.

He spotted Julia in the passenger seat. "Hi, Julia."

"Hello, David. Thank you for helping with the search." Her tone was stiff and formal, but I knew the words she spoke were true.

"Find anything yet?" I asked.

He shook his head. "No. Nothing so far. I think we should broaden the search. I'll keep moving farther east if you wanna look west out to the river."

I flicked my eyes in Julia's direction. She was chewing on the inside of her cheek. "You really think she could have gotten that far?" It was dark and overcast that night. If Olivia Desjardin had traveled as far as the river, we might not find her until it was too late. It had rained steadily over the past few weeks, causing the moderately tame waterway to move with more aggression. I didn't want to think about what might happen if she wandered down by the river's edge.

David shrugged. "I don't know. But maybe you should go straight out to the river just in case."

I nodded in agreement.

"Oh, I also wanted to give you this." He passed me a thick manila folder. "The paperwork from the State came back."

"What kind of numbers are we looking at?" I asked.

"At least fifteen million dollars over the past ten years."

"Jesus," I marveled.

"I know. Can I leave this with you to add to the master list?"

"Sure thing. I'll take a look at it in the morning."

"Sounds good." He exhaled deeply; it was cold that night, and I could just make out the steam of his breath. "I'll give your cell a call if I find anything." He gave Julia a jerky wave of goodbye before jogging back to his truck.

"What was that about?" Julia asked as I pulled the car out of park.

"It's nothing. It's just a case David and I have been working on."

"It doesn't sound like nothing. I haven't seen Cowboy that excited since high school homecoming."

"I really shouldn't talk about an on-going investigation."

Julia quirked an eyebrow. "Not even with me? We're supposed to be on the same side. I've given you council before, *and* I'm the one who got those charges against David dropped . . . unless you've forgotten already."

"I know you're one of the good guys, but I don't even know if there's anything to this case. It's still early. The moment we get a lead or make some connections, I promise to include you."

My words seemed to appease Julia for the time being. "That will be acceptable, Miss Miller."

My lips curved at the return of the formal name.

My phone rang. It was David. I answered, hoping for good news.

"Tell me you found her," I barked into the phone.

"I found her."

"Thank God."

Julia stirred in the passenger seat. "Is that David? Did he find her? Where was she? Is she okay?"

Rather than relay all of her questions, I handed my phone to Julia.

"David? Hi, yes. It's Julia. Mmhm," she hummed as she listened. "You did? She was? Good lord."

I could hear David's voice on the other end of the phone call, but I couldn't make out specific words.

"Alright. I'll be right there," Julia continued on the phone. "Thank you, David. I really can't express how grateful I am."

She hung up and handed the phone back to me. "David found her walking along the road near the elementary school. She used to be a teacher's aide when I was younger. She must have gone there because it was familiar."

"And she's okay? She didn't hurt herself?"

"He said she looked a little dirty and confused, but otherwise she seems okay. He's bringing her to the clinic right now. I said I'd meet them there."

I turned the police car down another road in the direction of the hospital. It wasn't much more than a walk-in clinic, but it was staffed twenty-four hours a day.

"I should send David something as a thank you," Julia said, thinking out loud as we drove to the hospital. "What might he like?"

"Besides a date with the city attorney?" I couldn't keep the bitterness from crawling into my tone. I sat stupidly in the drivers' seat actually feeling disappointed that I hadn't been the one to find Julia's mother. I wasn't the hero.

"That's not funny."

"I know it's not," I bit off. "How do you think I like working with a guy that's my competition?"

"Competition?" Her face pinched in confusion. "You know I'm not ... there's no competition, Cassidy."

"Yeah?" My breath hitched. It was the closest thing we'd come, outside of an elevator, to acknowledging our "arrangement."

She tucked a lock of dark hair behind one ear, a nervous habit perhaps, but I'd never seen this woman anxious about anything. "David's not the only police officer I should be thanking."

"You don't have to thank me. I was just doing my job."

"I've been..." She sucked in a deep breath, "pretty horrible to you since you got into town. And there's no excuse for that. My

171

actions have been selfish and self-serving. I shouldn't have taken advantage of you like that."

"You don't see me complaining, do you?" I rubbed the back of my neck. Her disassembling had me uncomfortable. I was used to Julia Desjardin being bossy and in charge. This vulnerable, yoga pants-wearing version of herself was like a stranger.

The in-car radio shrieked and we both winced at its volume.

"E-Three, this is Central. Come in, E-Three."

I grabbed the handset. "This is E-Three, Central. Go ahead."

"E-Three, I've got 10-14 at 87 Maple Ave."

"Central, be advised, E-Three is en route." I returned the radio to its holster. "I wish I could come inside with you," I sighed, "but I have to take this call."

"What's a 10-14?" she asked.

"Prowler."

Her eyes widened.

"It's probably an animal eating out of a garbage can," I dismissed.

Her mouth formed a half-smile. "Well once again, Detective, thank you for your assistance tonight." She unfastened her seatbelt and opened the passenger door. "I hope the rest of your shift is uneventful."

Chapter Fourteen

I heard the sharp, punctuated click-clack of high heels on cheap linoleum. I dragged my eyes away from a pile of paperwork to see Julia in the doorway, arms crossed and smirking.

"I had a feeling I'd find you down here." Her eyes scanned the modest police station. "I haven't been down here in years," she said, wrinkling her nose. "And now I remember why."

The two of us were alone. Lori had gone home earlier in the day, and the only noise in the station was the ticking of an old wall clock and the occasional squawk of the police radio.

I wiped my palms against the tops of my jeans. "What brings you down to the dungeon?"

"You. I was going to my car, and I saw lights on down here."

"And you assumed it would be me?"

"Only because you seem to be the most dedicated police officer in the history of the profession," she countered.

"What makes you say that?"

"This isn't your shift is it?"

"No. David's patrolling."

"Then why are you here?"

I felt a little like I was standing trial with all the rapid questions. "There's no air conditioning in my apartment," I shrugged. "And I have paperwork to catch up on."

"Paperwork?"

She stalked dangerously closer, each stiletto step sounding like a gunshot. When she bent to inspect the evidence on the desk, it was all I could do to keep from admiring the view down her dress shirt, unbuttoned to the third button.

She flipped through the documents on the desk while I held my breath and tried to maintain eye contact when all I wanted to do was lose myself in her cleavage. She had an amazing ability to render me a prepubescent teen.

"This doesn't look like your typical small-town crime paperwork." She righted herself along with my stack of papers.

I scrambled to my feet and uselessly reached for the paperwork. "Please don't mix those up. I need them in the right order." The pages were unnumbered, and I'd have no idea which documents went together if she jumbled them up.

Her unlined forehead furrowed, and she swept a defiant raven lock out of her face. "What is all this?"

I eased the papers from her hands. "Grant applications."

She rested her hand on a canted hip. "And what would you want with those? Are you applying for something?"

"No. It's for that case David and I are working on."

Julia arched an eyebrow, obviously waiting for more.

I let out a loud sigh and fell back into my chair. "Fine. But you might as well have a seat. This is a long story."

I gestured to the chair on the other side of the desk. The black leather upholstery was split in places, revealing an aged, yellow stuffing that might have been asbestos. Julia's facial expression indicated she had no intention of sitting in that chair.

"When does your shift start?" she asked.

"Ten. Just like every other night."

"Come out to the house; I'll be waiting for your story." She didn't wait for my response. She turned sharply on her red shiny heels and clacked her way out of the office.

Julia opened the door after the first knock as if she'd been waiting in the entryway for my arrival. She knew I'd show up, there wasn't a question about that. She pressed a glass into my hands, grabbed the front of my v-neck shirt, and pulled me through the doorway. Her lips were on mine, and I was pushed hard against the back of the door. She buried her teeth in my bottom lip and listened to the whimper that followed. She tasted like bourbon and lipstick. Before I could react, her mouth was gone and so was she.

The kiss left me vibrating. I drank down whatever was in the glass without thinking. I expected the fiery burn of alcohol, but it was plain juice. With a bewildered shake of my head, I followed her into the den.

The curtains were pulled open and moonlight shone in through the grand windows. It was too warm out for a fire, so the fireplace remained cold and dark. Only a few lamps illuminated the formal room. Julia took a seat on a red leather couch with a tumbler glass in her hand. She crossed one leg over the other and patted the space beside her, sparing me the mental anguish of deciding where to sit. Her work clothes had been abandoned for cotton sleep pants and a camisole, but her signature red lipstick remained.

"How's your mother?" I asked, taking a seat in the empty space beside her.

"Good. Safe. I insisted my father get an alarm on the doors and windows so he'll know if she wanders off again like that."

"That sounds like a good plan." I couldn't imagine what that would be like—to watch a parent deteriorate.

"How was your 10-14?" she asked.

"It was a bear. Eunice Brown didn't have her glasses on, and she thought it was a prowler," I laughed.

Her fingers stretched out, and she rubbed the pad of her thumb along the side of my mouth. "You've got some of my lipstick on you."

God, I wanted to kiss her. I wished I was bold enough to lean across the couch and pull her in for a kiss that she'd feel down to her painted toenails.

"So tell me about this case."

I shook my empty glass. "I might need a refill."

Her lips pursed and then broadened into a smile. "More apple juice, Detective? I know you're on the clock; I wouldn't want you to over-do it."

"You're right." I gave her a cheeky grin, sure to bring out my dimples. "Anymore juice and it wouldn't be responsible for me to drive."

"And then I'd have to insist that you stay the night." Short nails scratched down the length of my arm. "It would be irresponsible of me to let you get behind the wheel."

The intensity of emotions in that dimly lit room had my head swimming. I didn't need alcohol; Julia's presence was intoxicating enough.

"But back to your case," she smiled serenely.

The words roused me from the latest round of seduction chicken.

"You know how I've been looking into grant money and city improvement projects?"

She pulled her legs up on the couch, pulling them tight against her chest. "Like the roof on the new library," she nodded, remembering. "And your hypothetical city park."

"David thinks someone's been fudging on paperwork and pocketing grant money that should going to city projects."

She frowned. "But I already told you that most grants are reimbursements. The project gets built or the equipment gets bought, and then the Feds reimburse the city."

I nodded. We'd already gone over this the other day in her office. "But David's convinced someone's been able to cheat the system—a loophole or something."

"And what do you think?" Julia asked. She brought her glass to her lips and took a sip.

"I'm just helping out a co-worker," I said. "I don't have an opinion one way or the other."

"And yet you seem to be putting an awful lot of time into this — extra hours on the clock—which I'm sure you're not getting paid overtime for."

I fiddled with my empty glass, rolling it back and forth in my clasped hands. I wanted something stronger, but it was going to be a long night on duty. "It's not like I've got anything else to do with my days," I defended myself.

"You could be spending time with friends. Find yourself a hobby perhaps? Or a significant other."

I looked up at her sharply. I wasn't going to have this conversation with her. Not when she refused to go on a simple date with me, yet found it perfectly acceptable to kiss me senseless whenever she felt like it. I knew I was just as culpable, however, in this game she played; I could easily put a stop to this charade. It would be hard to avoid her altogether in a tiny town like Embarrass, but I could start by not showing up at her front door whenever she commanded it.

My look seemed to get my point across, so she continued our original conversation. "What proof does David have? I know he can be a little reckless at times, but this is unusual even for him."

"He found a receipt for forty police radios billed to the city."

Julia immediately made the connection. "And there's only three of you."

I nodded. "And he thinks it's just the tip of the iceberg. He's been hunting down paperwork on all kinds of capital projects through the City Clerk's office."

Julia's features creased in thought. "Believe what you will, but that money had to be spent on forty radios. The purchase order could be faked, I suppose, but it's all reimbursement. Money gets spent and a reimbursement check is issued by whatever agency awarded the grant. That's how these things work."

We both fell silent, trapped with our own thoughts. "What if the city bought forty police radios and then sold them at a higher price to neighboring agencies?" I suggested, just brainstorming and hoping something would stick. "Someone could make some extra cash that way, right?"

Julia shook her head. "The Feds would have never given that kind of money to Embarrass alone. Remember that a grant application needs to indicate a need or deficiency that the giving body deems sufficient in order to award the monies. What kind of justification does the grant application give for the surplus of radios?"

I felt like slapping my forehead. David and I had been so focused on the receipt he'd found that we'd failed to look at the original grant itself. We'd both jumped onto the next grant application instead of the original curiosity that had alerted him to the discrepancy in the first place.

"I'll look into that first thing after my shift," I vowed.

Julia clucked her tongue against the roof of her mouth. "Maybe after you get some sleep, Detective. Don't let this fools' errand wear you thin."

"You sound like you're actually concerned for my well-being," I deflected.

She rolled her eyes. "I'd just hate to see taxpayer money

wasted when you finally burn yourself out and aren't able to properly do your job."

"I'm actually paid through a federal grant and not city taxes," I chuckled, the irony not lost on me.

"Maybe someone's pocketing half your pay," she lightly laughed.

"Shit," I grinned, "if that's happening, I'd better solve this case right away."

Her returned smile was mild and complacent. "I probably shouldn't keep you any longer. I know you've got a long night of protecting and serving."

She was right, but I didn't want to go. I wanted to stay on her couch and continue to enjoy her company long after the sun had come up.

Julia stood from the couch and left the front den. I left my empty glass behind and reluctantly followed.

She stood near the front door, and I hesitated with her in the foyer.

"Thank you for the drink."

"Thank you for talking to me about your investigation," she returned.

"I should have included you a long time ago," I admitted. "You've been more than helpful tonight."

"Yes, me and my analytical brain," she softly laughed. "If you need to borrow it again, you know where to find me."

I walked out onto the front stoop. "It's a date."

She smiled curiously at me. "You're determined to get that date from me, aren't you, Detective?"

I had a smile of my own. "I'll wear you down eventually."

"Well, until that day happens ..." Her kiss was soft and just barely there, but I felt it all over like her lips were directly connected to my nerve endings.

I stumbled down the last step of the front concrete stoop. Julia covered her mouth and a laugh with her hand.

"When I took this job I had no idea it would be so glamorous." I tossed a donut hole in the air, but it knocked off my front teeth and bounced to the floor. I let this one escape rather than retrieve it. Who knew the last time the floor had had a decent scrub and wax.

"Police work's not all shootouts and car chases, you know." David popped another sugar-covered donut hole into his mouth. We were fueling our off-the-books overtime with donuts and hot coffee. David had us tracking down every major capital project the city had funded within the past five years and comparing it to our master list of federal and state-awarded monies.

"All you need is a mustache, and you'd be the perfect cliché," I joked.

"Yeah, and all you need is the mullet and a girlfriend and you'd be the perfect lady cop."

I cleared my throat and looked down at the desk.

"Holy shit," David exclaimed. "Are you gay, Miller?"

"I don't do labels," I grumbled at my hands.

"Shit, Cassidy. I was just playing. I didn't know."

I pushed out a deep breath and tugged at my ponytail. "It's fine, Addams."

"Hey, don't get me wrong. I'm totally cool with the gay thing. I've got a gay aunt."

I forced a smile to my face. "It's really fine, David. I've heard a lot worse."

"Yeah, but I'm your partner. You shouldn't have to deal with that kinda shit from me, too."

"Let's not make a big deal about it, okay?" I pushed. "You're sorry you're a dick. I get it."

His smile was sheepish. "Yeah." I was sure the combination of those dimples and long feathered eyelashes got him off with far worse. It was a good thing he was a decent guy. The authority that came from being a cop could go to a person's head.

"So back to this shit show," I said, eager to change the subject away from my sexuality. "Find anything new?" I asked.

"No. I've been staring at these numbers and this fucking fancy language for too long. Everything's starting to blur together."

I was experiencing the same thing. It was making my brain hurt.

"We need a fresh set of eyes to look over these budgets and grants."

"I don't know about that," David hesitated.

"I know you want this to be the Cass and David Show, but we're just beat cops." I shuffled the mess of papers on the desk. "I don't know about you, but I'm better at shooting my gun than I am hunting down a paper trail. These white-collar crimes are dicks."

David smiled. "Yeah, why couldn't they rob a bank like a normal criminal?"

"Or even run a drug cartel," I added with a laugh.

"Shit. I just had a thought."

"Uh oh. Don't hurt yourself." I idly licked sugar crumbs from my finger tips.

"What if it's Julia Desjardin?"

"What if what is Julia Desjardin?"

"What if she's our perp?"

"One, we don't even have proof of a crime having been committed," I asserted. "Two, that's ridiculous."

"Is it?" David posed. "Think about it. She's wicked smart. She knows all about contracts and criminal law."

"But embezzling? Money fraud? What does she know about that?"

"I bet she knows just enough that she could get away with something like this," he conjectured.

"Sure she's smart, but what about motive?" I pointed out. "Her family's already rich, and she probably makes bank as the city prosecutor. It's not like she needs the money."

"Her family's rich, but not *that* rich. We're talking about hundreds of thousands of dollars here, Cass. Millions maybe."

I found myself growing angrier and angrier at his accusation. There was no way Julia had stolen money from the city. She'd been the one helping me on this case, after all.

Fuck.

"You okay?" David asked. "I can practically see the gears grinding in your head."

I stood up and nearly knocked my chair over. I caught the back of the seat as it tipped and brought it back to all four legs.

"I'm fine. I've gotta head out though."

David's brow furrowed. "Is this because of what I said about Julia?"

I wanted to lie and try to convince him that everything was fine and that this had nothing to do with her, but it wasn't in my nature to bottle things up or avoid confrontation.

"It's complicated." Understatement of the year. "I'm going to ask her."

"And you think she's, what, just gonna confess when you bat those baby blues at her or what?"

"My eyes are brown."

"Shit." He grinned. "Even if you liked dudes, I still wouldn't have a chance, huh?"

"You're really a piece of work, Addams. Try not to eat all the donuts while I'm gone. I wouldn't want them to affect your girlish figure."

If Julia was involved with this, there had to be a good reason for it. I stood on her front stoop and knocked on the door.

I heard multiple locks being unfastened and the door swung open. "Detective Miller. This is a surprise."

"Are you embezzling money from the city?" I asked her directly. There was no reason to tiptoe around the question.

The pleasant smile fell from her face. Her shoulders straightened and she folded her arms across her chest. "So I guess you're not here to ask me out on a date."

"Fucking Christ, Julia. I just want the truth."

"No. I'm not stealing money from the city. And I'm going to do my best not to get angry with you for even asking me such a hurtful thing. I know you must be under a lot of stress."

I didn't know if it was her words or the way she was looking at me, but I felt something break. I felt it in my stomach first, a kind of nauseous rumble, but then it spread and intensified in feeling.

"Will you come in?" She took a step backwards.

I nodded, unable to form words because of the lump in my throat.

I kicked off my shoes without being told to and followed her back to the kitchen.

"Sit." Her words were gentle, but forceful.

I didn't have the energy to put up a fight.

I sat myself on a stool at the kitchen island and propped my head in my hands with my elbows resting on the countertop.

"Am I looking for something that doesn't exist?" I worried out loud. "At first I got involved in this investigation as a favor to David, but the deeper I get into it, the more I need it. It's like if I can find something wrong and fix it, it'll justify me giving up on my life downstate and running away to this little town."

I bit my lower lip. As long as I kept busy, I wouldn't have time to think about what if's and should have done's. I'd read about this in one of my PTSD self-help books. I tended to see everything in my civilian life as a "mission"—my work, my relationships. And I would drive myself crazy until the mission was complete.

Julia opened her refrigerator and took out deli meats, sliced cheese, and mayonnaise. "Is that what you really did? You ran away?"

"I don't know what else to call it. I thought a change of pace and environment would be good for me. But you can't run from yourself, no matter how fast your legs move."

She continued to silently busy herself in the kitchen.

"What are you doing?" I asked.

"Making you a sandwich."

"You don't have to do that."

She opened a bag of chips and poured some on the plate beside the sandwich. "I wanted to though."

I stood from my perch and ambled to the other side of the kitchen. Julia was packing things up and returning them to their places, but I stopped her movements.

"Thank you. For the sandwich and for listening."

"It's the least I can do."

"I just want to make a difference, you know? Working night shift isn't as fulfilling as I'd like, and it feels like every time I try to go above and beyond, I get shut down."

"Like this case with the police radios."

I nodded. "And I wanted to get some mobile fingerprint scanners for the department, but your dad said they were too expensive."

I hadn't wanted to bring up the mobile fingerprint reader again with the Chief, and all of my emails and messages to the Mayor had gone unanswered. I could have asked Julia to talk to her father on my behalf, but I didn't want to ruffle any more feathers, so I'd let the matter drop. I took heed of Chief Hart's reaction to me going over his head to mind the chain of command, keep your head down, do your assigned job, and nothing more.

Julia walked me outside where my bike was waiting.

"Where are you off to now?" she asked.

"I don't know. David's probably expecting me back at the station, but I need to get out of there for a while. Do you wanna go for a ride?"

She curled her lip. "On that death trap? Not a chance. Why would you even own one of those around here? It's not a very practical vehicle."

"But it's an adrenaline rush."

"Between the motorcycle and your clogged arteries, I'd say you didn't plan on living very long."

I tried to smile. It sucked. Normal people could casually throw around those kinds of words and phrases, but not me—not after I'd seen friends flown home in unmarked pine boxes. I tried to let her words roll off me. This was how civilians interacted. I knew she hadn't meant to offend me or make me upset. This was just how regular people talked to each other.

"Oh," I said, remembering, "I looked at that grant application for the police radios like you suggested."

"And what did your sleuthing reveal?"

"I figured out why we ordered so many radios. It was a collaborative grant application that included adjoining counties."

"So that explains the purchase of forty radios," she noted. "Case closed."

"Maybe." I wasn't convinced. "Is there any way we be sure those other departments actually got their radios?"

"You could always call them and ask," she suggested.

I wrinkled my nose at the idea. Calling up the other police, fire, and ambulance crews across the northern part of the state sounded like a lot of work. "Any other options?"

"I suppose it's probably public information under the Freedom of Information Act. You should be able to track down the serial number on each radio and see where it ended up."

I shook my head in wonder. "How do you know all of this stuff?"

"It's my job, Miss Miller. Now, I suggest you go do yours."

David had to use the squad car later that afternoon, so I drove my motorcycle to neighboring Babbitt to meet with their chief of police. Babbitt was a veritable metropolis compared to Embarrass. The police force was more than double the size of our own, and they boasted two stoplights and multiple fast food restaurants.

There was a fierce rivalry between the police departments of Minneapolis and St. Paul, so I was curious what it would be like with Babbitt's local force. Their chief of police was a tall, rangy man with an impressive mustache and a square haircut that made him look a little like Frankenstein's monster. I had called ahead to schedule a meeting with him, and a pretty secretary ushered me to his office when I arrived at the station that afternoon.

"It's nice to meet you, Detective Miller."

"Thanks for meeting with me on such short notice, Chief Plankton." A phone call to the neighboring police department might have worked, but a face-to-face visit was preferable. The other chief might not share departmental details with me over the phone without seeing my credentials.

"What can I do for you?" he asked, settling down in a chair behind his desk.

I sat down in my own chair and crossed my legs. "Your department received ten car radios from an OEC grant with Embarrass and several other departments, is that correct?"

"That's right. Your chief, Larry Hart, made us aware of an

available federal grant through the Office of Emergency Communications. All we had to do was raise half the money for our share of the radios and the grant took care of the rest."

"Do you remember how he contacted you? Was it face-to-face? Over the phone? Email?" I wondered if someone would have been able to pretend they were the Chief.

"I think it was a mass email to just about every chief in the area."

"You wouldn't happen to still have that message?" I asked.

"Probably not. After we received the radios, I wouldn't have had a reason to keep it, and our e-mail client empties the trash can after ninety days."

"What else can you tell me about the grant?" I asked.

The chief sucked on his front teeth. "Well, it was part of a post-9/11 initiative for interoperable communications."

"Interoperable communications?" I could barely get my mouth around the phrase.

"It lets all the emergency responders talk to each other."

I nodded. "And you needed the new radios?"

"Something fierce," he confirmed. "We're all small departments around here, but having the ability to communicate simultaneously with our fire and ambulance crews has been a great efficiency."

"Sounds like everybody won," I noted.

The chief made a humming noise of agreement. "I wouldn't be surprised if Larry ends up getting Chief of the Year from the MCPA because of it. You've got a good man over there, Detective."

The rest of our conversation was filled with idle chat about the area and how I was liking my job so far. Chief Plankton had no new or helpful information for me.

As I mounted my bike and headed back to Embarrass I was ashamed of the disappointment I felt that the investigation had reached another dead end. The radios were there, and they'd been purchased with a legit federal grant. Having this case had given me a purpose or at least justification for being in Embarrass. But now I was back to routine traffic stops and settling bar disputes. This was hardly the life I'd imagined for myself when I'd enrolled in the police academy.

Chapter Fifteen

I t was a clear night—beautiful actually—the perfect evening for fireworks. It took some convincing, but Chief Hart gave me the Fourth of July off. At first he'd denied my request, but he must have realized the reason behind me asking, because he changed his mind in the same breath. I tried to manage my triggers, and paramount among them was bright flashes of lights and the sounds of explosions. The night of the Fourth, I drove out of Embarrass and into the country to avoid aggravating my mental injuries.

I found myself taking the route to Julia's house just outside the city limits. The lights in her mansion were all off, but her car was out front in the circular driveway, so I knew she couldn't have strayed too far. It was too dark for gardening, so I knocked on the front door.

"Detective Miller." She looked beyond me and saw my bike parked outside. "Not working tonight?"

I didn't feel like talking. I just needed something to distract me —to help me forget.

I stepped her backwards into the house and shut the door with the help of my booted foot. She made no comment about my footwear or the possible scuff I'd probably left on the painted door with the inelegant action.

I flicked the top button of her blouse open and kissed at the bare skin that had been hidden there. My mouth left the area wet and slightly flushed, but not enough to leave a mark that would show up the next day. My intuition told me I'd be facing the city attorney's wrath if I'd done that.

I focused my attention on the next pearly white button and freed it from its strangling noose. More pale, olive-toned skin appeared beneath the white button-up. The beige bra was a letdown compared to some of the other undergarments I'd seen her in, but it couldn't detract from the pert flesh that I knew resided beneath the conservative garment.

I slid my hand beneath the soft cream blouse, but she stopped me, wrapping her fingers around my wrist. "Upstairs," she murmured.

I'd always thought you can tell a lot about a person from the way their bedroom looked. Julia's room was exactly as I expected. Everything had its place. Unlike my own studio, there was no dirty laundry on the floor, no bras hanging from anything that might serve as a hook, no stray socks whose partner had mysteriously vanished.

The furniture was uniformly dark and oversized, including the king-sized bed in the center of the room. I fell backwards onto said bed when the backs of my knees met the mattress edge. Julia placed her palm in the center of my chest and pushed me onto my back.

She shrugged out of her suit jacket and draped it over the edge of a high-backed chair in front of her vanity dresser. Next, she worked down the side zipper of an impossibly fitted skirt. The garment fell down her legs like a magician unveiling a metamorphosis illusion. She stepped out of the skirt and out of shiny black high heels.

From my place on the bed, I watched it all with mounting anticipation. Not satisfied being a passive onlooker, I inched myself to the edge of the bed and fumbled only briefly with the remaining small buttons of the sleeveless shell that had hidden beneath the tailored suit jacket.

With the buttons out of the way I was afforded an eye-level view of Julia's bra and the flat plane of her abdomen. I slid my hands beneath the open-hanging sleeveless shirt, avoiding the delectably rounded breasts the first pass, and up to smooth shoulders to completely remove the silk shell. Mindful that the shirt probably cost more than my living stipend, I layered it on top of her suit jacket despite the urge to ball it up and fling it across the room.

My hands glided up the soft swell of a round ass to settle in the small of Julia's back. I pulled her closer and she obliged. I pressed my face into the space between her precariously contained breasts. I inhaled the delicate perfume and the unmistakable scent of her arousal. She smelled spicy like sandalwood and cinnamon.

Julia inched closer until she stood straddling my thighs between her own. Her knees sunk into the mattress as she settled more comfortably on my lap. I raked my fingernails down the tops of her naked thighs.

I palmed twin breasts, not much more than a handful, that sat high and proud on her chest. I teased her nipples through the sheer material, coaxing stiff peaks to meet their potential.

I wrapped my arms around her waist, and in one fluid motion that exhibited my core strength, I lifted her from my lap and planted her back onto the mattress.

She released a soft, surprised gasp—the first sound emitted since the invitation upstairs. I couldn't recall having enjoyed shedding a woman's undergarments so much so. My fingers toyed only momentarily with the elastic waistband of her underwear before curling beneath. The lacy undergarment felt delicate beneath my slightly shaking hands. I was going to see Julia Desjardin completely naked. It was a sobering thought. When she arched her delectable backside off the mattress, it was the only encouragement I needed to slide the flimsy panties down her jutting hipbones and down her long, long legs. I resisted the urge to immediately taste her, exhibiting an ungainly amount of self-control.

When Julia sat up in bed to unfasten her bra, I placed my hands on top of hers. "Stop."

She arched a questioning eyebrow.

"I want to do it," I clarified.

I could hear the slight intake of breath before she nodded. I reached behind her; my hands slid along smooth skin until I felt the bra clasp. I unfastened the garment so it was only held up by the shoulder straps. I scooted a little closer on the bed so I could kiss along the tops of her toned shoulders. My suddenly steady hands slipped the two straps down her shoulders and off her slender arms, until the bra fell away, rendering her completely naked.

Her fingers curled around my wrist, and she dragged my hand down to cup her sex. We both groaned at the contact, and I gave her clit a rough rub. Her breath puffed out in an uneven exhale, and her eyes rolled closed.

Julia had not made a motion to remove any of my clothing. She had only stood in place, eyes lightly lidded and lipsticked mouth parted. It was then that I realized something: Julia Desjardin was a pillow princess.

I brought my hand away from her sex and back up to her breasts, leaving the one spot we both wanted me to linger. I walked my fingers over the exposed swell of her chest. I dipped lower and dragged my fingernail across a puckered nipple. I teased and toyed with the tender skin, but made no move to go elsewhere. I refused to do anything more than stroke my hand across her skin and kiss her, tongues teasing.

Her fingers clamped around my wrist for a second time. "Don't play games with me, dear." Dark eyes flashed in annoyance. "I always win."

"Maybe I don't mind losing."

Julia let her head fall back, affording me better access to her neck and collarbone. Her nostrils flared, her breathing sounded labored, and yet I had barely touched her.

I breathed in the woman perched on the bed from her raven dark hair, slightly mussed and falling across her forehead, and admired the slender, taunt body that seemed to defy age and gravity. I took my time, kissing the olive skin of her naked breasts, rotating from one breast to the other. I took a pebbled nipple into my mouth and flicked at the sensitive nub with the tip of my tongue.

I heard her quiet hiss. "Lower," she urged.

"I'm feeling a little overdressed," I murmured against her skin.

Julia was not an obtuse woman; I didn't have to provide her with a second hint before she quickly shed me of my clothes.

She pressed her fingers against my sternum. "Lay down."

"You're awfully big on giving me commands," I observed with a wry smile.

"Are you going to put up a fight?"

"Not until you tell me to do something I didn't already want to do," I said, meeting Julia's challenge with one of my own.

"Roll over."

"What's the magic word?"

"Do you want an orgasm, Miss Miller?" she clipped.

I barked out a laugh. "Good enough for me."

With some effort, I heaved myself off the far too comfortable mattress and rolled onto my stomach. I heard the sharp intake of air, and I realized what she'd discovered. Sometimes I forgot myself.

There was a noticeable pause before her fingers lightly dusted over the marbled scars she found on my back. I bit back a sob. No one except the doctors had touched them before. I even forgot about them sometimes since they were on my back. But the nightmares never let me forget completely.

She didn't ask me about the scars, but I knew her curious mind wanted to know the story behind them. There were more, less obvious and unseen, but I wasn't about to cry to this woman about what seeing my buddies being blown up to bits had done to my head, or how I re-lived that moment, night after night, re-witnessing the contorted looks of agony on their faces. Not all stories needed to be told. Part of moving to Embarrass had been to get off desk duty, but it had also been a new start overall. I couldn't handle one more sympathetic stare. I wanted to just be Cassidy Miller, city cop. Not Cassidy Miller, broken veteran.

Finally, I felt capable, confident fingers wiggle in the space between my knees and the mattress. Julia grabbed onto my lower thighs and pulled until I was up on my hands and knees.

"Much better."

"Julia." My voice wavered on her name in warning. I shivered when I felt hands ghost over my outer thighs to rest lightly on my hips.

"Don't worry, dear."

"I don't like surpri—" My words were cut off by a gentle, but firm smack to my backside. "The fuck?" I growled. I turned my head to look over my shoulder and glare.

She tried to look innocent, but her horns were showing. "I'm sorry. Should I warn you before I spank you?" she cooed.

"Or you could just not slap me," I snapped. "Ever think of that?"

Her short, manicured nails trailed over the place where her

palm had struck. She hadn't hit me all that hard, but I was sure my pale skin still showed a faint pink mark. Her hands left my backside and moved to rest on the inside of my thighs. She applied slight pressure on my inner thighs, coaxing my legs farther apart on the mattress.

I bit down on my lower lip when she spread me wider apart. If I'd thought I'd felt vulnerable before, simply lying on my stomach, this new position took that vulnerability to a whole new level.

The hands at my thighs tightened. "Are you ready for me, Miss Miller?"

Before I could respond or react, the mattress sunk and shifted beneath my hands and knees, and then suddenly Julia's mouth was on my sex. I breathed in sharply through my nose.

Julia licked the length of my slit. "Oh God," I quietly groaned when I felt the tip of her tongue just barely flick against my clit before sliding all the way back again.

She held hard onto my pale thighs, fingers digging in as if she worried I might try to run away. She flattened her tongue and licked again, tasting my arousal, already heavy between my thighs.

I felt the absence of her heat and the mattress moved again. "Why did you ... why did you stop?" I choked out, feeling equally annoyed and breathless.

I groaned again when she draped her naked body over mine and when her breasts flattened against my back. I could feel *all* of the city prosecutor this way.

"I didn't stop. I just changed my mind." Julia thrust her pelvic bone lightly back and forth, pressing against my sex from behind with each forward thrust. I could practically feel my arousal and her saliva, wet on the backs of my thighs.

"About what?" I was starting to feel the burn in my forearms from holding up my weight, but Julia's body felt too good pressed against my own, and I craved more.

195

Her breath was warm and it tickled my right ear. "How I'm going to make you come undone, dear."

"Oo-okay," I stuttered.

She placed a finger against the opening of my sex. She stroked up and down my wet slit, gathering my arousal. Slowly, she sunk her digit inside from the first to the second knuckle. She rotated her single finger like a corkscrew and was rewarded with my quiet mewls of appreciation.

Her free hand wrapped around my torso. She curled her finger up and sought out the slightly textured upper wall that she knew would make me scream.

The arm around my waist tightened. "Don't you cum," she growled into my ear. "Don't you fucking cum."

One finger followed another, and I whimpered at the delicious stretch. Her movements slowed to let me accommodate to the new intrusion before she resumed at a punishing pace.

The arm around my waist gave way, and a hand—hard and stern—pressed down in the center of my back, flattening me against the mattress while her other hand continued to assault me from behind.

"Don't cum," Julia warned again. "I want to keep fucking you like this all night."

The combination of her words and the magic of her punishing fingers caused me to cry out. I wasn't close to orgasm yet, but I knew how to get there.

"Please," I gasped, trying to arch into her unrelenting touch.

Her hand just above my ass kept me pressed against the mattress, denying me the freedom of movement I sought.

"Please, Julia," I pled. "I need to cum."

She fisted her hand in my loose locks and pulled them back as if in a ponytail. My head jerked backwards, my back arched, and my naked breasts jutted out, but I could finally lift my ass from the mattress to meet her thrusts with those of my own.

Julia gave a pained but approving noise as I pushed back against her, challenging her, forcing her, to fuck me even harder from behind.

"Julia." I gasped her name over and over again like it was the only word I could remember.

She slammed her fingers harder and faster. She let go of my hair and snaked her hand around my waist so she could pinch and stroke my clit between her fingers.

"Do it." The words were sharp in my ear. "Cum for me, Cassidy."

I fell forward and screamed into a pillow, my cries muffled by the thick down material. My arms finally gave out, my knees wobbled unsteadily, and I crashed onto the mattress.

"Holy shit," I gasped when my breathing came back under my control.

I thought myself in shape, but Julia had me rethinking that. I collapsed back onto the mattress, exhausted. I hadn't ever been so thoroughly fucked, and my muscles reveled in the aftermath. I was going to feel this woman in the morning.

Afghanistan, 2012

Our convoy bumps over the uneven terrain of a road that makes the potholed streets of my childhood town look like the autobahn. We've been at it for a handful of hours—military presence in a bumfucknowhere village on the edge of land that flip flops every other day between Taliban and rebels.

I'm squinting into the sun. My sunglasses struggle to cut down the glare over a shimmery horizon. The heat bouncing off the sand dunes creates squiggly lines in the air over the ground like snakes made out of vapor and steam twisting up toward the sky. I chew on a toothpick. It's been my constant companion since I decided to quit smoking. It's safer not to be a slave to nicotine when you could be picked off just for taking a cigarette break.

I scan the horizon with my M16 clutched in hands in dire need of a manicure, looking for anything out of the ordinary. I keep watch because it's my turn, but we all know this precaution has little effectiveness, especially when there could be a dirty bomb strapped to a goat that wanders into our area or a buried mine rigged to explode if you're unlucky enough to cross its path.

We try to be safe. We try to take precautions. But our reality is a world where chaos reigns the day and security is a politician's lie.

The insurgents' gunshots sound like firecrackers. *Pop, pop, pop, pop.*

"BOHICA," my LT groans. Bend over, here it comes again. We're about to get screwed.

A new kid, I think his name is Williams, is shaking in his Cadillacs.

"FNG," someone near me grumbles: fucking new guy.

It's Fourth of July in Minnesota, and I'm at my family's cabin on Armstrong Lake. My mom's made cherry pie and potato salad, and my dad is grilling burgers that plump up like ground beef baseballs. Barkley, my old golden retriever, is knee high in murky water, belly fur dripping with lake water, snapping at minnows that squirm away too quickly for his jaws.

My cousins throw pop rocks at the end of the pier as dusk settles over the lake. They snap and crack and light up like a firefly's butt. We run around with roman candles and sparklers, and my aunt Jean Marie yells at us to slow down and be careful.

My LT is yelling orders, but I'm too stunned to move. There's an explosion and the world falls out from under my feet, except that it's not the ground or the all-terrain vehicle that's moving; it's me. My feet and torso and two arms and legs are lifted from the force of the bomb, and I'm thrown against the stone foundation of a village building. The barked command of my superior is drowned out by the ringing in my ears.

This is how you're going to die, that voice inside my head tells me.

Our ride is scorched—twisted metal that belongs in a contemporary art museum, not a war zone—and there's a crater in the earth where there used to be straight road.

My gun is still miraculously attached to me, as are all of my external appendages. I've got my back to solid rock and my ass on the ground. On the other side of my primitive fortress, insurgents fire random shots into the sky. *Pop, pop, pop.*

"Unit Charlie, do you copy?"

"CFB," I bark into the radio. Clear as a fucking bell.

The LT shoots off a couple rounds of suppression fire so a portion of the unit can reposition without being hit by enemy fire.

My dad is lighting off confiscated fireworks. We're shooting bottle rockets across the lake. They squeal and shriek as they haphazardly zip through the sky.

Private Williams is screaming. He can't find his right arm.

I shot up in bed, breathing heavily as though I'd just run a great distance. Beside me, Julia roused from her own sleep.

I didn't know when I'd closed my eyes. Julia's bedroom was the perfect temperature, her mattress the perfect combination of sturdy and soft, and the warm body beside me smelled entirely edible. I hadn't meant to fall asleep, but I'd been so relaxed, so comfortable.

But even the most pleasant surroundings couldn't keep the nightmares away.

"Cassidy?" Her voice was thick and worry crossed her

features. She reached out and pressed the back of her hand against my sweaty brow. "You're burning up," she frowned.

I jerked away from the concerned touch. "I'm fine." I tossed back the blanket Julia had placed over me at some point in the night and scrambled out of bed.

Julia sat up. "Where are you going?"

"Home." I pulled on my jeans and hopped around a bit to get them all the way up my lean legs. "I didn't mean to fall asleep."

"I'm not exactly kicking you out of my bed, dear."

"I don't do sleepovers. Sorry."

Julia opened her mouth, but deciding against it, snapped her jaw shut. Her face clouded over, shuttering away the former worry I was sure I'd seen. "Well, please do be sure to lock the front door on your way out. I'd hate for a criminal to take advantage while one third of the town's police force is otherwise preoccupied."

I pulled my T-shirt over rambunctious blonde hair. I was embarrassed to have fallen asleep, but even more so that she had witnessed one of my nightmares. I knew I should thank her for the evening or kiss her or even say that I'd call her later, but my mortification had me keeping those sentiments to myself.

Chapter Sixteen

The front room of the Minneapolis police precinct was a cacophony of ringing phones and conversations too loud for the confined space. The noises caused the walls to seize, but I checked my nerves and strode up to the uniformed officer sitting behind the reception desk.

"Is Detective Gammon in?" I asked.

The male officer barely looked up from the morning newspaper, but I didn't have a problem with the lack of eye contact. I was sure I looked like a wreck. I'd ridden my Harley through the early morning hours, without detour, to reach the city. My hair was probably matted from my helmet, and I still wore the clothes I'd been wearing when I'd stumbled out of Julia's bedroom four hours earlier.

"Lemme see." He picked up the phone and dialed an extension. "Detective Gammon? Someone's asking for you." He grunted at Rich's response and hung up the office phone.

"He'll be right out," he informed me, finally looking me in the eye. If my disheveled appearance alarmed him, his emotionless face didn't let on. He nodded in the direction of an empty wooden bench. "You can have a seat over there."

I bobbed my head in thanks, but I chose not to sit down. I'd been on my ass for the past four hours and my legs could use the movement. I shoved my chapped hands into the front pockets of my tight jeans and began to pace.

Rich's dress shoes squeaked on the floor. His tie was loose around his neck and the sleeves of his dress shirt had already been rolled up to his elbows. "Cass? What are you doing here?"

"Can you help me get my old job back?" I blurted out. I could hear the desperation in my voice, but I was beyond caring. "Or *any* job?"

Rich's eyes swept around the front room. "Let's go back to my office," he said, lowering his voice. My shoulders crumbled, and he ushered me towards his cubical with a firm hand in the small of my back.

I slumped down in an empty chair and dropped my head into my hands.

"Can I get you something? Water? Coffee?" he offered, concern on his handsome face.

"Water would be great," I mumbled through my fingers.

"I'll be right back."

Rich's cubical was sparsely decorated. Unlike the other offices in the area, there were no photographs of a significant other and no crayon drawings posted to the carpeted partition walls. I picked up the sole framed picture that adorned his desk. It was a group shot— Rich, Angie, Brent, and me, faces smiling and arms thrown around each other's shoulders. We'd gone to a Twin's game late in the season, and Brent had practically fought a guy for a foul ball in the seventh inning.

"That was a fun day."

I looked up at the sound of his voice. Rich held out a Styrofoam cup to me filled with water. I took it and quickly drained it of its contents.

He sat down at his desk while I began to shred the cup into tiny pieces. "What's going on?"

"I'm going crazy up there."

He frowned. "Small-town cabin fever or something else?"

"Something else." My right knee bounced with pent-up energy.

"I was thinking about you last night," he admitted. "I was going to call."

"It's okay." I dug my short nails into the side of the foam cup and made half-moon imprints. "I probably wouldn't have answered."

The previous Fourth of July a group of us had gone to a St. Paul Saints baseball game. When the fireworks had started, I'd freaked out. It was embarrassing to think about now; I'd hidden out in the women's restroom and had refused to leave my stall the entire night. Rich and Angie had sat on the floor on the bathroom, keeping me company. My eyes started to burn at the memory. I held my breath and kept my eyes shut tight until the wash of overwhelming emotions abated.

Rich pulled at a stubborn hangnail. I could tell he was just as uncomfortable as I was thinking about that night. He cleared his throat. "Was it bad again?"

I let out a shaky breath. "It certainly wasn't good." I didn't want to go into detail, and he was a smart enough guy not to ask.

"You should come back, Cass," he said quietly. "We've got resources down here that I'm sure they don't have in that little town."

"If I can't be a cop, I don't know what I'm going to do," I admitted. I was a Marine, a soldier. I couldn't envision a future that didn't involve that.

Rich leaned back in his chair and rubbed both hands over his bald head. "I'll put a bug in the Captain's ear, but I can't promise you anything. I know he's been looking to fill the vacancy left when we had to let Officer Timmons go."

"Thanks, Rich." I let out a long breath; my chest felt lighter.

"Do you still have the key to my apartment?" he asked.

"Yeah, why?"

"Go there and get some sleep. You look like crap."

"I can't." I self-consciously fluffed at my tangled hair. "I've got to work tonight."

"Call in sick. Stay the night. It'll do you good."

"I can't," I insisted again, standing up on stiff legs.

"Why not?"

"Because if I stay tonight, I might never go back."

"And that's a bad thing because?" Rich pointed out.

I needed to go back. I *had* to go back; my mission wasn't completed yet.

"Detective Miller?" The curt, no nonsense voice rang across the rotunda of City Hall.

I stopped short of the staircase that would take me down to the police station. After leaving Rich's office, I'd dropped by Mickey's Diner in St. Paul for a burger and fries. Then it was back on the bike and back on the road. I'd returned to Embarrass just in time to grab a few hours of sleep before my shift.

My body reacted in an almost Pavlov's dog response to the sound of Julia's heels clicking against the floor. The dampness collecting between my thighs from the click clack against the hard surface caused me to grimace.

God, what had she done to me?

"Madam Prosecutor," I stiffly returned. "Another late night?"

I had nowhere to hide. When I'd last seen her I'd left her home angry and embarrassed. I hadn't shot out of someone's bedroom that quickly since the first time I'd had sex with a girl after experiencing a moment of Gay Panic. I felt ashamed for similarly abandoning Julia.

"I looked for you at the station earlier, but Lori said you hadn't been in today. I thought I'd catch you before your shift."

"Yeah. I was looking into getting a hobby."

I knew I was being rude, but my whirlwind round-trip to the Twin Cities had left me worn and frayed. Eight hours on a motorcycle had not been kind to my body or mindset.

"I got you something." She pulled a small paper bag out of her black briefcase and handed it to me. Inside, I found an ornament that spun on a loop of fishing line. "It's a dream catcher," she explained. "I picked it up this morning from the Bois Forte Heritage Center in Tower."

Its significance took me by surprise. I didn't know what to say or how to respond. I considered myself a fiercely proud person; admitting weakness or vulnerability wasn't in my nature.

"I-I'm sorry about last night," I stammered out. "I shouldn't have bailed like that."

She ignored my apology. It was clear she had her own agenda. "Once upon a time you told me you took this job as a favor. But you didn't say who the favor was for."

I couldn't meet her stare.

"Was Chief Hart the one giving out favors, Cassidy?"

"I ..." I blinked and tears clung to my eyelashes.

Julia wet her bottom lip. "Your nightmares," she said gently, "it's because of the war." It wasn't a question; she seemed to know.

The nightmares hadn't come for several months after returning to the States. They had nearly derailed my sanity and had prematurely ended my police career. I'd spent more time in the office of the city police's psychologist than behind the wheel of a patrol car. I'd graduated top of my class at the police academy, and now I feared I'd be stuck behind a desk for the rest of my working days. That was until my father, back in my hometown of St. Cloud, had reached out to his childhood friend, the Chief of Police in Embarrass, Minnesota. Working third shift in a small town in northern Minnesota was a far cry from the future I'd imagined for myself. It could have been worse though; I didn't have to sleep with a weapon under my pillow, and I could leave the house and go out in public, so I didn't have it as bad as some of the guys in my PTSD support group.

"I found something else you might be interested in." She pressed a stack of papers into my hands.

"More presents?" I said weakly. I didn't like the feeling that other people knew about my baggage. It was mine alone with which to deal.

"It's a grant through the Department of Homeland Security for those mobile fingerprint scanners you were telling me the police department needed. They're free. All you have to do is apply."

My mouth opened and closed a few times. "I-I don't know what to say."

"Thank you is always a good start, dear," she smiled.

"I don't know the first thing about writing grants." I was shocked she had remembered the brief conversation and even more surprised that she'd found a grant for me.

"It's okay. I can help you."

I shook my head and gathered my wits about me. "How about over dinner tomorrow night?"

"At Stan's?" She arched a critical eyebrow.

"Maybe I could cook for you," I offered.

"You know how to cook?"

"Actually, no."

She hesitated. "You know I don't—"

"It's not a date," I interrupted. I didn't know why labels bothered her so much. "It would just be two co-workers collaborating on a project after hours."

Julia raked her fingers through her hair. "I suppose I could be bothered to make you a decent meal. It wouldn't do if you had a heart attack from all that cholesterol you ply to your body. The medical bills alone would be a hardship on the city."

"Careful, Julia," I grinned knowingly. "Between the dream catcher and dinner, I might start thinking you actually care about my well-being."

"You're scaring me. It's like you're determined to cut off your fingers."

I gave Julia a crooked smile and wiggled the fingers on my right hand. "You're always so concerned about me keeping my fingers."

She rolled her eyes. "Give me the knife. I'll do it."

Julia had showed up at my apartment the next evening with an armful of bagged groceries. I'd protested her spending money, but she'd pointed out that she couldn't make a decent meal from frozen pizzas and boxed macaroni and cheese. I couldn't argue with her there. I had been meaning to go grocery shopping, but I hadn't been motivated to do the mundane chore. It was depressing filling my cart with lonely meals for one. Grace had suggested we do a once-a-week rotating dinner, but we hadn't followed through with that yet.

"No," I refused. "I want to help."

She stepped behind me, nearly pinning me between the counter and her body. "At least let me show you the right way to cut up an onion."

"I didn't know there was a wrong way."

"When you cut off your fingers, that's the wrong way."

She rested her hand on top of my knife hand and the other

wrapped around me to move the half mutilated onion out of my reach.

"Like this." Her warm breath ticked the back of my neck. If she truly wanted me to pay attention, having her body so close wasn't the best strategy. "Imagine your left hand is a hermit crab, and it's getting smaller and smaller as you cut the onion."

"What about these fumes? Any tricks for that?" I inhaled through my nose and it made an unattractive rattle.

"You're letting a little white onion make you cry? I thought you were tougher than that, Marine."

I wiped at my stinging eyes with the sleeve of my Henley top. "Fucking ooohraaah," I grumbled to myself.

There was a brisk knock at the door.

"This isn't over," I said, shaking the knife at the offensive onion.

I wiped my hands on my jeans and once more at my nose, and I opened the door to find David standing on the other side.

"Uh, did I catch you at a bad time?" he stammered.

I must have looked bizarre with my eyes red and nose close to leaking.

"No. Just losing a battle to an onion," I said, stepping back and ushering him inside.

He took a step into the apartment and froze again when he saw I had company. "Oh, hey Julia."

"David," Julia crisply returned. There was no place for her to hide in the studio apartment unless she ran into the bathroom.

"Sorry, I should have called first."

"It's fine." I wiped my hands on a kitchen towel. "Julia's helping me with a grant proposal."

David looked between Julia, me, and at all the groceries spread out on the counter top. Julia arched an eyebrow as if daring him to challenge my explanation.

"What's up?" I asked. "Are we still good for tonight?"

He nodded. "Yeah, I just wanted to drop off the extra set of keys for the cop car in case I forget and bring them home tonight."

"Cool man. Thanks."

"And if this rain keeps up, I could drop the car off at your apartment in the morning instead of City Hall."

"It's fine. I can walk."

"Are you sure? I know how you feel about getting wet," he grinned. "Delicate flower that you are."

"Very funny," I snorted.

"Okay, well I'll let you two get back to your dinner then. Sorry again for barging in. It was nice seeing you, Julia."

"Always a pleasure, David." Julia smiled tightly.

With a tip of his patrolman's hat, David left.

Julia took a sip of her wine and set her glass on the kitchen counter. "What did he mean he knows how you are about getting wet?"

I picked up the butcher knife and resumed dicing the onion. "It's an inside joke."

She hummed and looked unconvinced. "Maybe I should have a chat with Chief Hart about David's professionalism. He wouldn't want another lawsuit."

I rolled my eyes. "It was just a joke, Julia. Cops do that; we joke around."

"And why is he working your shift tonight?" she pressed. "You didn't do this because of our dinner, did you?"

"Nope. David offered to switch shifts once a week with me so I can actually have a social life."

"He *volunteered* to work third shift? Out of the kindness of his heart?" She arched an eyebrow.

"He's a good guy."

She made another humming noise and took another sip of her wine.

"What?" I set the knife down a little harder than I had

intended, and it made an ugly clanging sound. All of her noises and the looks she was giving me were starting to become aggravating. "You think he has an ulterior motive?"

"Not to be cynical, dear, but people usually only go out of their way to accommodate others when there's something in it for them."

"Like you and the dream catcher?" I pointed out. "And this grant application?"

Her lips thinned, but at least the humming noises had stopped.

"Seriously, there's nothing going on with me and David. He's just a good guy." I licked my lips. "Besides, it shouldn't matter to you if there was. There's no anti-fraternizing clause in my contract." It was admittedly a little pathetic, but I was purposely baiting her.

"Don't play games. You know how I feel about that." Her caramel eyes narrowed, and before I could react, her fingers were weaving themselves under my ponytail and tugging hard until my scalp felt the pull. My head jerked to one side from the violence of the action. I felt her canines rake down the sensitive flesh of my neck, and her breath was warm and wet on my skin. "I *will* mark you again, Detective."

I could hardly manage an embarrassing whimper.

She released her tight grip and my hand immediately went to my scalp to check for bleeding or other injuries. "Damn it, Julia," I growled. "Do you have to be so rough?"

She smirked, dark and knowing. "I don't think you'd like me half as much if I were gentle. You might lose interest if I treated you as though you were constructed from porcelain."

"I'm not a masochist," I grumbled, still rubbing my head.

She arched a defiant eyebrow. "You like the punishment, Cassidy. I can read it on your body as though it were written in black permanent marker. The only question I have is *why* you feel the punishment is warranted."

"Do you want to stay the night?"

Her eyes widened. I was sure she hadn't expected that question. "Oh, I ..."

"You know, to make sure the dream catcher works." I couldn't help the smirk that came unbidden to my lips. Julia was usually unflappable, but my invitation had brought a visible blush to the apples of her cheeks. Despite how many times we'd had sex, we'd never had a sleepover—nothing planned, at least. I'd fallen asleep in her bed on accident.

Julia wet her lips. "I wouldn't want to impose."

"Are you going to make me beg?" I huffed. She was clearly stalling.

"I ... I suppose I could stay. To make sure the dream catcher does its job," she was quick to add.

I pushed back my empty plate with a satisfied sigh. "Damn, Julia. If I was as good of a cook as you, I'd weigh three hundred pounds."

She finished the remaining bites on her plate and dabbed the corners of her lipsticked mouth with a paper napkin. "It's called *nutrition*, Miss Miller. I don't suppose they taught you about the food pyramid in school?"

"I'm sure they did, but I was too busy eating glue to pay attention," I winked.

I sipped wine out of a pint glass. I wasn't a big wine drinker; I preferred beer or hard liquor, but I'd bought the bottle on a whim during my last trip to the grocery store. I let the spicy, dry flavors wash over my tongue. From the way Julia had helped herself to a second glass, I sensed that I'd made a good choice.

My apartment was filled with the scent of food that hadn't been prepared in a microwave, and Julia sat beside me: eyes mirthful, white teeth flashing under painted lips, with her raven hair styled to frame her classically beautiful features. I could get used to this. I didn't think I'd ever seen her look so beautiful. But as I was quickly realizing, every new thing I learned about the guarded city attorney revealed a new, beautiful side.

"What?"

I blinked once. "Huh?"

"You're looking at me like I've grown a third eye." Julia's eyes narrowed in suspicion.

I shook my head hard. "Sorry. My mind was wandering."

She set down her nearly empty glass. "Perhaps you should try to get some sleep, dear."

"Yeah, uh, I think you're probably right." I stood up awkwardly from the island countertop. Over the past two days, I'd barely had half a dozen hours of sleep. "I'll clean all of this up first," I said, motioning to our dirty plates and utensils.

Julia waved a dismissive hand. "They'll still be here in the morning. Now go get ready for bed."

When I emerged from the bathroom, teeth scrubbed and face washed, Julia was in the kitchen, elbow-deep in sudsy water. She had shed her clothes from the workday. Her black pencil-skirt and cream-colored dress shirt were now carefully folded on the cushion of the overstuffed easy chair in the nook that I referred to as the living room. A delicate demi-cup lace bra sat on top of the pile.

I swept my eyes up her slender, toned legs, now bare, up to the barely visible underwear that peeked out from the bottom hem of one of my military-issued T-shirts. The soft material contrasted with the sinfully sexy white and black underwear. The shirt wasn't ill-fitted, but it hung more loosely on her thin frame. She was smaller than me, narrower shoulders and more feminine curves where I was long, sleek, and lean.

"That shirt has never looked so good," I openly admired.

Julia spun on naked heels, looking startled as if she hadn't heard me come out of the bathroom. The surprise faded when she realized my praise. She smiled softly and tucked a lock of hair behind her ear. "I hope you don't mind. I didn't really come prepared for a sleepover."

I crossed the room, dissatisfied with the distance between us. I toyed with the bottom hem of the short-sleeved shirt. "Maybe I just mind that you're wearing clothes at all," I husked, feeling braver than usual.

"That's a nice line," she smirked. "Been thinking about it long?"

"It just came to my head. You must be particularly inspiring."

I regarded the kitchen sink, filled with hot water and soapsuds. Everything about the setting felt overly domestic: the homemade meal, Julia doing the dishes, and her wearing my clothes. I should have been panicking, but instead I found the situation comfortable. Natural.

"I thought you said those could wait until morning?" I said, nodding to the half-cleaned dishes.

"You question me too much, Detective." Julia's hands found the straps of my a-frame tank top. They were damp from the dishwater. She gave a sharp tug on the clothing, and my breath caught in my throat. "And you're also wearing too much."

Outside, someone's dog barked incessantly. Inside my apartment, Julia's breathing came in quiet, deep inhalations that told me she was sleeping. She slept soundly, but for me, sleep never came so easily. My work schedule had altered my already unpredictable sleep patterns, and I didn't want to dream tonight. But watching the rhythmic rise and fall of Julia's chest was sure to lull me to sleep eventually.

Julia slept on top of the covers because of the muggy heat in my un-air conditioned apartment. I was sure this was as close to roughing it as the city prosecutor ever got. The moon cast strange shadows on her bare legs—dark stripes from the dividers of the window over my headboard.

I traced my hands softly down the curve of her hip. My touch was soft so as to not disturb her sleep. I traveled the distance from the twisted narrow waist up a gently swelling thigh, down a jutting hip that made its presence known even beneath the satin of her underwear.

Julia stirred and I pulled my hand away. She rolled over on the mattress and faced me. Her dark eyes looked confused. "You're still awake?"

I allowed myself an unnecessary, indulgent touch and brushed a sweep of hair away from her forehead. "I'm fine," I quietly insisted. "Go back to sleep."

Her eyes fluttered closed once again. She looked young without her dramatic makeup. She never looked overdone, but without the smoky eye shadow or the crimson lipstick she looked human. Mortal. Vulnerable.

"I can feel you looking at me," she said with eyes still closed. "Stop that."

"Where should I look instead?" I posed.

"How about the backs of your eyelids?" she suggested.

I ran the tip of my index finger over her lips and lightly grazed the small white scar that dipped into the top of her lip. "Tell me this story."

She gently grabbed my wrist and pulled me away from her scar. Our enjoined hands rested in the valley between her breasts. "Will you tell me about yours?" she countered.

I shut my eyes tight and felt a single tear escape the corner of my eye. Her fingers reached up collect it before any others could threaten to follow.

"Another time, perhaps," I heard her say.

I rested my head on her sternum and kept my eyes closed. I felt raw and vulnerable, something that didn't settle well with me. I fought the instinct to run, like I'd done on the Fourth of July when she had observed my nightmares. The way she held my hand was enough to make me stay.

She cleared her throat, and it reverberated through her chest. "I was six," she started. "It's probably my first memory, or at least the one that's stuck with me. I was standing at the end of the pier at my family's cottage, pretending to fish or some nonsense."

A choked laugh bubbled up my throat and escaped before I could stop it. I could practically feel the heat of a pointed glare digging into the top of my head. "I can't even imagine what you find so funny," she said sternly.

I rested my chin against her collarbone. Her eyes were dark. "I'm having a hard time visualizing you, even as a child, doing something so rustic as fishing."

Her nostrils flared and her mouth curved down. "I grew up in northern Minnesota, Miss Miller. I climbed trees and tore the knees of my jeans and went fishing with leeches just like any other child. I wasn't always like this."

I nearly asked her what had changed her, but I imagined that was another story for another time, and one she wouldn't share so freely.

"Is it safe for me to continue without further interruption?" she asked.

I smiled, nodded, and pressed my lips tightly together.

She sighed and annoyance crept into even the exhale of breath. She raked her fingers through her dark locks, pushing them away from her face before continuing.

"My brother Jonathan wanted to use the fishing pole, but I told him he was too young and too small. We fought about it, and he pushed me." She touched her fingertips against the small, white scar.

I wanted to jump in with another question. I hadn't realized she had any siblings. But knowing her annoyance at being interrupted, I saved the building list of questions for later.

"I fell and hit my mouth against a metal pole on the pier." I felt her shrug beneath me. "It could have been worse, I suppose."

I drummed my fingertips against her collarbone. "Thank you."

"For what?"

"You, opening up like that."

Her lip curled up. "It's just a story from my childhood, Detective. It's no great secret."

"We're naked in bed together, Julia," I deadpanned. "I think you can drop the formalities."

A playful grin appeared on her beautiful mouth, and it warmed me like a beam of sunshine. "You say that as if I could forget you're naked."

The mattress dipped beneath me as she moved, and her fingers tugged on a sensitive nipple. I reflexively slapped her hands away, causing her eyes to narrow. This was a woman who did not like to be denied what she wanted, and it made my heart pound a little heavier to know that, at least in this moment, it was me that she wanted.

I woke up in an empty bed. I rolled over and buried my face in the pillow. I shut my eyes and breathed in. I thought it smelled like Julia's perfume, but I was probably imagining it.

"For a cop, your taste in coffee is appalling."

My head jerked up when I heard her voice. I thought she'd left before I'd woken up.

I turned my head as far as it could go. The end of the mattress sank as Julia sat down with a cup of coffee in her hands.

"It's probably appalling *because* I'm a cop," I retorted. "You should drink the mud they tried to pass as coffee in the military."

Her hair was slightly mussed from sleep and her naturally beautiful face was makeup-free. My T-shirt was gone, folded carefully on the chair I called my living room; she'd changed back into her clothes from the previous day. The cream-colored blouse was slightly wrinkled, but her walk of shame would be far classier than anyone else's. She always looked so polished in her immaculately tailored suits, but I think I liked her best like this, visibly disheveled, but only just so.

She passed me her mug, and I sat up in bed to take a sip. I inhaled and let the rich scent warm me.

"You should go back to sleep. You've barely had the equivalent of a nap."

I hadn't had any nightmares. Maybe that was the secret—long, sporadic naps. Or maybe it had more to do with the woman who had slept beside me.

"I want to make you breakfast."

"Your refrigerator is practically empty, dear."

"I know. But what about breakfast at Stan's? I'm sure he could make you an egg-white omelet if you're worried about calories."

"I should really be going. I have to go home and shower."

"I've got a shower. Hot water and everything."

She smiled mildly. "I'm sure you do. But I certainly can't go into work in the clothes I wore yesterday."

"You really think anyone would notice?"

"*I* would notice, Miss Miller. And when I'm in a meeting with the District Attorney later today, I'd like to feel at my best, not like I just stumbled out of your bed."

I held up my hands. "Okay, you win. You present a very persuasive argument, Madam Prosecutor."

She leaned forward and I did the same until our lips met. I swabbed my tongue against her lower lip, but she sighed and pulled back.

"What's wrong?" I covered my mouth with one hand. "Do I have morning breath?"

She stood up and tugged at the bottom hemline of her knee-length skirt to straighten the lines of the garment. "No. But you're quickly becoming an indulgence, Miss Miller. And I don't know how to feel about that."

Chapter Seventeen

"**I** brought donuts."

A collective cheer erupted between Lori and David when I walked into the police department later that day. Chief Hart's office door was closed, so I suspected he was either in a meeting or was out on a complaint.

I set the pink cardboard box down on an open desk, and David attacked the container like a scavenger after roadkill.

"Free donuts. What's the special occasion?" he asked around a mouthful of pastry. "Did you get laid last night?"

"It was just dinner," I blushed.

He sat on the edge of the desk and folded his arms across his bullet-protected chest. "Is there any funny business going on between you and the city prosecutor that I should know about?" he smirked. "Don't get shy on me, Miller."

My eyes fell to the floor. "We're working on a grant together." That part wasn't a lie. "She's helping get some free equipment for the department."

"Oh yeah? Like what?"

"It's for a portable fingerprint reader," I said. "Like if we pull someone over who doesn't have their ID, we can scan their prints to verify they're the person they say they are and check it against any outstanding warrants."

"Awesome," he grinned. "You wouldn't believe how many townies don't carry their licenses on them. I'd write them all tickets, but I've probably get sued again."

"And I'm sure Julia would love you for that," I laughed.

David wiggled his eyebrows suggestively. "When you put it like that, maybe it would be worth it."

My nostrils flared. "Uh huh."

"Mind if I take a look?" He licked the sugar from a bear claw off of his fingers.

I handed David the unfinished grant application and continued to silently stew. It wasn't fair. I wanted to announce on the local radio station that Julia Desjardin was spoken for. But I'd be facing her wrath if I ever did that, and I had no idea how receptive the people of Embarrass would be.

David made a noise.

"What?"

"Nothing. I just ..." His forehead scrunched in thought. "Julia said these fingerprint scanners were free?"

"Yeah. Cool, right? It's part of some Homeland Security communications program—non-disaster preparedness stuff."

His lips silently moved as he continued to read.

"Is something wrong?" I asked.

The concern remained cemented to his face. "I don't know. I could be totally wrong, but this looks like the same grant application we used to get those police radios from the OEC."

"It shouldn't be. The radios weren't free," I reminded him. "That was a fifty/fifty match program."

"Was it?" David looked up from the paperwork and caught my gaze. "We were *told* it was a match program, but did you actually look at the original grant application?"

My eyebrows crunched together and I bit my lower lip. "Only to see which other agencies participated so I could confirm they got their radios."

"Do you still have a copy of that application?"

I nodded. "Back at my apartment with all the other paperwork from that case." I hadn't gotten around to shredding or recycling any of the files after the investigation had reached a dead end. It was another one of those depressing chores like grocery shopping that I had been avoiding.

"Are you busy right now? Can we go look?" David's face had taken on an eager, almost manic look. "This could be huge."

"Yeah, sure," I shrugged. "Just don't mind the mountain of dirty dishes in the sink. I'm not a very good housekeeper."

David arched an eyebrow at me. "I'm a dude who lives alone. I think I can handle a little clutter."

I unlocked the front door of my apartment and did a quick visual scan to make sure there was nothing embarrassing or incriminating out in the open before I opened the door wider to let David in. I picked up a wet towel from the floor and flung it over the back of a chair.

"I thought chicks were supposed to be neat freaks," David remarked.

"You've clearly never lived with a girl," I shot back.

To be fair, I wasn't a total slob, but my bed was unmade and the remnants of dinner with Julia were still visible in the kitchen area. I might not have religiously vacuumed, but I did have a habit for keeping meticulous files. I had stored the paperwork from our joint investigation in one of my empty moving boxes. There was a neat stack of boxes, some still with packed-up belongings, near the foot of the bed. I crouched down and separated the box labeled "Summer Stuff" from the rest of my things.

I removed the top from the box and sifted through the folders to find the file for the radio information. I thumbed over the documents, but the longer I searched, the deeper the crease between my eyes became. "Where is it?" I mumbled.

My murmuring drew David's attention. "What's up?"

"I can't find it." I sat on the floor and began looking inside each individual file folder. Maybe I'd accidentally put the police radio grant application inside of another file. "It should be in this box."

David's duty belt creaked as he crouched beside me to peer into the box. "Here, let me have a look."

"I'm not overlooking it," I snapped. "It should be in here, but it's not."

"Did you bring it to the office? Maybe you left it on a desk?"

I shook my head. "No. I always remembered to put it back. And I haven't had to look at the radio file since I went to Babbitt."

"Is that the last time you saw it?"

"I'm not a little kid who misplaced her backpack, David." My irritation continued to build. Why couldn't I find it?

David held up his hands in retreat. "I'm sorry. I'm just trying to help."

I ran my fingers roughly through my hair. "I know," I grunted.

"Who else knows about these files? Who's been in your apartment that might have seen this box?"

"You, my friend Rich, Grace Kelly." I ticked off the few names. "Julia." I shot him a warning look. "And don't even think it. Julia didn't touch these files."

"Can you be sure?"

"It's not her, so drop it."

"Do you have a crush on the city prosecutor, Miller?"

"No." Yes. Obviously. But I wasn't letting that color my judgment.

"Okay, okay," he conceded. "I won't keep trying to implicate her. It's not really a big deal anyway. I can go over to the City

Clerk's office and get another copy of the grant. They keep the originals on file."

We returned to City Hall with renewed energy. I knew we should both be exhausted: I hadn't slept much that week and David was working his normal shift after taking my night hours. David took a detour into the City Clerk's office on the first floor while I descended the stairs to the police station to wait.

A few minutes later, David returned to the basement looking wounded. "I think I'm getting rusty. The ladies in the City Clerk's office wouldn't let me see the file. They told me to get a warrant."

"That's weird. You didn't have any problems getting copies of those files before, right?"

David winced. "Yeah, but last time I might have suggested I'd buy the Assistant City Clerk dinner if she got me those files."

"Let me guess—you didn't follow up with her and now she's pissed."

His sheepish grin was my answer.

I pushed out a deep breath. "Okay, so that resource is no longer reliable, what else?"

"We could see if the Office of Emergency Communications has record of the original application?" David proposed.

"That's smart. Do you want to call or should I?"

"If a dude answers, I'll give you the phone," he said. "If it's a chick, then I'll do the talking."

I pulled up the appropriate number on the computer screen. Referencing it one more time, I dialed the number. "You really like using sexual persuasion to get what you want, don't you?" The phone began to ring, and I handed him the receiver.

"It's served me well so far," he noted with a grim grin.

"What if a girl answers, but she's gay?" I pragmatically pointed out. "Your wile charms aren't going to work then."

"I'll just try to make myself sound really butch."

I suppressed the urge to roll my eyes. "Charming."

David switched over to what I'd describe as his Cop Voice when someone answered the phone. It was deeper and more authoritative. "Uh, yes. This is Sergeant David Addams of the Embarrass Police Department in Embarrass, Minnesota. I'm calling in regards to a grant we received a few months ago for the purchase of new police radios. I'm curious about the nature of the grant."

His call was redirected a few times until we'd been transferred to the appropriate office. Each time he repeated his story and questions.

I leaned in, trying to pick up a few words from the OEC office, but they sounded muffled like Charlie Brown's parents.

"You don't?" He frowned. "Could you at least confirm if it was a match grant or if it was fully funded?"

I held my breath and waited for the answer.

"Okay. Thank you. You've been very helpful." He carefully returned the phone to its cradle.

"Well?" I asked, impatient. His face was unreadable.

"The woman on the phone said they don't keep those kinds of records for very long—too much paperwork."

My face fell. "So they don't have our grant application."

He shook his head. "But she did she tell me that every grant that has come out of their office in the past year for emergency communications has been fully funded."

I swallowed hard. "So that means ..."

A grin slowly took over his handsome face. "We're back in business."

Wendy Clark was a busy woman—too busy to be bothered to reply to my repeated e-mail requests and voicemails to view the paper-work on the city's general fund. Her negligence had me in the

Office of the City Clerk for the second time of my short employment. We had confirmation that the interoperable radios should have been free through a grant with the OEC; now we required tangible evidence that neighboring agencies had actually paid the city of Embarrass for the free equipment. To do that, we needed to look at the records for the city's general bank account.

Wendy Clark was an older woman, probably in her early fifties. Her dishwater blonde hair was permed in loose curls that fell just above her shoulders. She was deeply tanned and wore minimal makeup. As city clerk, she was one of the most powerful and influential women in the city, but her wardrobe didn't match the title. That day when I caught her walking out of her office, she wore khaki shorts and a polo shirt.

"Mrs. Clark," I called after her. "I need to look at the city's bank account statements."

"This isn't the First National Bank, Miss Miller," she clipped.

I forced out a laugh as if she'd told me a hilarious joke. "No, I know that. It's for a case David and I are working on. We need the account information for the city's general fund."

I bet this woman was unbeatable at poker. Her face didn't move. "Then I guess you'll also need to get a warrant."

If I could melt the city prosecutor, I should have been able to at least coax a smile out of the city clerk. But she clearly wasn't having any of it. I wished I had Rich with me; that kid could sell ice cream in winter. He and David should team up: between David's Boy Scout manners and boy-next-door good looks and Rich's unique brand of bad boy charm, they would have been able to get away with anything. But all I needed was one lousy bank statement.

"Did I do something to offend you?" I asked.

"This has nothing to do with if I like you or not, Miss Miller. This isn't high school. I'm simply not allowed to give you that account information."

"When I get the warrant, you'll have to fork over the information anyway," I pointed out, "so why don't you save us all some time and give me those transaction records?"

Her thin lips were pressed into a straight line. "I'll see you when you have your warrant, Officer."

David was sitting in the same place I'd left him when I returned to the department.

"I should have sent you to sweet talk the City Clerk."

David looked up from a game on his cell phone. "She's ornerier than hell isn't she?"

I flopped down in a tired chair that looked older and more damaged than me. My boots immediately went on top of David's desk. "Whatever happened to Minnesota nice?"

"I think she's from Illinois," he grinned.

"Well that explains it."

He pulled a stack of forms out of a wall cubical. "Guess I'd better start on the warrant paperwork."

It took a few days of impatient waiting, but a judge finally granted our warrant and the City Clerk's office released the account information for the city's general fund. I had assumed it would be easy to notice a dozen or so five-figure deposits, but it wasn't like the city's general fund was used to fill up a car or buy groceries. Nearly every deposit, transfer, and withdrawal was in the tens of thousands of dollars range. I'd underestimated how many fiscal transactions a town made on a daily basis, let alone trying to uncover multiple deposits that had been made months ago.

We had a rough date from the original radio purchase order, but no way of knowing if the local agencies had paid Embarrass before or after that date. Narrowing down a timeframe when the deposits most likely occurred had helped expedite my research, but from the moment I saw the size of the file, I knew it was going to take a while.

I tossed a highlighter pen onto my kitchen island. My apartment had once again become investigation central. I had suggested asking Chief Hart directly what he knew about the OEC grant, but David had insisted that more than ever we required secrecy. Chief Hart was currently our number one suspect. According to every local chief I'd been able to get a hold of, he had been the one who'd e-mailed the local emergency responders about the collaborative grant application. My gut told me that Chief Hart had nothing to do with this. I owed him this job, so I owed him the benefit of the doubt. But if he wasn't responsible, then who was?

"The money's not here, David. It never went into this account." I'd gone over the spreadsheets again and again for the months over which the payments should had been made, but I'd found no record of the money ever being deposited into the account.

"It's there," he insisted. "We just haven't found it yet. Or maybe there's a special bank account that was created specifically for the radios."

Maybe, but I was starting to lose hope.

"My eyes are starting to cross," I complained.

"Mine too." David checked the time on his watch. "Shit. I've got my shift soon." He stood from the kitchen stool. "Call me if you find anything?"

I nodded and went back to the never-ending spreadsheets. I had been expecting a searchable excel program, not the mountain of paper the Assistant City Clerk had dumped on the spare desk in the police department. I didn't know if she was still annoyed because of David's failure to follow through on dinner and she wanted to make things more difficult for us, or if there was something else going on.

I dialed Julia's number before my apartment door had even closed with David's departure.

"Hey," I said when she picked up.

"Always so eloquent, Miss Miller."

"What are you doing?" I asked.

"Finishing up some work at City Hall. Why?"

"Do you want to come over?"

Julia's laughter filled my ears. "Is this what a third-shift booty call sounds like? You call me at four o'clock in the afternoon?"

"We don't have to do anything. We could just talk."

"Isn't that what we're doing right now?"

I bit my lower lip. I missed her. I missed her beautiful face. But I couldn't say that, not without risking scaring her off. "Maybe you could help me with the case. I think we're at another dead end."

When David and I had discovered the discrepancy with the OEC grant, I had filled in Julia on all the new details. She was smart, she knew the city and proper procedures, and we needed that. Plus, it gave me an excuse to talk to her.

"What's wrong?" she asked.

"If the money's not in the city's general fund, how do we prove any wrongdoing?"

"There could be another bank account specific to the police department," she noted.

"David suggested that too," I said. "But do I really have to look over the bank records of *every* account associated with the city?" I could hear the whine in my tone.

"No, dear. Just ask one of the other cities for the account number they made the deposit to."

"You're a genius. I knew I kept you around for a reason," I breathed. "I never would have thought of that on my own."

"Stop working," she ordered. "I know they don't pay you nearly enough for all the extra work you put in."

I set down my highlighter marker even though she couldn't see me. "Will you come over if I promise to stop working?" I could hear her hesitate. "It would only be until my shift starts."

"Fine," she relented. "Give me half an hour to wrap things up. Then you can work a little overtime on me instead."

It was hard enough to go into work each night, without knowing that Julia was in my bed. We'd both fallen asleep after dinner, and as much as I wanted to stay with her curled in my arms, I couldn't neglect my shift. I quietly locked up my apartment, trying to be considerate of the woman sleeping in my bed and the residents of the two other apartments in my building. I need not have been so careful, however, as I bumped into Grace Kelly Donovan coming home as I was leaving for work.

"Hot date?" I teased. I rarely saw her out of her apartment after dinner time.

"Hardly," she scoffed. "Just another late night at the newspaper."

"I hope there won't be any surprises waiting for me in the morning."

She held up her hands and smiled. "Your secrets are safe with me, Cassidy. I promise, no more front page stories."

I wiped at my forehead in an exaggerated manner. "Phew."

"How *is* Julia, by the way?"

I'd never been good at lying. My friends said it was one of my most endearing qualities. Instead of pretending like I didn't know why she was asking that question, I stayed silent.

"Is she still in there?"

I shifted my body and strategically positioned myself between the closed door and Grace, even though without x-ray vision she wouldn't have been able to see into the apartment.

"Yeah, she is."

"You two have gotten close, huh?" she pressed.

"Is this on or off the record?" My tone was sharp, but her question had blindsided me, and I was left feeling defensive.

"Oh, totally off the record." She held up her right hand as if taking an oath.

I was keenly aware that Grace's job was one step short of gossiping, and I could guarantee that a relationship between the aloof city prosecutor and the rough-around-the-edges new police officer would be considered a legit news story.

"I can't really speak for her, so you'd have to ask Julia."

"You're really going to pretend that you're not the reason why Julia Desjardin smiles?"

I shrugged and tried to look noncommittal even though my chest constricted at the thought that I could make someone happy. "Maybe she got tired of frowning all the time."

"And this rare phenomenon just happened to coincide with you moving to town." Grace looked unconvinced. I was no lawyer; I needed Julia here to spin a masterful explanation that would satisfy my neighbor's curiosity.

"Stranger things have happened, I'm sure."

"Yeah, like the city prosecutor being gay."

I bristled. "That's ridiculous." I needed to end this conversation immediately, but this was no fighter jet and there was no ejection button.

"Not so ridiculous when I see Julia disappear into your apartment in the middle of the afternoon, promptly followed by the sounds of two women having sex." Grace made what I thought was a particularly smug look. "The walls are thin in this building, Cassidy."

I couldn't really deny that. I sometimes heard Grace's workout videos before my evening shift.

I swallowed hard as I gathered my thoughts. "Look, it's okay to tease and poke fun of me about this, but don't drag Julia into it. You know Embarrass is too small to handle this kind of news; it could ruin her."

"What about you?"

"What about me?"

"You're not worried about your reputation?"

"I'm already an outsider," I dismissed. "I don't have any disillusions that Embarrass will embrace me as one of their own. But this is Julia's home. Don't ruin that for her."

"I told you—no more stories."

"So you're not going to say anything? I'm not going to wake up tomorrow to see I made front page news again?"

"Not by my hand," Grace avowed. She shook her head and barked out a laugh. "I can't believe you seduced the most unapproachable woman in town."

I grinned. I wished I could have taken credit for that, but it had actually been the other way around.

"So are you two, like, dating? Or just fooling around?"

"I honestly have no idea." I let out a deep breath and rocked back on my heels. It was kind of refreshing to have someone to talk to this about. "I kind of let Julia take the lead on this one, and I'm just along for the ride."

"Well from what I've heard through the walls, it sounds like it's been a fun ride."

I could feel the heat of my blush reach the tips of my ears. "We'll try to keep it down in the future."

"Oh, don't hold back on account of me," Grace insisted. "At least *someone's* getting laid in this building."

"There's always Rich, you know." Not that I approved of my

friend going out with my neighbor. Grace Kelly was too much of an innocent, and he was too much of a commitment-phobe.

"Yeah, right. Like he even remembers who I am."

"He's a little thick sometimes, but you shouldn't underestimate yourself, Grace. You made quite the impression on him."

Her face had taken on a faraway look, and as uncomfortable as it made me to talk about Rich in that way, it at least got us off the topic of Julia and me.

"If it's any concession, I think you're good for her."

"How do you mean?"

"There's something different about her lately," Grace mused. She tapped her fingers against her bottom lip, looking deep in thought. "She hasn't been as ... chilly when we run into each other."

A small smile fluttered onto my lips. "I should get to work. Thank you though, for your discretion."

Grace waved me off and went to unlock her apartment. "Yeah, yeah," she muttered. "Damn that moral compass of mine."

Julia was still sleeping when I came home at the end of my shift. I wanted nothing more than to slip into bed beside her, but I needed a shower first. Around bar time, I'd gone on a call to the Ice House —a dive bar near the harbor—where I'd had a beer spilled on me by an angry patron who'd put up a fight when the bartender had cut him off. It wasn't any fun coming home smelling like beer and cigarettes, especially when I hadn't even gotten a buzz.

I took a quick, skin-scalding shower to scrub away the third shift grime. When I turned off the shower, I heard sounds coming from outside the bathroom door. I didn't bother to full dry off; I rubbed a towel roughly over my hair and wrapped the damp cloth around my still dripping torso.

Julia was nearly dressed in her outfit from the previous day when I came out of the bathroom. She sat at the edge of my bed, slipping back into her shoes.

I tucked my lower lip between my top and bottom row of teeth. "Taking off?"

She gave me a cursory glance. "I have to go home and shower and get ready for the day." She ran her fingers through stiff, sleep-matted hair. "Did that lead pan out?"

My shoulders slumped. She had more willpower than I gave her credit for.

"I guess so. We're waiting for the judge to grant us another warrant so we can get the account information from the issuing bank."

I had called Chief Plankton in Babbitt to get the account number where they'd direct deposited the radio money to. It had taken him a few days to hunt down the information I needed, but when I got the number, I started on the warrant paperwork right away. I knew it would be a waste of time to ask Wendy Clark to volunteer up that information.

I was thankful Chief Plankton hadn't asked why I was still asking questions about the police radios. It was premature to tell him about our findings, especially since at this stage, everyone was still a suspect—even the other towns' chiefs. David had pointed out that all of the neighboring law enforcement might have been working on this together. I didn't want to feed into his conspiracy theory, but even I had to admit that anything was possible.

"Can I see what you've got?" she asked.

"Sure."

Julia pulled her reading glasses out of her work briefcase. Her gaze poured over the e-mail I had printed out from Chief Plankton. "Babbitt's chief must have made a mistake. This isn't one of the city's accounts."

"Do you know every account number by heart or something?"

233

"It's not like I memorized *pi*. If you see numbers enough times, they stick in your brain."

"You wouldn't happen to know what this account is associated with, would you?"

"No." She shook her head and her raven locks fluttered around her face. "But I can tell you one thing—this number sequence doesn't belong to a commercial account. It's a private bank account."

I frowned. "And that's important because ...?"

"Think about your own bank accounts. I assume you have a checking and a savings account?"

"Yeah, back in Minneapolis." Not that there was a lot of money in either of them.

"And not only are the numbers associated with those accounts different, but they're also structurally different, right? Checking accounts are usually a successive string of seven numbers and saving accounts have hyphens, kind of like a social security number."

"This is all news to me," I admitted. "I do everything online."

Julia made a noise. "Which is probably why this went unnoticed for so long. People don't recognize those kinds of details anymore because of digital transfers and direct deposit."

"So you're saying that like the difference between a checking and saving's account, that there's also a difference between personal and business accounts?"

"Exactly." She stabbed her finger against the piece of paper. "And according to this, the other police agencies didn't deposit a quarter of a million dollars into the city's bank accounts. It went into someone's personal account."

"But whose?"

"Go get yourself a warrant, Detective, and find out."

"So you think I've got something here?"

"It's certainly not nothing," she confirmed. She glanced at her watch. "Damn it," she cursed. "I'm going to be late."

"If you're already late, then what's the hurry? Cancel your work plans and play hooky with me," I urged.

She pushed out a long breath. "God, that sounds nice."

I tugged at the knot between my breasts which held up my damp towel. The material loosened until the towel slipped and fell to the floor. Julia's caramel eyes drank in the view. I took a barefoot step towards her.

"Do you need anymore convincing?"

The tip of her tongue flicked against the cleft in her bottom lip. "I really shouldn't."

"Which is exactly why you should," I countered.

"Aren't police officers supposed to be positive influences? Help you decipher between what's right and what's wrong?" she asked in an amused tone.

I wasn't going to back down, but she wasn't making a move towards the door, either. I made a big show of turning my head this way and that. "I don't see any cops in here."

She retrieved my duty belt, which I'd discarded on the floor before my shower. She fished the handcuffs out of their compartment and let them dangle from one finger. "No?"

A slow smile spread across my face.

"You're shittin' me. *More* numbers?" David groaned in frustration. "When are we going to get a break?"

Our second warrant—the affidavit to acquire information on the bank account the neighboring cities had deposited money into —had finally been approved by the judge. I'd also received confirmation from two other towns' chiefs that they'd direct deposited money into that specific account number as well. Unlike the information on the city's general fund, this file had come electronically. It took only a few taps of the keyboard to find the proof we needed. We now had the physical evidence that proved other cities had paid money for communication equipment that should have been free.

The one essential detail we didn't have, however, was a name. There was no personal information on who had opened the bank account: no name, no date of birth, no home or business address. The only identifier we had connected to the account was a nine-digit number.

"This sequence," I said, tapping the computer screen. "That's got to be a social security number, right?"

David gave the number a second look. "Looks like it."

"How do we figure out who it belongs to?"

"I have no idea. The Internet?"

"I know who'll know." I pulled my cell phone out of my pocket and searched for the number I had only recently programmed into my contacts. She might have continually refused to go on a date with me, but at least she'd finally given me her phone number.

The phone rang so many times, I was worried the call would go to voicemail. "Detective, this had better be important," she said in lieu of a hello. "I have quite the busy day. Against my better judgment, I was forced to call in sick yesterday, and now I'm playing catch up."

Despite Julia's censuring words, I could detect the warmth in her tone. I wanted to call her bluff and point out that she hadn't been complaining about taking a day off when she'd had me hand-cuffed to my bed, but David was sitting right next to me.

"I've got a question," I said.

"Yes. I want to make out with you."

I flicked my glance in David's direction and cleared my throat. "I've got a *work* question," I clarified.

"Go ahead."

"Information on that personal bank account came back, but there's no name associated with the account, just a social security number. Now what?"

"Just a social security number?" she echoed.

"They're doing a stellar job of covering their tracks," I complained.

Julia hummed. "If that's the case, it very well could be a fake social security number, or it might belong to someone who's dead. You can easily get that information from the Social Security Death Index."

"And if it's a real number, and the person is still alive?"

"Then you need a warrant to petition the Department of Social Security. Make sure you're precise in your affidavit detailing why you need the information."

"So I guess this means more paperwork?" I groaned.

I could hear the smile in her voice. "Better get back to work, Detective."

Chapter Eighteen

T he last time I had taken a bike ride out of the city had been in the wake of a vicious nightmare on the Fourth of July. Tonight, I drove into the countryside and beyond Embarrass' city limits to erase the memory of that night. What a difference a few days made. The investigation was finally coming together, and I was starting to feel good about my role in this town. I was more than just a babysitter with a badge.

I drove past Julia's house with a passing glance at the massive manor. The lights were all out and her car was missing from the driveway. I had the night off, and I thought about calling her, but I would have to pull my bike over for that. The pavement felt too good beneath my tires to stop, however, so I kept driving.

The farther north I drove, the more relaxed I became. If I kept driving northeast, I'd eventually hit the Canadian border. I didn't think I had that much gas in the tank, but it might be fun to try.

I continued to ride along the abandoned county highway until I came across a black Mercedes parked on the narrow shoulder. I slowed down and idled my bike in the middle of the empty road. I flipped the visor up on my helmet.

"Julia?" I called out into the dark. "Julia?"

After no response, I rolled my bike to the shoulder and parked it behind Julia's car. Intent to investigate, I pulled a travel flashlight out of one of my saddlebags and used it to peer through the tinted windows of her car. I could make out nothing except for her black leather briefcase on the passenger seat, but there was no sign of the driver herself.

I retrieved my cell phone from the inner pocket of my leather jacket and dialed her number. The first call went immediately to voicemail. I didn't start to worry until the second attempt was forwarded straight to her recorded message as well.

I crouched down and inspected the loose gravel near the driver's side door. The ground was still damp from the rainy summer we'd been having, and I could make out the precise holes of aggressive stilettos that had sunk into the earth. I followed the evenly spaced divots into a dense patch of forest, which led me to a grassy path. At the end of the trail I found a weathered cabin perched beside a small lake.

The cabin couldn't have been more than one thousand square feet. There were no lights on inside, so I used my flashlight to peer through the dirty windows. With still no signs of life, I continued to follow the matted path. A few yards away I discovered a short series of wooden steps that led down to the lake and a floating pier. I found Julia sitting at the end of the wooden dock. Her chin rested on her knees and her arms were wrapped around her shins. She looked like she'd come straight from City Hall. She'd cast off her shoes, however; the heels were caked in thick mud.

"You didn't answer your phone."

"There's no cell reception out here," she responded, not turning her head away from the waterfront.

The rubber-band croak of bullfrogs echoed in the background, and I heard a random splash from a fish breaking the surface of the inland lake.

"What is this place?" I took a tentative step out onto the aged pier.

Julia pulled her legs tight to her body. "My family's cabin."

"Your family has two mansions *and* a cabin in town? Isn't that a little overkill?"

"My family has money. And when you have money, you buy things," she said with a simple shrug. She turned her head to regard me finally. "How did you find me?"

"I'm a good detective. But maybe a better question is what you're doing out here?"

"It's my favorite place in town." She paused and looked back at the water. "It might be my favorite place anywhere."

I gingerly sat down on the dock beside her. I didn't trust that my added weight wouldn't sink us into the lake. The boards creaked and groaned, but the old wood didn't fail.

"Are you cold?" I asked.

"No. I'm fine."

I shrugged out of my jacket and laid it on Julia's erect shoulders.

"I'm really fine."

"Just take the jacket, Julia."

She ended her protest and pulled the jacket closer and tighter around her body.

I rested my weight on my palms and looked up. "Do you know any constellations?" Far away from the light pollution of any major city, the night sky was sprayed with distant stars and galaxies.

Julia breathed out. "Just a few of the major ones: the Little Dipper, Orion's Belt, Cassiopeia, Andromeda."

"Andromeda? I don't think I know that one."

"It's my favorite."

"Will you tell me about it?"

Julia fluttered a small smile in my direction. "Andromeda was Cassiopeia's daughter. She boasted that Andromeda was more beautiful than the Nereids. As punishment, Poseidon sent a sea monster to ravage the shoreline of the family's kingdom. Andromeda was chained to a rock as sacrifice to appease Poseidon, but she was rescued by Perseus before she was killed."

"*That's* your favorite constellation? It's ... a little heavy."

"I know. But a part of me relates to her." She sighed. "We should talk about something less serious." She flipped her hair away from her eyes. "Like politics or religion."

I rubbed at my arms absently.

"Now *you're* cold," Julia frowned, noticing the action.

"I'm fine." I picked at the splintering boards of the wooden pier. "The dream catcher," I started with some trepidation, "how did you know my nightmares had been because of the war?"

"My brother, Jonathan, went to Afghanistan, too, but he never came back. He survived—bodily," she clarified, "but the boy who returned wearing his soldier uniform wasn't him. He'd changed. And the nightmares ... I recognized it in your eyes that night when you..." She coughed delicately. "Anyway, he ... he took his own life in the end." She straightened her back. "My family was obviously grief stricken. I was living in St. Paul at the time, and I came back to Embarrass to mourn with my parents and bury my brother in the family plot. And I guess I've just never left."

I knew I would never find the right way to express my regret, but I tried the obvious words anyways. "I'm so sorry. I didn't know."

"Why would you?"

"Grace told me—"

"Grace Kelly Donovan is a horrible gossip," Julia snapped. The hard lines of her features softened as she reigned in her anger. "I know the entire town thinks I'm angry with my family—that they're the ones keeping me on a tight leash, and that's why I'm such a bitch." She shook her head. "But the truth is, they're not keeping me here. I'm doing that to myself. *Fear* is keeping me here.

241

And if I'm angry all the time, it's only because I'm disgusted with myself for not being braver."

Small birds or bats, I couldn't tell which, swooped low over the lake, picking off insects as they flew. They hovered so close to the water's surface that their bodies actually bounced off the lake.

"I got too comfortable—too content—staying in this little bubble where there are no surprises," she continued. "Honestly, the last time I was surprised was when I saw you at Stan's diner that first morning." She softly laughed at the memory. "You should be flattered. No one's been able to surprise me in years."

I didn't know how to react to Julia's soliloquy. She'd revealed so much: the death of her brother, the reason she stayed in town, the reason for her anger. It felt like a gift that I didn't deserve. All I could offer in return was my own story.

I cleared my throat, and Julia looked up to meet my steady gaze.

"When the bomb went off, it felt like I'd been stung by a million bees."

"The marks on your back?" she correctly guessed.

I nodded. "You take a part of that place back with you. For me, I literally did. There's probably rocks still embedded in my skin."

She licked the tip of her tongue to the scar at her lip. "What happened?"

"My team had received intelligence about a key al-Qaeda target. I didn't expect to find anything though—you get hundreds of leads, and maybe one pans out from the lot of them. This one panned out. We were supposed to bring the target to a safe house in this little mountain village. But when we got there, the house was empty and the radio was broken. We were too far behind enemy lines. Our interpreter tried to get what we needed to fix the radio or find another one, but a dirty bomb killed the target. I don't know if they did it on purpose or if he was just collateral damage.

When the bomb hit, we scattered. I didn't know if anyone else made it out alive."

I stopped for a moment to gather my thoughts. I hadn't told anyone this story in what seemed like a very long time.

"It was just me, my buddy Terrance Pensacola, and this insurgent named Amir. My plan was to use him as a hostage to get us safe passage if it came to it. We sought shelter in a bombed out building that provided adequate cover from the sun and from hostiles. We were stuck there for days with minimal rations. A piece of shrapnel had bit Pensacola in the calf, and I was worried he was going to lose his leg or his mind if we stayed much longer, so I got him out of there under the cover of night. We hoofed it along a main road, but stayed out of sight if any car went by. We needed a ride to get back to base, but at night it was damn near impossible to tell the friendly cars from the bad guys."

I took a much needed breath.

"Did Terrance make it?" she asked.

"He lost both of his legs."

"But you saved his life," Julia said gently.

"Yeah, I guess so." I often thought about if I'd actually done him a favor. Pensacola had survived the ordeal, but his was the kind of injury that made me wonder if he would have rather come back to the States in a box. They'd called me a hero for saving him, but few things felt heroic about what we'd had to do to survive.

"Have you ever been in love?" Her question took me by surprise.

"I'm sure I've been in *like* before. But I'm not so sure about the other thing," I said truthfully. "What about you?"

"No," Julia answered without deliberation. She hugged herself when a cool breeze passed over the water. "Never in love."

"There's still time."

She smiled a little too sadly for my liking.

I touched the side of her face. Her caramel-colored eyes fluttered close, and I could hear the barely audible sigh. Julia's face was normally a mask—a disguise of foundation powders, crimson lipstick, and dramatic eyeliner and shadow. But with the careful contact, her emotions were laid bare for my eyes only. I became witness to the hurt and the pain that she religiously wore like a mantle, not unlike myself.

"Will you come to bed?" she asked.

"With you?" I felt ridiculous for having asked the question, but I didn't want to assume anything—especially not with this woman.

Julia nodded. "I don't feel like being alone tonight."

I stood and brushed the debris from the back of my jeans. I held my hands out to her, and for once, she accepted the help.

"It isn't fair," she murmured.

I lifted my head from the pillow with some difficulty. "What's not?"

"You eat nothing but cheeseburgers and pizza." She raked her nails down my naked torso, leaving pink, raised trails. "I so much as look at a carbohydrate, and I bloat up."

"I find that hard to believe." I slid my hand along the smooth expanse of her exposed thigh. "Your body is amazing."

"Thank you." Julia smiled softly and tucked blonde sweeps of hair behind my ear. "You never did tell me how you found me tonight."

"I wasn't looking for you," I said truthfully. "I was just driving."

"I guess that radar I implanted in your brain is working."

"Would it be okay if we just ..." I flipped the ends of her hair through my fingers. I wasn't sure how she'd react to my question.

"If we just what, dear?"

"Slept?" It had been a tough week, and even though the investigation was going well, I still felt drained.

"Of course." She brushed her lips on a spot just below my earlobe, causing a shiver to ripple down my spine. The simple action had me reconsidering my request.

"Are you sure?" I asked.

Her chuckle vibrated against my neck.

"You've done this before."

She knew what I meant. Obviously we'd had sex before, but there had been women before me.

"Yes."

I rolled over onto my side and tucked my hands under the pillow. "Who? When? What was her name? What were *their* names?"

"You ask a lot of questions." It was too dark in her bedroom to interpret the expression in her eyes, so I couldn't tell if she was annoyed or amused.

"It's what makes me a good cop."

"It was college," she vaguely revealed. "But there was no one of consequence."

I tried to shove down the jealousy that bubbled just under the surface from her admission. I didn't want to think about someone else touching her skin and making her back arch off the bed. I tried not to picture an anonymous woman kissing behind her knees or in the crook of her elbows. I didn't want to mentally see a stranger's mouth mapping her body and traveling the distance from her breasts to her belly button and below.

"Stop stewing, Detective."

I cleared my throat. "Am I that obvious?"

"Your face is an open book, dear." She touched the side of my face, and she stroked the pad of her thumb across my cheekbone. "I bet you're a terrible liar."

I swallowed hard at the lump in my throat. Gods, I could fall hard for this woman. Even now, it was probably too late to put on the breaks. "The worst," I croaked out.

She didn't turn the question around to ask about my previous experiences. Maybe it didn't matter to her, but it bothered me that she wasn't as curious as I had been about her.

"Don't you want to know about me?" The words felt needy and juvenile, like it was important to know I had the power to make her jealous as well.

"Not really."

I didn't know what to say to that.

"It's your past that's made you the woman you are today, Cassidy." Another pass of her thumb across my cheek and I would melt into a gooey puddle. "But I'm more interested in the woman in my bed, not the girl she'd been before."

"Good answer," I said thickly.

She pulled her hand away, and I instantly missed the heat of her touch. "You should get some sleep."

I wasn't tired anymore. Every nerve ending in my body was ready for a round with this goddess. It was imperative I erase all traces of previous lovers. I slid my bottom lip out, ready to protest.

"I have an early morning."

I tucked my lip back into place. "Okay."

The mattress dipped and the crisp sheets rustled as she moved beside me, wiggling and shifting to get comfortable. One hand rested lightly on my thigh and the other fisted in my defiant curls. I sucked in a sharp breath when she tugged my hair at its roots and her fingers curled around the tender flesh of my inner thigh. Her words said one thing, but apparently her hands didn't want me to fall asleep. But then the fingers twisted in my hair relaxed, and she began to stroke the top of my head as if trying to tame the chaotic mess in my brain.

There was no dream catcher hanging above us, and the last time I'd slept in Julia's bed I'd experienced one of my worst flashbacks. Such troubled thoughts were certainly writ on my face.

"Just sleep, Cassidy." Julia smoothed down my hair. "I'll be right here."

I shut my eyes. Home is where you can sleep.

I slept so soundly that night, I forgot where I was in the morning. That hadn't happened in a long time. Forget the dream catcher, all I needed was Julia Desjardin.

The woman in question was no longer beside me, and the sheets were cool to the touch on her side of the bed. I rolled onto the empty space beside me and was rewarded with the scent of her light perfume.

The clock on my phone told me it was morning, but the curtains in the room had been drawn so that no sunlight would wake me. The clothes I'd worn the previous day had been folded and sat in a tidy pile on a bench at the foot of the bed. The sight had me grinning. Someone really needed to help the city attorney cut loose, and I was happy to take on the job.

I slipped into my clothes from the day before and pulled my tangled hair into a loose bun. The door to the master bathroom was slightly ajar and I could see the warm glow of light peeking around the door's edges. I knocked softly on the door and pushed it open without waiting for a response from the other side.

"God damn." The words slipped out of my mouth without filter.

Julia was leaning over the vanity sink and applying mascara to her already dramatic eyes. I raked my eyes up and down her tantalizing body. Her skin was flawless, not scarred, like mine. She looked too perfect for words in only a delicate lace bra and panty set. Standing on her tiptoes as she bent over the vanity to lean closer to the mirror, her calf muscles were even more defined than when she wore high heels. Her back arched, her shoulder muscles flexed with movement as she carefully applied makeup, and her lacy underwear perfectly hugged her backside. I bit my lip at a mental image of me ripping the light blue undergarments from her body.

She regarded me via the mirror. A carefully manicured eyebrow rose on her forehead. "Need something, Detective?"

"More like need *someone*, Madam Prosecutor."

Maybe I should have been more reserved or kept my emotions more in check, but the moment was too powerful, too intimate, to not step behind her and wrap my arms around her slender waist. My hands seemed to naturally curl around her hipbones.

She set her mascara tube on the vanity counter. "I have a very busy morning."

"What does that mean?"

"It means you can't distract me."

"Then maybe you should have put on clothes."

I dropped kisses on her naked shoulders. I did what felt natural with no filter or second-guessing my actions. Her skin tasted clean and not like the sweaty residue after sex. I resisted the urge to lick the expanse of her neck.

What we were doing felt very coupley, and I hoped she didn't mind. I really hadn't had a boyfriend or girlfriend in high school, and dating had been far off the radar when I was enlisted. There had been attractions and hurried sex in semi-private locations, but I'd never had the luxury of waking up in bed next to someone. I didn't know how to date. I didn't know how to be in a relationship. I could add that as yet another grown-up skill I'd missed out on.

I grinned into the kisses when I saw her eyes flutter close. Her hands came to rest on top of my hands. Maybe it was just me, but it felt like things had changed overnight. We hadn't only spent the night together; we'd both shared secrets and memories that neither of us had wanted to re-live. I was discovering that while sex could be intimate, words and conversations could be even more so.

She spun around in my arms so we were face to face. With us both barefoot she was a few inches shorter than me, but not by much. Her hands fisted in my mess of blonde curls, and she crushed her mouth against mine. She tasted sweet and minty.

Before I could do anything except for kiss her back, she was letting me go and pushing her hands against my collarbone.

"Go downstairs so I can finish getting ready."

"But—"

She gave me a stiff shove. "Now."

"Fine."

"Make yourself useful. There's coffee grounds in the freezer and the coffeemaker's on the kitchen counter."

"Yes, ma'am."

Her tongue flicked across her bottom lip. "I think I may like that title even more than Madam Prosecutor."

"I'll call you whatever you want," I grinned.

She tugged at the belt loop of my jeans. "Go. Before I change my mind again about having a busy morning."

I bounded down the stairs and busied myself with the task of making coffee. After a brief investigation, I found a travel mug and filled it with coffee for Julia to bring to work. She appeared a short while later in an outfit that left me wanting to ditch the rest of the day.

The light grey dress was sleeveless, displaying her long, lean arms. The neckline was modest, but not prudish. A wide black belt cinched around her small waist, flowing out to slightly flaring hips. The skirt was fitted with a respectable side slit, and the bottom hemline stopped just above the knee. I repressed the desire to let loose a wolf-whistle. I could anticipate her reaction if I'd done so—she'd narrow her eyes and chastise me for the unrefined action.

249

I handed her the coffee mug. "Black, right?"

She effortlessly slipped into black heels without having to bend over. "Yes. Thank you."

I leaned against the kitchen counter while she grabbed her briefcase and finished getting ready for the day. "I have to pick up my bike from your cabin. Do you have time this morning to drive me there?"

"I wasn't planning on making you walk, dear."

A light rain had started by the time we left Julia's home. We drove out farther into the country to her family's cabin with only the sound of intermittent windshield wipers filling the void. It wasn't an awkward silence, though. It felt almost natural, just as it had in her bathroom while I'd watched her get ready for work.

Julia pulled off the county highway and onto a long dirt pathway that led to her cottage. The Mercedes bumped down the unpaved road, and it reminded me a little of driving down the remote village roads in Afghanistan. But instead of being surrounded by piles of sand and rock, I saw evergreen trees, and instead of being elbow tight with sweaty Marines, I had a gorgeous, perfumed woman in the driver's seat. I was worlds away from that life.

Her eyes squinted as she pulled the vehicle to a stop. "What is he doing out here?"

"Who?"

"My father." Julia shut off the engine and the wipers stilled. "That's his car."

A charcoal grey luxury car, an older model Jaguar, was parked next to my motorcycle.

"I can't imagine what he'd be doing out here though. He always hated this place, but especially after Jon died."

"Did your brother ..." I didn't know how to ask the invasive question without being obtuse. "Did he ..."

"He took his life out here, yes," Julia answered before I could form the complete question. "My father used to store hunting rifles out here, and Jon kept his own guns in the locked cabinet as well. My father wanted to bulldoze the place afterwards—burn it to the ground and salt the earth. But this place belonged to my mother's family, and she wouldn't allow it."

"Who owns the deed now?" I thought about Olivia Desjardin, the frail woman in the red cardigan.

"It's still my mother's," Julia answered. "Her family had the money. My father came from far humbler origins. But he's always been a very ambitious man. He only tolerated the very best from us. I think he was disappointed when Jonathan enlisted—like being a soldier was somehow only for poor people with no futures."

I must have made a face because she was quickly separating her opinion from her father's: "*I* never thought that though. Serving one's country is about the most selfless thing a person can do. I've always thought of it as a valiant act—almost romantic, like something from another time."

We climbed out of her car and walked to the cabin's front door. Julia tried the handle. Finding it locked, she singled out a key from her collection. She unlocked the door, pushed it open, and walked inside. "Father?"

I hovered just outside, not wanting to insert myself into a family matter. Plus, I thought the Mayor was almost as intimidating as his daughter.

"You can come in, Cassidy," Julia called to me.

I took a tentative step past the threshold. The inside of the cabin better resembled my studio apartment than either of the Desjardin homes. The furniture was sparse: a worn couch and a card table with four folding chairs around it. In one corner was a wood-burning stove that flickered with life despite the mid-July mugginess.

Julia picked up a piece of paper she found near the woodstove.

251

"What is it?" I asked. Her features seemed to have visibly darkened.

She crushed the paper in her fist. "It's nothing." She lifted the lid of the woodstove, and a plume of grey smoke escaped before she could toss the balled up paper inside.

She coughed and closed the lid. "Great. Now I smell like smoke." She wrinkled her nose. "I'll have to take another shower and pick out a new outfit before I meet with the City Council later this morning."

I placed my hands at her hips. "You smell good to me."

"You probably think the fryer at Stan's smells good."

I grinned and nodded with enthusiasm.

"I can't show up to work smelling like campfire." Julia ran a hand through her hair and tried to look annoyed, but I could tell she was having a hard time feigning the emotion when I was touching her with such familiarity.

"You could shower at my place," I offered. "It's on the way."

"I appreciate the noble gesture, dear, but there's still the matter of my clothes. And before you go suggesting I borrow something of yours, I'm sure I don't need to point out that you and I don't share the same taste in clothes."

"Maybe you should keep some things at my apartment." My eyes instantly darted to the floor when I realized what I'd just suggested. "You know, in case you ever smell like campfire again."

Instead of issuing an immediate refusal as I had expected, Julia's head tilted to one side as though she was actually considering the offer and its implications.

"Why don't you stop by my house before your shift tonight, and we can talk about it then."

My head snapped up. "Really?"

"I'll expect you for dinner at 7:30 p.m."

Chapter Nineteen

My grin was nearly too big to fit on my face when I walked into the police department later that day. David made no comment about my obvious good mood this time. He waved me over to the computer and desk where he was sitting.

"Miller, you've gotta see this."

"If it's another dancing cat," I remarked, "I'm not interested." I pulled an extra chair up to the desk and sat beside him. "What's up?"

"I've been looking over that bank account that the radio money was deposited into. And I think I found the fucking Mother Load." He pointed at the computer monitor. "Look at these other deposits."

Our warrant had given us access to the account's deposit, transfer, and withdrawal information for the past five years.

"Jesus Christ," I mumbled as I looked over the numbers. "Look at the size amounts for the deposits in this thing."

"That can't be for more radios, right?" David posed.

I slowly shook my head. The month we were looking at had deposits totaling millions of dollars.

"I knew it!" David slapped his hand down on the desk. "Who knows what other illegal money is in this account." He practically vibrated with energy.

"You two knuckleheads mind telling me what this is all about?" Chief Hart called from his office.

Both David and I snapped to attention.

"What's that, Chief?" David yelled back.

"Did one of you contact Social Security?"

Uh oh.

"We've got to tell him," I said under my breath.

"But he's still a *suspect*," David growled back.

"Got to tell me what?" Chief Hart stood in front of our shared desk with his hands resting on his gun belt.

My lips twitched. I couldn't do this. I wasn't any good at lying.

"Nothing, Chief," David quickly covered.

"I just got an e-mail from Social Security about a warrant they received from this police department requesting information about a person of interest," Chief Hart announced expectantly.

I couldn't keep my father's oldest friend in the dark about this investigation any longer. Even if he had something to do with the embezzled grant money, we'd have to confront him eventually.

I opened my mouth.

"Don't do it, Miller," David warned. "It's too soon."

"We can't keep this under wraps anymore, Addams," I snapped back.

Chief Hart looked lost by our conversation, and it made me feel incredibly guilty. "Sir, over the past month, David and I have been following up on a federal grant that allowed our department and neighboring agencies to purchase new interoperable communication systems."

"The Homeland Security grant," Chief Hart noted with a nod. "I know it well; I headed that up."

I cleared my throat uncomfortably. "We recently discovered that the feds provided those radios for free."

"No they didn't," Chief Hart argued. "It was a collaborative match grant."

"That's what you told the other departments' chiefs," David said sourly.

"Because that's what I was told," our boss countered. "What are you implying, Addams?"

"Chief, we really need to see that email from Social Security," I insisted.

He waved his hand towards his open office door. "Sure. Go ahead."

David practically stampeded into Chief Hart's office. I was eager to read the e-mail, too, but I showed more physical restraint.

I sat down behind Chief Hart's desk and maneuvered the mouse to pull up the email from Social Security. It was curious that the e-mail had been sent to Chief Hart's work address instead of David's or my own, but we had the message and that was what was important.

"What does it say?" David asked. "Whose social security number is it? Who does the bank account belong to?"

My eyes scanned over the email as I took in the new information that our warrant had procured. "Oh no," I muttered.

David leaned over my shoulder to better see the computer screen. I felt nauseous, and I didn't know if it was from his overpowering cologne or from the contents of the email.

William J. Desjardin was at his home when we arrested him later that day. David was the constant professional as he read the Mayor his Miranda rights, but I could tell from the brightness in his already brilliant blue eyes that he was geeked by the arrest. For myself, I was more subdued. Even as David lowered the Mayor's head and guided him into the back of the patrol car, I couldn't help worrying how this arrest would affect Julia and me.

The clock on my microwave glared at me in neon green. How long would it take for news to reach the city prosecutor that her father had been arrested? I roughly rubbed my hands over my face. It should have been me. I should have been the one to call her. But here I was, hiding out in my apartment like a coward. She didn't deserve this; *I* didn't deserve her.

I imagined Julia in her kitchen when she received the call. Maybe she'd left work a few hours early to get started on dinner for tonight. Her hand would grip the phone tighter, sure she'd misheard the caller's words. After hanging up, she would calmly pull the roast, potatoes, and baby carrots out of the oven, wrap everything in plastic wrap, and put them in the refrigerator. It was easier to shut down and not feel anything rather than take on your emotions. I was a professional at it.

The microwave clock told me I still had another hour until Julia was expecting me. I pulled on my leather jacket like donning body armor to prepare for war.

I grabbed my helmet, phone, and keys, and nearly ran into Julia on my way out the door. She looked startled for a moment, but her features slipped into nonchalance when she recovered from the initial shock. Her smoky eye makeup looked more dramatic than ever. I doubted she had reapplied it only to confront me. This had been for me, pre-arresting her father.

"I was just on my way to see you," I said, tucking my motorcycle helmet beneath one arm.

"It looks like we had the same idea."

I cleared my throat. "Weird day, huh?"

"You arrested my father."

I glanced to my right and then to the left. There was no sign of Grace or my landlady, but if they were in their apartments they'd be able to hear our conversation as clear as if we'd been putting on a performance in their living room.

"We should discuss this inside."

Julia didn't wait for a second invite. Our shoulders brushed as she pushed past me.

She turned on her heels. Her dark grey jacket, skirt, and black blouse were as stormy as her mood. "My father is a good man. Whatever you think he did, he must have had a good reason for it."

"Did you know?"

"Know what? That my father was allegedly stealing money from my hometown? No. Of course not."

"*Alleged?* Your father's social security number was connected to the bank account the money for those police radios was deposited to."

"Because he's the mayor," she said stiffly.

"It's a personal bank account, Julia. You saw the numbers yourself. And, you were the one who told me the difference between personal and commercial accounts, remember?"

"Maybe there's higher interest rates in a personal account than a commercial account," she tried to reason. I knew what she was doing; she was a lawyer. But I couldn't tell who she was trying to convince of her father's innocence—me or herself.

"That still doesn't explain why neighboring police departments were told the radio grant was a matching funds program. Regardless if your father was using this account for his own personal slush fund or for city business, the actual money in the account should never have existed."

My logic for once was sound, and I could tell she knew it, too.

"And we found more. More money," I continued, feeling myself becoming agitated the longer we talked and the more she denied his culpability. "I wouldn't be surprised if half of the failed grant applications in this town had actually been awarded, and went right into your father's pockets."

Julia slipped her hands beneath the collar of my leather jacket until her fingers curled around the worn material.

I stiffened at the contact. "What are you doing?"

"Come on, Hero. Save me," she breathed.

"Julia." I struggled on the name. I could feel her hold tighten.

"Isn't that your job, Detective? Isn't this what you do best?" Her caramel-colored eyes flashed. "How are you going to save the day now?"

Julia kissed me hard. Her mouth was unforgiving, and I tried to not think about the motive behind the kiss. She tugged my lower lip between her top and bottom rows of teeth and bit down. It wasn't hard enough to draw blood, but it would be swollen and tender later.

My knees wobbled while she pulled me towards the closest piece of furniture—the overstuffed easy chair. She struggled only briefly before shrugging out of her three-quarter length suit jacket. I reached for the top button of her black, silky shirt, but her fingers wrapped around my wrists to stop me. Her mouth never left mine, and she yanked my arms down and pinned them at my sides. Her strength surprised me as I found myself being shoved backwards and falling into the easy chair.

She stepped out of her high-heeled shoes and reached for the hidden zipper of her form-fitting skirt. The material clung to her like a second skin; it was so tight, I didn't know how she could maneuver in it. The zipper went south and the skirt fell down her thighs and long legs to pool at her ankles in an expensive heap. She sidestepped the circled material and left it on the floor next to her high heels. My eyes traveled the length of her legs, from her bare ankles up to her slightly parted thighs.

My breath hitched when she settled on my lap. Her thighs straddled me, leaving her legs deliciously open. The bottom hem of her black shirt crawled up her thighs to reveal a glimpse of dark red underwear. We'd been in this position before in my police car. I knew what was expected of me.

I reached between our bodies. My fingertips brushed against silk as I slipped her panties to the side.

"No."

I recognized the cold, angry emotion splashed across her face. It was how she'd looked at everything in this town before I'd been able to soften those edges. It hurt to see that hardened mask had returned and to know that I was partially responsible. But what had she expected me to do? Her father was a criminal; I couldn't just look the other way because she was the most beautiful and complex woman I'd ever met.

I didn't know what game she was playing, so how could I ever know the rules? I dropped my hand back onto my lap.

Although she was half undressed, I still wore my leather coat, and she appeared satisfied to let me continue to wear it. She grabbed the lapels once more and tugged the jacket open at the neck. The movement caused the material encasing my arms to seize, effectively restricting the movement of my limbs. She could do whatever she wanted to me, and I would be powerless to stop it. This helpless, trapped feeling was not foreign, and it should have triggered me. But I trusted her—even now—and that feeling alone kept the flashbacks at bay.

She dipped her head and jet-black hair fell across her face. I ached to brush it behind her ear, but I worried she'd only slap my hand away. Her lips ghosted against the side of my neck, and I tensed when I felt the familiar scrape of teeth against my pulse point. We'd done this before, too, and I knew how it turned out for me. But her touch remained soft, and her lips fluttered lightly against my skin. I let out a deep, tension-filled breath and relaxed farther into the chair.

A hand wiggled beneath my T-shirt, and she lightly raked her fingers down my abdomen. That same hand moved up to cup my breast over the bra. She squeezed, her touch remaining firm but light. I clenched onto the tops of her thighs and her movements beneath my T-shirt immediately stilled. Her eyes narrowed in warning until I released her toned flesh. With nothing else to cling to, I curled my fingers around the arms of the chair. I had a gorgeous, half-naked woman straddling my lap, but apparently I wasn't supposed to do anything about it.

She slowly slid down my body until she was on her knees in front of the stuffed chair and me. I swallowed hard under her predatory stare. She ran her palms up the outside of my legs, across the tops of my thighs, and up my inner thighs. Perfectly manicured nails trailed over the seam of my jeans, and I chewed on my lower lip in anticipation.

The button of my jeans was popped, and it felt like the air had been sucked out of the room. The zipper followed and my hips naturally canted up so she could pull my jeans down my hips and thighs. I did it without thinking and without questioning why this was happening, much like I'd done the first time she'd burst into my apartment, only months ago.

She tapped her fingertips against the inside of my thighs, and I spread my legs farther apart. "Good girl," she hummed. She never spoke much when we had sex, but when she did, I could feel her words like an electric prong to my body.

Her hands were warm and dry against the vulnerable flesh of my inner thighs. She leaned forward and pressed soft kisses against me, starting at the insides of my knees and slowly working up. My legs quivered as she blazed a wet trail closer to my sex.

I clenched the arms of the easy chair to resist raking my fingers through her soft hair. Everything about this exchange told me I could look but not touch. She brushed the pad of her thumb over my underwear, focusing dedicated pressure on my clit. My hips jerked at the touch, and her generous mouth curled up on one side in a mischievous smirk.

I sucked in a sharp breath when she leaned forward and brushed her tongue against my clit through my underwear. Her teasing was torturous. She was gorgeous. She was perfect. But I didn't know if I could continue because of the cloud hanging over us. The easy decision was to tangle my fingers in her dark hair and hold her where I needed her the most—that's what my selfish body wanted, at least. My brain said otherwise.

Her fingers traveled the short distance to the elastic waistband of my underwear. Her fingertips dipped beneath, and she tugged upward rather than removing the garment. The material pulled taut against my sex, pressing into my clit.

"Julia," I gurgled out.

Her dark eyes flicked to my face, but her mouth latched onto my clit over my underwear. I felt a finger press into me through the cotton material.

"Oh, God."

She wasn't playing fair.

I curled my fingers around her shoulders. "We should talk," I somehow managed to pant. I dug my fingernails deeper into her blouse when she swiped my clit again with the flat of her tongue.

Her eyes fluttered closed. "We will," she said thickly. "Later."

Her finger pressed more firmly against me. I thought she might tear through my underwear. I strained against her single finger, but I would get no satisfaction with my underwear serving as a stubborn barrier. She pressed two fingers against me and wetly suckled my clit.

Any hope I had of mounting a continued complaint was erased when her fingers curled under the waistband of my underwear and she began to drag the garment south. My underwear briefly stuck between my thighs—my body's final act of resistance —before she slid the cotton undergarment down my thighs and past my knees to fall at my ankles.

Naked from the waist down, I was completely at her mercy. Her palms rested lightly on the tops of my thighs, but I felt anchored to the chair. I yearned to touch her in some way, but I resisted knowing how she'd reacted earlier.

She stroked her fingers through my closely cropped hair. She cupped my sex and settled her fingers on either side of my clit.

"Jesus," I panted. My legs twitched as though electrocuted.

She leaned forward and blew warm air over my already over-stimulated parts. My fingers went to her hair, and I dug my nails into her scalp. She slid a finger solidly inside of me and curled the digit up. I breathed out harshly in uneven, ragged gasps. This wouldn't take long. She'd already teased me to a fervor.

When her mouth reconnected with my clit, it was all over.

"Cumming, Julia. Fuck, I'm cumming."

My head fell backwards. I bit my lower lip and a quiet whine escaped my throat.

She used her thumb to wipe at the corners of her mouth. "Do you still want to talk, dear?" She looked unfathomably dignified for just having had her way with me.

I straightened myself in the chair. My clit throbbed, but I was hardly finished with her. "Later."

My response seemed to surprise her.

I regained use of my legs in impressive fashion. I shot my arms forward and curled them under her armpits. A surprised noise escaped her throat as my inertia had her tumbling backwards. It was inelegant and her tailbone struck the floor as I scrambled to top her. My mouth covered hers before she could voice a complaint. I hesitated for only a moment, worried I'd been too rough, until I felt her lips pushing up to meet mine and her hands wrapping around my biceps.

I tore off my jacket, glad to finally be free of the garment. Her hands fisted the material of my shirt and then tugged at the bottom hem. I stopped kissing her long enough to dip my head so she could remove my shirt. It joined the rest of our clothes on the floor.

I held myself up in a frozen push-up. The wood floor felt gritty against my palms, and I grimaced at the thought of what she must be feeling on the backs of her thighs. I wasn't much of a housekeeper, but in my defense, I hadn't anticipated any of this.

"We should go on my bed."

She canted her hips up into me. "No."

The sun had set long ago, and Julia gathered her clothes from the floor. She reassembled her armor with her back to me.

"Do you really think he's innocent?" I asked quietly from my place on the bed. We'd eventually made our way back there.

"That doesn't matter." Julia carefully buttoned up her dark blouse. "I have to defend him in court. He's my father."

"But won't that be a conflict of interest?"

"I'm going to resign as city attorney." She looked over her shoulder at me. "And I'm sorry, Cassidy. But I'm going to win this."

Chapter Twenty

Dav_id was already in the courtroom when I skirted inside. As the arresting officers, we were afforded seating in the front row, right behind the prosecuting attorney—the seat where Julia normally sat. Even if I hadn't been subpoenaed, I still would have shown up for this trial. Other people in town must have had the same idea. The courtroom had been sparsely populated when David had been sued a month earlier, but there wasn't an empty seat for Mayor Desjardin's trial.

The jury box was empty, meaning the Mayor was to receive a bench trial. I assumed that he wouldn't be on the witness stand at any point, based on his constitutional right to avoid self-incrimination. Julia was smart; she'd never allow it. This was not to be an impeachment.

The arraignment had happened earlier in the week. Because of his position as mayor, William Desjardin had been granted an initial appearance before the judge not long after David and I had made the arrest. He'd pled not guilty and he'd paid his bail, although the judge hadn't set bond very high. Maybe if the presiding judge had known about the size of the Mayor's personal bank account, he would have reconsidered setting bail so low.

The District Attorney's office had talked about the possibility of a change of venue, but I'd heard from Grace Kelly Donovan that Julia had deemed it unnecessary. That bit of information had me worried. I didn't know why she wouldn't want to try the case in a neighboring county to give her father the fairest trial possible. It made me think she had an ace hidden up her designer sleeve.

The District Attorney's office had sent in an Assistant D.A. to try the case. I didn't recognize him from around City Hall or town. My first impression of the man was that his suit was poorly tailored. On wardrobe alone, Julia would have this guy beat. More unsettling, however, he looked scared, bringing to mind the eighteen-year-old kids I'd witnessed getting dropped off in the middle of a sand-smothered war zone.

Until the date of the criminal trial, I had done my best to immerse myself in work, even more so than I had before the arrest. I didn't run into Julia—not at the grocery store, not at Stan's, not at City Hall, and most certainly not at one of our homes. It was clear that we were avoiding each other. But even though I sought ways to escape her physical presence, she was still there. It was the worst at my apartment—the defiant spider plant that thrived despite my ignorance of horticulture and the dream catcher that hung from the headboard of my bed. I could have easily thrown them both away, but they remained, as did my vivid memories of her.

I tried being mad at her, but I just couldn't do it. Every time I thought about what I'd do in her situation—if my own dad had been accused of a crime—had me doing the same thing as her. Blood was the thickest bond of all.

Julia knew how to make an entrance. She walked into the courtroom with her father shuffling behind. Her head was held up, chin slightly elevated. Her black hair shone in the natural light of

265

the courtroom, and her heels clicked on the laminate flooring. The volume of the courtroom seemed to lessen with the click-clack of each step until the room was practically silent when she reached the defendant's table. It was like a teacher walking to the head of the classroom.

"All rise," the court bailiff instructed.

The presiding judge, a handsome man with a square jaw and salt and pepper hair, walked out of his office to take his place at the front of the courtroom. Julia's entrance had already silenced the capacity crowd, so the judge had little wait before he could begin the trial.

I lost focus during the Assistant D.A.'s opening statement. His voice was monotone like my seventh grade health sciences teacher, and he used unnecessary multisyllabic words to basically explain that it was his job to convince the judge that William Desjardin was a bad guy. Because ours was a criminal prosecution and not a civil case, the ominous of burden of proof was the prosecution's responsibility. Mayor Desjardin was innocent until proven guilty.

As the Assistant D.A. gave his opening statement, which he'd probably practiced in a mirror to himself, my eyes were on Julia. From my seat I could really only see the back of her head and a sliver of her profile, but it was still a nice view.

When the Assistant D.A. finished his speech, the judge opened the floor to Julia. She didn't stand from her seat as her counterpart had done.

"Your Honor," she said, raising her voice in volume, "I will not be presenting an opening statement at this time."

A quiet murmur erupted among those seated in the gallery. The judge struck his gavel block. "Order," he called. "Ms. Desjardin, are you sure you'd like to forfeit that right?"

Julia inclined her head. "Yes, your Honor. The Defense will not be giving an opening statement."

I shifted anxiously in my chair. What was she up to?

The Assistant D.A. looked similarly perplexed, but he regained his composure and continued the presentation of evidence by calling a number of witnesses to the stand. Both Chief Hart and David gave testimony for the prosecution as representatives for the police department. I was glad that David had been subpoenaed as the arresting officer instead of me. I had been dreading the thought of being cross-examined by the defense's attorney in front of all these people.

It turned out, however, that I didn't have anything to worry about. Each time the Assistant D.A. finished questioning one of his witnesses, Julia refused the opportunity to cross-examine the individual. With each rejection, the courtroom became collectively more and more anxious, myself included. Her strategy was unorthodox and unsettling.

I didn't know how to be angry with her. I was more worried for her than anything. She'd resigned as city attorney as soon as City Hall had opened for business the day after her father's arrest. What would happen after the trial? Would she return to being the city prosecutor or had she forfeited that job? And if she was no longer defending the city, would she move away? All of these questions and more plagued me as the prosecution continued to lay out its case and Julia refused to participate in the trial.

At the end of another line of questioning, the judge cleared his throat. "Ms. Desjardin? Your witness. Again."

Julia didn't look up from her legal notepad. "No questions at this time, your Honor." She sounded almost bored.

The judge looked as confused as the rest of us. He turned his attention back to the Assistant D.A. "You may call your next witness, Mr. Woodson."

The Assistant D.A. worked the knot on his necktie. "The prosecution rests, your Honor."

The courtroom seemed to hold its collective breath as we waited for Julia's response. She had done virtually *nothing* all day in court. I half expected her to ask for a motion to dismiss the charges, arguing that we had failed to prove our case, but that request never came.

The judge swung his gavel. "Court is in recess. We'll reconvene at 10:00 a.m. tomorrow morning." He trained his gaze on Julia. "Ms. Desjardin, I expect you'll have a defense ready by then?"

"Of course, your Honor."

As the courtroom emptied, the former city attorney gathered her yellow legal pad and other loose notes and carefully filed them away in her black leather briefcase. Her father said something to her too quiet for me to overhear. Her red lipsticked mouth thinned, and she shook her head hard.

He leaned forward as if to say more, but she snapped her bag shut. "I said *no*," she growled out.

Mr. Desjardin shoved his wooden chair back into place. "Fine. I'll see you in the morning," he grumbled before stalking out of the courtroom.

I walked up to the defense table on shaky legs. "What was that about?" I shoved my hands into the back pockets of my jeans.

Julia scowled. "Not that it's any of your business, but he invited me out to dinner."

"I hope it wasn't to celebrate."

"Of course not. That would be premature."

"Especially since you did nothing at all today to win your case."

She jerked her head up and leveled me with a steely gaze. "That's your opinion."

"What game are you playing at, Julia? Are you even *trying* to defend your father?"

"I wouldn't have resigned from my job if I was going to let him go to jail."

"Why not? It seems like the perfect scenario to get you out of this town. No more job. Your dad in some white-collar prison."

Julia's eyes narrowed. "What do you want from me, Cassidy? Because it sounds like you actually want me to win this case and beat you."

"I don't," I denied. "Your father embezzled a shitload of money from the city, and he has to face the consequences."

"I'll see you tomorrow in court, Detective."

I didn't want to be dismissed so easily, but David snagged my arm before I could go after her. "Come on, Miller," he said. "No fraternizing with the enemy."

I tried to form a protest as he dragged me away. "But I—"

"I need lunch and you're buying."

We stopped off at Stan's after court had adjourned for the day. The diner was filled with others who had also attended the unusual court proceedings. David dug into his cheeseburger and fries while I picked at mine.

"What do you think she's up to?"

David jammed a few fries into his mouth. "Julia?"

I nodded.

"Discredit the witnesses, introduce a new suspect, and create doubt," he listed off around a mouthful of greasy starch. "At least that's what they do on all of those lawyer-crime TV dramas."

"I've never heard of a defense attorney not doing anything with the prosecution's witnesses though," I thought out loud. "It makes me nervous—like this is the calm before the storm."

"Uh huh." I didn't think David was actually listening to me. He at least didn't share my concerns. "You gonna eat that?"

I pushed my plate in his direction. "Go ahead. It's all yours." I couldn't eat. My stomach was too knotted with dread.

That unsettled feeling still hadn't left when I showed up at the courtroom the next morning. I hadn't been able to sleep before my shift when I'd returned from lunch with David; my brain refused to shut down. I kept thinking about Julia's strategy. There had to have been a reason why she'd refused to cross-examine any of the prosecution's witnesses. I was thankful to have work that night to keep me busy, because for once, my war demons weren't bothering me. Instead, it was the not knowing when it came to this case and Julia that assured I wouldn't sleep well.

"You look spooked," David remarked out of the side of his mouth. The courtroom seemed even more populated on day two of Mayor Desjardin's trial.

"Because I am," I admitted. "I still think Julia's up to something."

"What makes you say that?"

"You were here yesterday. It was like she was purposely trying to lose."

"Maybe she realizes what a strong case we've built against her dad," David suggested. "Maybe he refused to plead guilty, so she's helping move along the inevitable."

My eyes followed the shapely figure of Julia Desjardin as she entered the courtroom with her father. She ignored me, chin held high, just as she'd done the day before as she reached the front of the room. "That would be the best case scenario."

"And the worst case?" David asked.

"We're fucked."

The judge entered the courtroom, and all conversations came to an end. Everyone rose from their seats and waited for him to sit down in his chair before returning to theirs.

He adjusted his reading glasses at the end of his nose. "Court is now in session. We will return to the case of the City of Embarrass versus William Desjardin. Ms. Desjardin, you may call your first witness."

Julia rose gracefully from her chair. I turned in mine to watch her in profile. Her face was stony and emotionless. "Your Honor, the Defense calls Detective Cassidy Miller of the Embarrass City Police Department to the witness stand."

David elbowed me in the ribs. "What the fuck?" he quietly hissed.

"I don't fucking know!" I scrambled to my feet, unprepared. David had been called to testify the previous day on behalf of the prosecution and police department. Julia had refused the opportunity to cross-examine him. I had no idea what she hoped to accomplish by dragging me to testify.

I stumbled up to the witness stand and nervously raked my fingers through my hair. The bailiff swore me in, and I took my seat beside the judge.

Standing behind the defense table, Julia looked poised. She took a moment to review her notes before her caramel-colored eyes looked in my direction. When our eyes finally locked, I saw only determination reflected in hers.

We were fucked.

"Your Honor," her voice rang out, clear and assured, "I'd like to identify Detective Miller as a hostile witness."

A collective murmur buzzed in the courtroom. I didn't know how savvy the gallery was on criminal law or trial lingo, but they at least gathered that something was happening. By identifying me as a hostile witness, Julia was acknowledging that my testimony would not be favorable to her father's defense. But more importantly, it gave her the power to ask me leading questions that normally would not be allowed.

The judge struck his gavel to call for quiet. "Please proceed, Counselor."

"Detective Miller," Julia began, "how long have you been a police officer?"

I squirmed in my chair. The first question was a softball, but it still made me anxious. "A little over a year."

"And of that year, how long have you been employed by the city of Embarrass?"

I glanced in the direction of the Assistant D.A., but he wasn't even looking at me. His head was buried in his briefcase. "About two months."

David's words from lunch the day before flashed in my head: *Discredit the Witness.*

Julia pressed her palms flat against the wooden table. "Can you walk us through how you and Sergeant Addams came to connect the Defendant to these alleged crimes?"

There was that damn word again. Alleged. I kept my inner monologue to myself, mindful of my environment, and took to the task of talking about the case. It was largely the same response that David had given the day before, but slightly different from my point of view.

"Sergeant Addams approached me with a concern about a purchase order for forty police radios. We both found it to be suspicious because our police department is only three people."

"But you discovered later that those forty radios were for police departments in other towns, is that correct?"

I frowned. Julia was intimately familiar with this case because of me. She was asking leading questions, which normally wasn't allowed, but I'd been named a hostile witness which gave her the power to lead me in whatever direction she wanted to. I proceeded to answer her question, careful with my words as though treading through a mine field.

"Correct. As part of the investigation I visited the chief of police in Babbitt. He told me he'd received notice from Chief Hart about a collaborative grant opportunity for communication equipment available through the Department of Homeland Security."

"So it was Lawrence Hart who approached the neighboring agencies about this opportunity."

"Yes. At the time." I frowned. Julia was making it sound like

Chief Hart had done something wrong when he'd only been following the Mayor's directive. *Introduce a New Suspect.*

"But upon questioning Chief Hart, we were informed that Mayor Desjardin had directed him to reach out to neighboring police and fire departments about the radios, and that he'd been told by Mayor Desjardin that the grant was a match program instead of it being entirely free." I wasn't going to let her throw shade on the Chief. He hadn't done anything wrong; he'd been manipulated just as much as the other cities' emergency responders had.

"Miss Miller," Julia coolly stated, "I'll ask you to only answer the questions I've asked and to stay on topic."

I flicked my gaze over to the judge who only nodded his head in agreement.

Yup. Fucked.

Julia cleared her throat. "So your investigation hit a dead end. The group grant accounted for the unusually large purchase order."

"Yes." She knew the story better than I did.

"Tell me, Detective Miller, when did the case resume?"

"I, uh, when the paperwork on the radios went missing."

"Went missing?" Julia echoed. Her voice lilted up almost comically, but she knew all of this.

"Yeah. I was keeping it in my apartment, and when we went to look for it, it was gone."

"Is it standard procedure to keep paperwork for an on-going investigation in one's home?"

"Well, no." I cringed. She didn't have to try very hard to discredit me. I was doing a bang-up job on my own. "But the investigation had come to a dead end."

"So you lost the files."

I couldn't very well say that I thought someone had stolen them. It sounded too much like a conspiracy theory. "I don't know what happened to the paperwork," I settled for. "We called the Office of Emergency Communications directly, and they were able to confirm that the grant for the radios had been entirely funded. Not long after that, Sergeant Addams and I petitioned the Freedom of Information Act to obtain the original grant application. Mayor Desjardin was named as the issuing agent."

"But surely you had more than just a name on a piece of paper, Detective. As Mayor, it wouldn't be unreasonable for William Desjardin to be listed on the application," Julia pointed out. "Isn't it possible that the Defendant filled out the grant application for the fully-funded police radios, but then Chief Hart told other police agencies it was a collaborative match program?"

"It's possible, but not likely," I noted. "We later discovered that the bank account that other cities had been provided wasn't the city's general fund. In fact, it didn't belong to the city at all. It was a private bank account that further investigation revealed belonged to Mayor Desjardin. If Chief Hart was the person responsible, why would Mayor Desjardin have fiscally benefitted?"

Julia smiled prettily, and I hated her a little for it. "I'm not the one on the witness stand, Detective. It's not my job to answer your questions."

I looked again in the direction of the judge to get some backup, but his stoical face indicated I was still on my own.

"Can you walk us through how you discovered the personal bank account that allegedly belongs to the Defendant?" Julia continued.

Alleged. I bit my tongue and kept my comments to myself. I was an officer of the court, and I would respond appropriate to my position.

"The OEC grant indicated that no money should have been exchanged for the forty police radios. We had the word of several police chiefs, but we needed tangible proof. While looking through the city's general fund to confirm that each neighboring agency had paid for their share of the police radios, we came up empty. The money wasn't there. Rather than look through every bank account associated with the city, the former city attorney suggested we ask the other agencies directly for the specific account number where they'd deposited the radio money to."

Julia visibly stiffened at the reference to herself, but I kept going. "It turned out to be a private bank account—one belonging to Mayor Desjardin. The Mayor misled Chief Hart and the police chiefs of surrounding towns into thinking it was a collaborative match program and he pocketed their money."

"Detective Miller," Julia snapped. "I'll warn you only one more time to stick to the questions I've asked. I don't need you to ad lib."

"Ms. Desjardin," the judge interjected. "Your witness is repeating testimony we heard yesterday from Sergeant Addams. Does she have anything new to contribute?"

"I do, your Honor," I spoke up without Julia's prompt. "Sergeant Addams and I also discovered that money from the Carnegie Foundation had been deposited into the Mayor's bank account, amounting to millions of dollars. When we followed up with the Foundation, they confirmed our suspicion that the money had been earmarked for the construction of a new public library. Mayor Desjardin never told anyone that the city had been awarded the grant, and instead the Community Foundation ended up footing the entire bill."

A murmur arose in the courtroom at my admission. That was something David hadn't mentioned in his testimony yesterday. I sat up straighter in the witness box. It was a tenuous connection, and the prosecution had suggested we not mention anything about the discovery until we investigated further, but I wasn't going to let Julia get to step three—Create Doubt. Her father was guilty.

The judge struck his gavel to silence the chatter.

Julia wet her lips and looked down at her notes as the court-room settled down. "How did you discover that the OEC grant for the police radios was fully funded, Cassidy?" Her voice had audibly softened, and the use of my first name took me by surprise.

I furrowed my eyebrows. "I didn't. *You* did. You found that grant for the mobile fingerprint readers, not me."

Julia gave me a slow, sad smile, leaving me more confused than ever. "Thank you for your candor, Detective." What was she up to?

"Your Honor," her voice raised in volume as she addressed the entire courtroom, "as you well know, until recent events, I was employed as city attorney for this town. As such, I was an officer of the court, just like any police officer. The OEC grant that has become central to this investigation was acquired by myself without a warrant. It's true that there was no need at the time for a duly signed affidavit as it was unconnected to any on-going investigation, however, because it has been used as *the* motive that spurred Sergeant Addams and Detective Miller to look further into this matter, any evidence found as the result of this illegal search should be considered Fruit from the Poisoned Tree and therefore cannot be used in this prosecution."

I turned to the judge; I had no idea what she was talking about. His dark eyebrows were high on his forehead, however, indicating that he did.

"But I wasn't doing an investigation when you found the OEC grant," I uselessly blurted out.

"Moreover, at the point this became an official investigation," Julia continued, ignoring my plea, "Detective Miller and Sergeant Addams needed a warrant as well. The formal investigation tech-nically started when Detective Miller contacted the neighboring communities and discovered they'd been told the grant program wasn't fully funded." Her heels pounded on the marble tiles as she stalked from the witness stand back to the defense table. She produced a stack of paper from a beige folder. "The Embarrass police first procured a warrant to look at the city's general fund weeks after Detective Miller's initial visit to the chief of police in Babbitt."

My head dropped into my hands. I now knew what this meant — if the radio information was inadmissible because the OEC grant had been obtained without a warrant, then all the dirt that David and I had dug up on the Mayor would be suppressed. And the only reason we'd discovered the Carnegie Foundation money was because of the radios.

I suddenly realized Julia's defense strategy and why she hadn't bothered to cross-examine any of the prosecution's witnesses. She had only needed to call one witness to the stand to have the charges against her father dropped—me. There would be no closing arguments from either side of the aisle. Julia had gotten her father acquitted on a fucking loophole.

The gavel cracked, sounding loud and hollow in my head. "Case dismissed."

I ran the eight miles down Main Street and back to clear my head. It was the hottest part of the day, and I really shouldn't have chosen that time for a brisk jog downtown, but I wasn't going to be able to face the day's events if I didn't first expend some anger. I moved my legs at a faster pace than I normally would have on a distance run. I needed to exhaust myself, to expend my frustration. By the time I'd finished, there was sweat dripping from my elbows.

I collapsed in the stairwell that led up to my apartment. It was stuffy in the windowless corridor, which didn't help my heat fatigue. My tank top stuck to my back and stomach, my sweat like an adhesive. I still had to work third shift that night, but I didn't know how I was supposed to return to my job as though nothing had happened.

To say that Julia's betrayal stung would be an understatement. She'd succeeded in securing her father's acquittal and had made me look like an incompetent cop in one, efficient blow. The people of Embarrass knew their mayor was corrupt, but in their eyes, he'd go unpunished because of procedural failures.

I hadn't signed up for this. Embarrass was supposed to be a break for me; it wasn't supposed to add to my mountain of troubles. I could run myself into the ground, but I'd never shed this anger. I knew myself; no amount of sweat would cleanse me of these emotions. I needed to see Julia.

I kicked off my running shoes and left them on the floor in the middle of my apartment. As I shimmied out of my sweat-soaked running clothes, I noticed the small bruises on the outsides of my thighs. I didn't know if they were from Julia's fingers or her mouth, but probably both.

After a quick shower and change of clothes, I drove my bike out to Julia's. I didn't call ahead because I hadn't wanted to give her the opportunity to avoid me. But now that I was standing on her front stoop with the house tall and silent before me, I started to question my plan.

I ran my fingers through my wet hair, manually untangling the mess that had formed under my helmet. I didn't know what I was going to say to her. I had no practiced speech running through my head; I was running on pure, barely-checked emotion.

I fished my phone out of the front pocket of my jeans and dialed Julia's number, but every time the call went straight to voicemail. Her throaty recorded message assured me that if I left a detailed message, she'd call me back at her earliest convenience. Bullshit.

I knocked on the door until my knuckles felt raw. "Julia!" I hollered at the door. "You can't avoid me forever!"

I took a calming breath and tried her number again. Like all the other times before, the call was transferred directly to her voicemail.

"So help me, Julia!" I yelled up at the silent house.

I hit redial, and when I heard her recorded voice again it suddenly struck me: she wasn't dismissing my calls; she didn't have cell service where she was.

I found her sitting at the edge of the old wooden dock at her family's cabin on the outskirts of town. She was still wearing her outfit from court. Her feet were bare and a pair of red lacquer soled heels had been discarded beside her. She dangled her legs over the edge of the dilapidated pier and her toes skimmed across the water's surface.

I stepped onto the dock and the wood groaned beneath my weight. I couldn't have snuck up on her if I'd tried.

"Don't jump." I tried to keep my tone light, but the words got caught in my throat.

She didn't look away from the water. "You really are a good detective."

"You didn't hide very hard." My steps continued to creak and water lapped at the sides of the floating dock as I walked closer until I stood directly behind her.

"I was talking about my father's case."

She was holding something in one hand, and it took me a moment to realize what it was: a hot dog.

"I thought you didn't eat that junk."

She dabbed at the corners of her mouth with a napkin pulled from a pocket in her trench coat. "I won't tell if you don't."

"Why did you do it?"

"He's my father," she said as though it explained everything. "He's my blood."

"But you knew he was guilty."

She sighed heavily. "That morning, here at the cabin when we saw my father's car, I found the missing grant application. He must have had access to your apartment since his office is paying the rent. I knew you were close to catching him, but I still burned it."

I swallowed hard from the weight of her confession. "I could have you arrested for obstruction of justice."

"I know."

"I'm going back to Minneapolis."

Julia's head swiveled on her neck to finally appraise me.

"For good," I decided. "I can't stay in this town and do my job knowing what I know."

"I'm sorry you feel that way." Julia returned her gaze to the water. She finished the last bite of the hot dog and daintily brushed the crumbs from her thighs, destroying the evidence of her dietary indiscretion. "What will you do there?"

"Go back to my old precinct, I suppose. Try to get my old job back." I hadn't heard from Rich since I'd shown up at his office, but there had to be something available.

"And your nightmares?" she asked.

"They've gotten better since I got here," I admitted with a slow, thoughtful nod. "I'll probably be stuck behind a desk again, but I'm hopeful with a little work they'll put me back on active duty. But even if they don't, I have to go back. I ... I can't stay here."

Julia was quiet.

"Good luck, Detective," she finally said. "I wish you all the best."

Chapter Twenty-One

Grace Kelly Donovan stood at my front door with baked goods cradled in her hands. "I made you something for your trip."

"Pie?" I arched an eyebrow. "I don't think I'll have room for that in my saddlebags."

"Then we should eat it now." She walked past me and into the studio. "Oh!" she exclaimed when she noticed the state of my apartment. "You're already packed."

I shut the apartment door. Packing up my belongings hadn't taken much time or effort. I didn't own much, and I had barely unpacked from the original move to Embarrass. It was a good thing I hadn't yet recycled the boxes.

I didn't have an apartment lined up in the Twin Cities or even a job, so the plan for now was to crash on Rich's couch in his one-bedroom apartment until I figured things out. His place was little more than a dirty bachelor pad, which made it perfect in the interim. There would be no threat of getting too comfortable or over-extending my stay.

I hadn't told my parents that I was giving up on Embarrass;

they'd figure that out soon enough when I shipped them my half a dozen moving boxes. They worried about me, as good parents tend to do. I'd given them a lifetime of anxiety just between my time in the service and becoming a cop. I knew my childhood bedroom would be waiting for me if it ever got that bad.

The way things were so up in the air made what I was doing feel a whole lot like running away. But in a way, that's what I had been doing since high school graduation. With no real long-term plan in mind, I had simply shuffled from one bad decision to the next.

I pulled open a drawer in the kitchen and produced two forks. Nothing in the kitchen belonged to me, not even the salt and pepper shakers. They'd all been here when I'd first moved in.

"What are you going to do with that?" Grace asked. "Are you going to put it on your bike?" The spider plant Julia had once gifted me sat atop the radiator near a window. I hadn't known what to do with it while I packed up my life into cardboard boxes.

"Leave it."

"But that's plant genocide," she lightly teased.

"I told her I was no good at keeping those things alive."

"Told who?"

"Julia."

"She's the reason you're leaving." It wasn't a question.

This wasn't a conversation I wanted to have. "Let's just eat some pie, okay?"

I tossed my fork into the nearly empty tin. Together, the two of us had torn through the majority of the pie.

"I can't believe we ate all that," Grace groaned.

I rested my hand on my slightly distended abdomen. There was strawberry-rhubarb pie crammed into every open space in my stomach. "Never let me eat my emotions again, okay?"

Grace continued to pick at the baked pastry, but she didn't eat more. The tines of her fork made tiny impressions in the flaky crust. "I won't be able to do much about that when you're back in the Cities and I'm still here."

"I'm sorry. I know it's pretty shitty of me to be leaving like this."

Grace finally abandoned her fork, and she leaned forward in her chair. "Truth time: why are you going? Were things really that bad here?"

I did miss living in a bigger city where there were more activities, and I missed my friends from my old job, but life in Embarrass honestly hadn't been so bad. I'd made a few friends, had a few laughs, and I'd genuinely liked my job. Being a cop was emotionally taxing, but when you could see the good you'd personally been responsible for, it nearly made up for the headache of a bad shift. I had once thought the same thing about my military service until the fighting had turned into a war of attrition.

I tried to be as honest with Grace without revealing too much. "I need to go back to my life in Minneapolis. The past few months were like a vacation from my old life, but it's time I go back and finally confront my fears."

"What about Julia?"

I wasn't expecting the question, and my normally schooled features probably showed as much. "What about her?"

"Isn't she one of your fears? Shouldn't you face her?"

"I never said I'd face them all at once," I smiled sadly.

Rich was still at work when I arrived in Minneapolis, but I had a key to his apartment from the few times he'd needed someone to feed his cat. Jack—named after the hard liquor—was as ornery as they came. I wasn't a cat person, and Jack seemed to sense that. He eyeballed me with a look of clear disinterest and distain when I let myself into Rich's apartment and dropped my duffle bag on the floor in the entryway.

"Hey cat," I greeted.

Jack sniffed at my bag, but apparently after deciding I wasn't worth his attention, he lifted his tail, turned, and walked away.

Not bothering to change my clothes after the long bike ride or to start unpacking my bag, I inspected the contents of my friend's refrigerator.

"Jackpot," I said to myself as I grabbed a six-pack of St. Pauli's Girl out of the fridge. I cracked open the first victim and kicked my feet up on a coffee table that was in dire need of glass cleaner. If the water rings on the table's surface were any indication, Rich had never heard of coasters. I fished the remote control out from between the couch cushions and flipped through the channels in search of something mindless.

A few hours later I woke up to the jangle of a heavy key ring and the belligerent swearing of my friend. On the neglected television, an infomercial tried to convince me that their product could remove stubborn stains.

"Fucking Christ, Miller!" I heard Rich complain from the entryway. "Think you could have put your bag someplace where I wouldn't trip over it?"

Rich's steps were punctuated by the creak of leather and the metallic jangle of his gear. It sounded more like the swagger of a gunfighter's spurs in the Wild West than a Minnesotan police officer. He plopped down next to me on the couch, took off his gun belt, and tossed it onto the coffee table next to the six empty beers. The green empties were lined up like they were meeting the firing squad later.

"I see you made yourself comfortable."

"I was thirsty," I said in self defense.

"Could have at least saved one for me," he complained.

I stood and started to clear off the coffee table. "Sorry," I grumbled. "I'll buy more in the morning."

"Take a load off, Mama Cass." Rich patted the cushion beside him. "You're not here to clean."

"Then why *am* I here?" I openly lamented. I dreaded this part —the moment when I stopped running and started realizing I had no idea what to do with my life.

"How about we start with a simpler question?" Rich sagely posed.

"Like what?"

"Like what do you want on your pizza? I'm starving, dude."

Rich was already awake and rummaging around the apartment when I woke up on the couch the next morning. The remnants of last night's pizza were still on the coffee table along with a few more empty beer cans we'd discovered not doing a very good job of hiding in the refrigerator.

I inhaled through my nose and ran my hand over my face. "Shit. What time is it?"

I felt disoriented by the change of location. I hated that feeling when your brain believed you were someplace, but upon opening your eyes, you discovered you were someplace entirely different. It used to happen to me all the time when I first got back to the States. I'd wake up thinking I was still on base in Afghanistan only to open my eyes to the posters on my childhood bedroom.

"It's almost 11:00 a.m.," Rich informed me. "You can crash in my bedroom if I'm being too loud out here. The sheets shouldn't be too gross."

I sat up, groggy, and re-secured my ponytail, which had loosened itself throughout the night's sleep. "No, I'm good."

"You look like death warmed over." Rich shook his head. "Are you sure you wanna drop by the station this afternoon? The Captain can wait, you know."

I couldn't stay on Rich's couch forever, but I'd gotten back to town less than twenty-four hours ago.

"I need to keep my brain occupied," I said. "And the sooner I let Cap know I'm back and I'm serious about wanting my old job back, the sooner I can get back to active service."

I knew getting rehired wouldn't be easy. There was a mountain of paperwork to fill out and meetings with the police department's shrink to re-evaluate me. And even if I could convince the appropriate people I was ready to patrol again, there would be a significant probationary period with more psychological evaluations and supervised shifts. I'd probably have to go back to my old PTSD meetings and do things like keep a journal.

I hadn't ever considered what it would take to get my head right; I simply kept running away, hoping I could continue to avoid my problems. Grace's words haunted me. Had I made the right decision in leaving Embarrass? Or should I have stuck it out? There were better resources in the Twin Cities to help me deal with the worst of the nightmares and flashbacks, but coming back to this place had meant running away from something—*someone* —again.

I glanced at my cell phone on the coffee table. It had remained silent and unused since I'd left Embarrass. I hadn't heard from Julia after I'd left her at her family cabin, but I hadn't reached out to her either.

Rich sat down beside me on the couch. "It's up to you, I guess." He shrugged helplessly. "I just don't want you to push yourself too hard too soon, you know?"

"I know," I nodded. "And I appreciate that, buddy. I really do. But it's time Cassidy Miller got back to her life."

"Great. Now you're referring to yourself in the third person," Rich teased.

I gave him a playful shove. "Shut up."

~

I pulled at a loose thread on the couch. The more I tugged, the more it unraveled. I tried to yank it free, or at least snap the thread off, but it continued to lengthen despite my efforts.

"Why don't we talk about why you're here instead of destroying my couch."

I abruptly dropped the string as though it had burned me and sat on my hands to keep from picking at more loose threads.

"I'd like to return to active duty," I said. "And the Captain says I need your okay before I can do that."

The police department's psychiatrist was a long-limbed man with thinning red hair. He wore his glasses down low on his nose, which made me want to push them up the bridge of his nose. He flipped through papers that were stapled together at one corner. "According to your file, you requested to be taken off active duty back in May. Why?"

I was glad my hands were pinned beneath my thighs so they couldn't shake when I spoke. "That's when the nightmares got worse."

The papers in his hands rustled again. "You're referring to your PTSD, correct?"

I swallowed. "Yeah."

He continued to look at my file. "Cassidy Miller, active service in the Marines since 2004, awarded the Navy Cross in 2012." He flashed me a quick smile. "Congratulations."

It felt like a strange thing to be patted on the back for. I'd dragged a gravely-wounded buddy over sand dunes and rock piles for days until we'd been picked up by another convoy. "Thanks."

"Have the flashbacks and nightmares stopped?" he asked.

"No. Not entirely." I could have lied, but that wouldn't have done either of us any good.

He set down the file on the coffee table between us. I itched to scoop up the documents and read what had been written about me. "So why now?" He clasped his hands over one knee and crossed his legs. "If the nightmares are why you voluntarily removed yourself from active duty and they persist, why do you want to come back now?"

"Back in May I was scared—terrified, actually. I didn't know what was happening or how to control the flashbacks."

"But now you can?"

"I'm getting there." I sucked in a deep breath. "I know what my triggers are, and I work to avoid them. And recently I've been able to sleep for entire stretches without the reoccurring nightmares."

He made a thoughtful noise and picked up a yellow legal pad. He scribbled some notes on the paper. I wondered if he was writing about me, or if he'd simply remembered something he wanted to pick up from the grocery store later.

He looked over the pad of paper at me. "What do you think changed?"

I hesitated. I hadn't wanted to talk about her. This meeting was supposed to be about police work, not my private life.

"After I left MPD, I was working in a little town up north. There was ... a girl. A woman. The nightmares got worse for a short time, but then they got better."

"And you think this woman had something to do with that," he conjectured.

"I don't know," I sighed. "It could have been a coincidence."

"Is that what you really think?"

"No."

"Then what do you think explains it?"

"I really don't know," I said, my frustration at his pointless questions mounting. "Maybe I was too tired from all the sex to have any dreams."

The psychiatrist frowned and he tapped his pen loudly against his pad of paper. "Miss Miller, I'm here on your behalf. You requested this evaluation in order to be reinstated to active duty. I would strongly suggest you take this meeting seriously."

"I'm sorry," I quickly apologized. "I'm just not comfortable talking about her."

"Why not?"

Fuck. I bit on my lower lip. I could feel the sting at the corner of my eyes. "She betrayed me."

He looked unmoved or unimpressed by my admission. "Is she the real reason you've come back?"

I cleared my throat and collected myself. "Part of the reason."

"And the other?"

"It wasn't real up there, you know? That wasn't my life."

"But being in the Twin Cities is?"

"Yeah, maybe."

A quiet bell chimed and the psychiatrist smiled. "That's all of our time today." He shifted in his chair. "This was very productive, Miss Miller."

"So you're going to reinstate me?" I asked hopefully.

He gave me a measured smile. "Not after only one session. But today was a good start."

Chapter Twenty-Two

I teased the delicate underwear down her thighs. The material stuck to her skin, already damp with arousal. Her thighs pressed around my ears, muffling out the explosions I heard elsewhere. I brought my hand up to her concave stomach and her fingers joined mine. Touches that had once been greedy and forceful had now become languid and gentle. There was nothing rushed or desperate in this exchange.

I lathed my tongue the length of her slit and felt her shudder around me. She arched off the bed, words of praise and encouragement falling in my direction. My tongue divided her slick heat, eager to taste more and make unchecked noises tumble from her slightly parted mouth.

I held her lips open and suckled softly on her exposed clit. Her heels thrummed against my bare back, and I squeezed out the imagery of her digging the stilettoed heel of her shoes into me.

"Right there," she sighed. Her hips bucked into my mouth. "Stay right there."

"Never leaving," I murmured against her skin.

Her movements stilled beneath me, and I looked up at her

achingly beautiful face. Her raven-black hair had fallen across her forehead.

"But you did, Cassidy." Her voice sounded rough. "You left."

I woke up from my dream to hushed whispers.

"She only goes from my couch to the police station and then back to the couch," the voice whispered. "No, it's nothing to worry about. She just needs to get all of this pouting out of her system. No. She hasn't mentioned her name since she showed up. Yeah, I figured as much."

I slowly opened one eye. I was on the couch, and Rich was on the phone in the kitchen. I didn't know what time it was, but it couldn't have been too late because the alarm on my cell phone hadn't gone off yet.

"She went back to work nearly the day she showed up at my apartment. Uh huh. That's what I said, too."

My other eye opened and joined the first in being awake. My dinner plate from the previous night was still on the coffee table next to two empty beer cans. Yellow cheese sauce and a few neglected elbow macaronis were cemented to the plate.

"She's tough. She's been through worse."

I sat up and ran my fingers through my hair. My body felt stiff, but two beers wouldn't have had that impact on me. All the garbage I'd been eating lately, combined with inactivity and sleeping on a lumpy couch, was starting to catch up with me. I tugged the rubber band from around my wrist and pulled my hair into a ponytail.

I bussed my dirty plate and the two empties and went into the kitchen. Rich was leaning against a counter, sipping coffee from a mug in one hand and holding his phone in the other. He smiled and mouthed "good morning" when I walked in. I grunted in response and dropped my dish in the sink with the saucepan I'd left soaking overnight.

"I'm due some time off soon." Rich continued with his phone call and I helped myself to coffee, topping off his mug first before I took the rest of it. "Are you sure?"

I wasn't one hundred percent sure who he was talking to, but I had a pretty good idea.

"Yeah. That would be awesome. I'll show you around." He chuckled into the phone. "You think so, eh? Well, maybe I just want to show *you* off."

Yup. I knew exactly whom he was talking to.

Rich's eyes flicked in my direction. "Cass is up; I should probably get going. Uh huh. I will. Yeah. Me, too. Bye."

He ended the call and turned his attention on me. "Good morning, Princess."

I brought the coffee mug up to my mouth. "Speaking of princesses, was that Grace Kelly Donovan?"

"No."

"You're a terrible liar."

"Said the pot to the kettle," he countered.

"You have a tell. Your smile gets too big for your face."

"Okay," he conceded with a sheepish grin. "It was Grace."

"How is she?"

"Good. She told me to smack you for not calling when you got here. She was worried when she didn't hear from you."

I winced. It was weird being accountable and having people care if I was safe or not. "She's a keeper, Rich," I said, deflecting.

"I think so, too." He cast his eyes to the countertop. "She, uh, she might come down for a visit."

"Lemme guess," I smirked, "you want me out of your apartment by then."

Rich jerked to attention. "No way. I told you before, you can stay on my couch as long as you need to."

"Thanks, buddy." I didn't plan on cohabitating with Rich for much longer. I needed my own space, and I didn't want to overstay my welcome with my friend. I was going to be receiving another psych evaluation in a few days and hopefully get back on the force —active duty—not riding desk. But even if it came to that, I'd take the desk job. Maybe later, when my dreams didn't plague me so graphically, I could become a real police officer again.

"Besides," he said, his mouth curving into a mischievous grin, "she said she's getting a hotel room."

"Don't ruin her, okay?" I sighed.

"Not planning on it." He paused, waiting for something. "C'mon, Miller. Don't you want to know?"

"Know what?"

"How Julia is."

"No," I lied. She was all I could think about, and my dreams the past few nights were evidence of that. "You wanna go to the shooting range with me later?" I asked, changing the subject. I needed to get some hours in with a gun as part of my road to reinstatement.

Rich made a face. "Is that my punishment for saying her name out loud?"

"This has nothing to do with her," I denied. Embarrassment chased me to the pantry, and I poured myself a bowl of cereal.

"See?" he poked. "You can't even say her name out loud."

I shoved the spoon into my mouth. "That's because it's not polite to talk with food in your mouth."

"I'm sure your mom would be so proud," Rich rolled his eyes. "Speaking of which, have you talked to your parents lately? Do they know you're here?"

"No," I mumbled guiltily. I used my spoon to moved my cereal around in the bowl. My packing boxes had probably recently arrived at their house with no warning or note of explanation.

"That seems like something you should do."

"I know," I sighed. "But it's hard. I feel like such a disappointment. My dad says I've got no stick-it-to-it-ness. I run away before I can ever fail. I don't follow through," I said, repeating my dad's well-practiced speech.

"You did two four-year-long tours in the fucking Marines. You were top of your class in the academy. You're a decorated war hero, Cass!" The more Rich spoke, the more agitated and aggravated he became. "Where's the disappointment in that? Show me one thing you haven't followed through with."

My cell phone chirped, interrupting Rich's rant. Both of our eyes fell to the screen.

"It's my mom," I said. "I didn't know she even knew how to text."

"What's it say?"

I frowned at the text message. "My boxes arrived at their house, and she has no idea what's going on."

"Jesus, Rookie. You didn't even tell them you were shipping them your shit? Forget about the firing range today," he ordered. "You're visiting your parents."

St. Cloud was about an hour and a half away. The house I grew up in was on a long residential street with generous lawns, houses not situated too closely to neighbors, with a thin patch of woods in the back. My mom was out front hanging damp laundry on the clothesline when I rolled my bike into the driveway. She held up her hand to her forehead, using it as a shield from the overhead sun. I could see the concern and confusion writ on her lined face until I dismounted my bike and tugged off my helmet.

"Cassidy!" She dropped her wicker basket on the freshly mowed lawn and rushed toward me.

I stood awkwardly in the driveway and shook out my hair. "Hey, Mom," I greeted.

The air was forced out of my lungs when two strong arms wrapped around my ribcage and she squeezed me in a fierce hug.

"I didn't know to expect you," she sternly chided. "I haven't even started on dinner and the house is a mess. I haven't dusted in days. And look at me." She ran her hand over her short hair and plucked at the front of her worn T-shirt. "I've been cleaning windows and doing laundry."

Everything about this moment was so warm and familiar and perfect. It was home. I swallowed down the large lump in my throat. Everything was going to be all right.

I hugged my mom tightly in a second, unexpected embrace. "You look great, Mom. Perfect as always."

She lightly slapped my shoulder when I released her. "Why didn't you call? When your things showed up this morning I thought you'd died."

I ducked my head, feeling properly shamed. "I'm sorry. I know I should have called."

"You're right. You should have. I thought we raised you better than that."

The cross look on her face softened. "You should go say hello to your father. He's back in his work shed. I'm gonna go start dinner," she said as she bent to retrieve her discarded laundry basket. "Remind your father that he promised the Potters he'd mow their lawn while they're away this week."

"Sure thing," I said, already falling back into the familiar routine.

My mother left me in the front yard and made her way to the house with the laundry basket propped on one hip. Her still-flustered mutterings about me not calling and my god damn motorcycle was music to my ears.

My dad's work shed was an old pole barn in the backyard

where he used to store his snowmobiles until he'd messed up his lower back and couldn't ride anymore. Now he spent most of the day out there, tinkering on some handyman project. He was leaning over a metal vise, his back to the door, and his body blocking my view of whatever he was working on. The bottoms of my boots scuffed the cement floor as I entered.

"Nancy, can you get me two double A batteries from the house? I think I saw some in the junk drawer."

"Hey, Dad."

My father straightened his back. "Cassidy." He turned on his heel to face me.

I rocked back and forth in my boots. Unlike my mom, my dad wasn't a hugger. But even if he was, that wasn't my go-to reaction with him. My father and I had never been close. We'd had little in common as I was growing up, and when I'd come back from war—damaged goods in his eyes—the distance between us had only grown. He was too young to have fought in any previous war. His older brothers, veterans of Vietnam and currently living with the after effects of Agent Orange, could relate to what I was dealing with when I returned from Afghanistan. But my dad couldn't wrap his brain around an illness like PTSD that was invisible to the eyes.

Not knowing what to do with my body, I shoved my hands into the back pockets of my jeans. "Mom wanted me to remind you to mow the Potter's lawn."

His grey eyes blinked behind his reading glasses. "That's right."

"I could do it if you're busy," I offered.

He nodded solemnly. "That would be a big help. Thank you, Cass."

. . .

It shouldn't have taken long on my dad's riding lawn mower to take care of the Potter's lawn, but I kept having to stop when other neighbors wandered into their yard to say hi and ask questions I didn't have the answers to:

How long are you in town for?

What have you been up to?

Are you staying out of trouble?

How have you been?

After taking care of the Potter's yard, I took a shower and rummaged around in my room for something clean to wear. My packing boxes were stacked in the garage, but I found a shirt and jeans from high school that I could miraculously still wiggle into.

My bedroom smelled the same—a little mustier—but mostly the same. The bedspread on my double bed was the same and so were the posters on the walls. Framed pictures of me with extended family or friends I hadn't seen in a decade covered every available flat surface. My swimming medals and trophies from high school still lined the top of my dresser. My Navy Cross was still in its box in the sock drawer.

There was a tentative knock and the white wooden door of my bedroom creaked open. "Cassidy, baby?" It was my mom. "Dinner's almost ready."

"Ok. Thanks, Mom."

She hesitated a little longer in the doorway. "Are you staying longer than that?"

I ran my fingers over the cool metal of the silver cross and the textured material of the attached blue ribbon. I blinked away the tears. "Yeah, Mom. I think I am."

Dinner was a lasagna my mom had frozen earlier in the week. She continued to fuss and apologize throughout the meal about not having something more special for me to eat. But my glass was filled with two percent milk and my plate was overflowing with my mom's lasagna and green beans from the garden. It didn't get much better than that.

The questions started when dinner was winding down.

"What happened in Larry's town, Cassidy? Why did you leave?" my dad asked.

I pushed out a long breath. I knew this was coming. I wondered if Chief Hart had told them anything after I'd left Embarrass. "It's a long story."

My dad frowned, dissatisfied with the brevity of my answer. "Larry went to a lot of trouble to get you that job, you know. He was probably bending a lot of rules and regulations letting you be an active officer after what happened."

Hidden from view under the dining room table, I clenched my left hand over my knee. "I know, Dad. But it's better for me in Minneapolis, trust me."

"He told me about the investigation."

"Then you know what happened," I said dully. "And why I couldn't stay."

"Some," he admitted. "He said a lawyer manipulated the system to help a corrupt politician avoid jail time. Sounds more like something that would happen in the Sin Cities, not northern Minnesota," he snorted.

I ran the pad of my thumb over the tines of my fork and watched the tiny indentations they made in my skin. "She was just protecting her dad. There's nothing wrong with that."

My dad snorted. "From what Larry tells me, the girl's a real piece of work. It's probably better you got out of that place when you did."

I balled my paper napkin up and tossed it on my plate. The legs of my chair shrieked as I stood up.

"Where are you going?" my mother said in a panicked voice.

"I need to get back on the road."

"But you just got here!" she protested. "I thought you'd at least stay the night."

I stared at my father. "I thought I'd stay longer, too," I regretfully admitted.

"Pat, say something to your daughter," my mother urged.

My father remained silent and unmoved. He continued to eat his dinner.

I bent to kiss the top of my mom's head. "Thanks for dinner, Mom. It was wonderful. I'll send for my things in the morning."

Chapter Twenty-Three

F inding a new apartment in Minneapolis had been relatively easy; there was a vacancy in my old apartment complex. It wasn't the exact same apartment I had been living in before Embarrass, but I liked the familiarity of the building and the neighborhood. Convincing the property manager to rent to me without having been reinstated yet with the city police was harder. But, I'd been a good tenant before, so they took a good faith chance on me, plus two month's rent upfront.

In the wake of my brief visit with my parents, I had my boxes shipped to Rich's apartment, and shortly thereafter, I moved into my new place. It was larger than my studio apartment in Embarrass and even after I'd unpacked my boxes, the space still felt empty. I'd come back from Embarrass without only one new possession—Julia's dream catcher. I hung it over the headboard of the bed in the partially furnished apartment.

My phone rang nearly the moment I hung up the ornament. My heart seized, thinking it might be *her* calling, but the organ unclenched when I saw Rich's idiot face flash on the screen. I hadn't heard from Julia since I'd left: not a phone call, not an email, not even a text message. I still thought about her plenty though.

"What do you want?" I said in lieu of greeting.

"You're a real panty dropper, Rookie," Rich shot back.

"Hello, *Richard*," I tried again. "Miss me already? I only moved out today."

"Yeah. You got me there. You totally classed up the place," he snorted. "Your beer pyramids were a nice interior decorating choice."

"What's up?"

"We're going out tonight."

"No."

"Yes."

"I just moved into my new place today," I sighed, dropping down to sit on the end of my bed. "The last thing I want to do is go out."

"It's been almost a month, Miller. You can't keep hiding out with your frozen pizza rolls and cheap beer."

"Why not?" I bristled.

He ignored my question. "Clean your ass and comb your hair or whatever it is that you do to make yourself presentable. We're going out and finding you some tail."

"Some tail?" I echoed. Oh, lord.

"Yup. And you're in luck, Rookie. I'm gonna be your Wingman."

The club was busy for the middle of the week, especially considering classes hadn't started up at the university for fall semester yet. But at least I could relax somewhat. Going out during the school year kept me on edge, knowing that a good percentage of co-eds in the bars I went to were probably underage and using fake IDs to get served. It was hard to turn that mindset off and not be a cop unless I was blind drunk myself.

I stood at the bar nursing a beer and shredding the label out of boredom while Rich was in the bathroom. It didn't escape my notice that he'd brought me to the club where I'd first met Julia. It hadn't been our usual hangout when I'd lived in Minneapolis the first time, but now I was back—to what end, I didn't know. Maybe Rich thought it would give me closure to that chapter of my life. Maybe he thought since I couldn't face Julia directly, this club would pass as a surrogate. Or maybe he just remembered the high volume of attractive young women who frequented this place. I could practically picture his wide, innocent grin and hear his words: "Just taking one for the team, Rookie."

"Well, look what the cat dragged in," a low, husky voice announced behind me.

I turned and couldn't contain my grin. "Angie."

I gave my friend a tight hug. She was significantly shorter than me, so the hug turned more into me assaulting her with my armpits. We had talked on the phone when I'd first moved back to the city, but our paths hadn't physically crossed until now.

"What are you doing here?" I asked, holding her at arm's length.

"Rich told me he was dragging you here tonight," she supplied with a sly grin. "I didn't want you to have to deal with him on your own."

I pulled her back in for another hug. "Thanks. He's a little much to take sometimes."

"Agreed." Angie scanned the club when I finally released her from the hug. "So we're finding you someone to take home tonight, right?"

"Jesus, Ang. Not you, too."

Her mischievous grin was wide. "C'mon, Cass. I'm sure you had fun playing house up there, but the chicks in the Twin Cities have got to be better than whatever they had up in bumfuc-knowhere."

I made a noncommittal noise. I'd told my closest friends just a glimmer of what had happened in Embarrass and why I'd returned to Minneapolis. They hadn't pried beyond the surface, however, knowing me to be a private person. They were just happy to have me back.

"To be honest, I never thought you'd stick it out up there forever; I knew you'd be back."

I couldn't agree with her. When I'd taken the job in Embarrass, I hadn't thought much about how long I'd be there—not ten years, not ten weeks. I knew too well how unpredictable the future could be. All I'd cared about was getting to stay an active-duty cop.

About an hour and two beers later, I was talking to a cute blonde and starting to feel a little more like myself. She was about my height, and I found it encouraging that she touched my forearm a lot when she talked. She'd told me her name once, but her voice had gotten lost among the pounding bass pouring from the dance floor, and I wasn't eager to embarrass myself by inter-rupting her soliloquy about if Taylor Swift was a feminist or not to ask her name again.

My eyes wandered, not completely out of boredom, just habit, and I caught Rich's attention across the room. Even though he'd been the one to drag me to the club, we hadn't actually spent much time together. He'd abandoned me nearly the moment we arrived, but I'd managed to entertain myself in the interim. He raised his beer bottle in salute to me. I could practically hear his voice in my head: "Finish her!"

I was about to suggest to the girl that we go someplace more conducive to conversation—like an all-night coffee shop or my new apartment—when I saw a hand slide a slip of paper across our cocktail table. I looked up and met brown eyes. The woman had dark, close-cropped hair, reminding me a little of Grace Kelly Donovan. I didn't know who she was, but she looked at me like I should have.

"I'm supposed to give you this," the mystery woman said.

"Getting numbers and you don't even have to try," the Taylor Swift fan frowned.

I opened up the slight slip of paper. There were numbers written on the inside, but it wasn't a phone number. It was a bill.

"She said you'd know what it was about," the stranger lingered a moment longer.

"Where is she?" I demanded. I licked feverishly at lips that had suddenly gone dry.

The messenger nodded in the direction of the main bar, and my eyes connected with warm caramel. She stood, leaning against the bar top, looking unapproachable and untouchable in a little black dress.

I grabbed the paper off the table and, leaving my drink and the two women behind, I crossed the length of the club until I was standing in front of her.

I shook the piece of paper in her face. "What is this about?"

She took a careful sip from her funnel-shaped glass. "I thought that much was obvious."

"A dry cleaning bill? *Really*, Julia?"

Her tongue flicked out and touched the small scar at the top of her lip. It was an involuntary movement, but I couldn't help being drawn to her one visible flaw.

"What are you doing here?" I demanded.

"I moved here."

I blinked. "Minneapolis?"

"St. Paul," she said, looking bored. "I think it's more quaint."

"Wh-when?"

"Not too long after you left."

"Why didn't ... I mean, how am I just hearing about this now?"

Julia shrugged. "I didn't want you to think I was doing it for you."

"Oh."

"Let me be frank. You were *a* reason for the move," she admitted. "But I did it for me. I realized I couldn't stay in Embarrass forever."

"What about your family? Your mom?"

Julia chewed on the inside of her lip. "I'm fighting my father for custody. I'm trying to become her legal guardian so I can have her moved to a home in the city. He doesn't deserve her."

"Because he's a criminal?" I retorted, my anger getting the best of me.

Julia's temper was slower than mine to appear. I hated the control she had over her emotions.

"After you left town, I did some digging on my own." She pushed out a deep breath. "My father was having an affair with Wendy Clark, the city clerk. That's why no one realized that grant money was being deposited into my father's private accounts until you and David came along."

I didn't know what to say. Embezzlement *and* he was cheating on his wife?

Julia toyed with the stem of her martini glass. "After the trial I advised him it would be in everyone's interest if he resigned as mayor."

"And he actually listened?" I snorted in disbelief.

"Not at first," she said. "But then I reminded him that while he had survived the criminal trial on a technicality, there was nothing stopping a civil court from trying him. I told him if that happened and he was still mayor, he'd have to find a new lawyer."

"But he still has all that money." I didn't bother hiding my bitterness.

"I told him to give it back," she said with a small shrug. "If he returned it all, we'll probably never know. But at least the neighboring towns got their money back as did the Community Foundation. I suggested to Meg Peterson at the library that she meet with Peter Lacroix to discuss which city improvement projects might benefit from the new funds."

I thought about the city architect's little girl, Amelia, and smiled. Maybe she'd finally get her lighthouse.

"My father is a proud man," Julia continued. "Better he live out the rest of his days reviled and disgraced in Embarrass than in some white-collar crime resort prison."

"You really think he'll stay in town?"

"I do. He's never lived anywhere else; Embarrass is his home. And he's stubborn and arrogant enough to believe he can win back people's esteem now that he's done 'the right thing.'"

"And all is forgiven?" My skepticism was palpable. I couldn't imagine the people of Embarrass going back to business as usual after this betrayal. Yet, here I was, having an amicable conversation with Julia after what she'd done in order to win her father's trial.

"Cassidy," Julia started. I hated the way my traitor knees buckled when she said my given name. "I know you must still be angry with me."

"Anger is the least complicated thing I feel for you," I cut in. Anger was easy; I could be mad. I knew how to handle that emotion. It was everything else in combination that had me twisted in knots.

She frowned and cast her gaze to the bar top. I could tell that my tone had hurt her, and I hated the resulting guilt. How could I still be so attracted and so invested in her wellbeing after everything that had happened? I must truly be a masochist.

"How have you been?" she asked. Her voice was so quiet, it almost got lost in the din of the busy bar. "I thought I'd hear from you after you left ... but then nothing."

"I know. I've been really busy," I excused myself. "A lot of getting myself right again." I sucked in a deep breath. "I'm going to therapy again—group and individual—for my PTSD. With a little re-wiring of my brain, I'm hopeful I'll be back to my regular beat soon. I've come to accept that I won't ever be *cured*, but I don't have to be a prisoner to my nightmares and flashbacks anymore."

"That's really great, Cass," she said softly. "I mean it."

"How about you?" I asked, turning the question on her. "What have you been up to?"

She wrung her hands. "It took a little while to find something suitable, but I found work at a nonprofit legal defense fund."

"That's really great, Julia," I said in earnest. "I'm happy for you."

She nodded thoughtfully. "It feels nice to be doing good. And it's a challenge, too. "

This conversation felt like closure—it felt like an end to something rather than a rekindling. And I discovered that I didn't like that at all.

I toyed with the thin slip of paper that was Julia's dry cleaning receipt. "Is this a coincidence? Or have you been carrying this bill around with you on the off-chance that we'd bump into each other?"

"Your bald friend said you'd be here tonight."

"My bald friend? You mean Rich?" My gaze traveled around the club until I found him in a near corner having a drink with Angie. Our eyes met and he shrugged his shoulders, knowing he'd been caught. But even from this distance he didn't look too upset about being found out.

Julia hummed. "When I got his call this afternoon, I wondered how he'd gotten my number or how he'd even known I'd moved here, but he said that Grace Donovan had told him."

I shook my head in disbelief. "Those assholes," I mumbled under my breath.

"Would you like to go on a date, Detective?"

I snapped my eyes back to Julia's beautiful face. "A date? I thought you didn't *date*?" I knew I was being an idiot. Why couldn't I say yes and allow myself to be happy with this amazing woman?

Julia appeared unaffected by my stubborn resilience. She carefully set her drink on the bar top. "Let's just say I've found a reason to rethink how I go about my life." She licked again at her upper lip. "You saved me from a lot more than the rain and a broken car, Cassidy Miller. And I think it's only fair that I return the favor."

"And what exactly do I need saving from?" I stubbornly asked.

"Yourself, obviously."

Obviously.

"Is it wrong that all I want to do right now is kiss you?" I blurted without filter. "I know I should be mad at you, and I still am," I verbally acknowledged. "But why does it feels like everything will be better, everything will be forgiven, if I can just kiss you?"

Julia quirked an eyebrow. "Do you want to test out your theory?"

"More than you know." So much for maintaining a poker face; I was all in.

She threw her arms around my neck, letting her forearms rest on my shoulders while both of my hands came to rest on her hips. "Then what are you waiting for, Detective?"

"I'm an unemployed former cop," I said, smirking. "No more fancy titles."

"Well, that's a relief," Julia laughed. "It was honestly becoming tiresome having to call you that all the time." Her vibrant eyes twinkled even under the dim lighting in the club.

At the edge of my consciousness I heard the shrill shriek of a wolf whistle cut through the pulsing bass of the DJ's music.

Rich.

There'd be time to chew him out later for his subterfuge. Right now I had a gorgeous woman to properly kiss.

And a first date to plan.

About the Author

Eliza Lentzski is the author of lesbian fiction, romance, and erotica including the best selling *Winter Jacket* and *Don't Call Me Hero* series. She also publishes urban fantasy and paranormal romance under the penname E.L. Blaisdell. Although a historian by day, Eliza is passionate about fiction. She calls the Midwest her home along with her partner and their cat and turtle.

Follow her on Twitter and Instagram, @ElizaLentzski, and Like her on Facebook (http://www.facebook.com/elizalentzski) for updates and exclusive previews of future original releases.

http://www.elizalentzski.com

Made in United States
Troutdale, OR
04/27/2025

30924175R00179